THE EYE OF THE BEHOLDER

Margie Orford was born in London and grew up in Namibia. A Fulbright Scholar, she was educated in South Africa and the United States, has a doctorate in creative writing from the University of East Anglia and is an honorary fellow of St Hugh's College, Oxford. She is an award-winning journalist who has been dubbed the Queen of South African Crime Fiction. Her Clare Hart crime novels have been translated into ten languages and are being developed into a television series. She is President Emerita of PEN South Africa and was the patron of Rape Crisis Cape Town while she lived in South Africa. She now lives in London.

@MargieOrford

'Margie Orford has a quietly understated,
beautiful literary style'
Peter James

'The acclaimed "Queen of Crime fiction" in South Africa
takes a further step into the dark . . . *The Eye of the Beholder*
is sure to play a key role in the ongoing debate about what
women and men are, and can be, for each
other in these violent times'
Jacqueline Rose

'A hard-hitting, affecting novel about women who
refuse to allow men off the hook'
Declan Burke, *Irish Times*

THE EYE OF THE BEHOLDER

MARGIE ORFORD

CANONGATE

This paperback edition published in Great Britain in 2023 by Canongate Books

First published in Great Britain in 2022 by Canongate Books Ltd,
14 High Street, Edinburgh EH1 1TE

canongate.co.uk

1

British Library Cataloguing-in-Publication Data
A catalogue record for this book is available on
request from the British Library

ISBN 978 1 83885 687 8

Typeset in ITC Legacy Serif by Palimpsest Book Production Ltd,
Falkirk, Stirlingshire

Printed and bound in Great Britain by Clays Ltd, Elcograf S.p.A.

MIX
Paper from
responsible sources
FSC
www.fsc.org   FSC® C018072

For my sister Melle (24 September 1966 – 14 November 2021),
who was always my champion

and for Ellah Wakatama and Rebecca Servadio, who believed

To attempt to speak of what has been, would be impossible.
Abyss has no Biographer –

– Emily Dickinson

Cora. Maybe he shouted after her. *Cora*, a command. *Cora*, a plea. Maybe it was just an echo in her head, but this time Cora wasn't listening. This time she wasn't stopping. This time she was running. The cold air rasped in her chest as she zigzagged through the pines down to the lake with his panicked dog at her heels. She glanced towards the distant houses hunched against the winter. They were shuttered and lightless. No sanctuary there, no witnesses either. She slipped on the icy footbridge, caught hold of the wooden railing and stopped herself just before she went over. She saw where the branches, submerged in the ice, had snagged a rodent's small corpse.

The dog whimpered – a forepaw cut deep. Cora's wounds were hidden: the still-felt pressure of his hand, a vice on her arm, his other hand around her throat. The roar of her fury when he told her that she was delusional; she just did not see things right.

That was when she remembered that she knew how to fight, how to bring a booted heel down hard so that his hold on her loosened for the fraction of a second she needed to get through the door, lock it, get out, get away.

A series of harsh cries made her look back: crows flying up from the trees behind the cabin, but no other movement. He was not following, he couldn't follow – not yet, at least – but she had seen what he was capable of and she was taking no chances. She scrambled to her feet and sprinted to her car hidden in the fir trees and tore the door open. She was in, but before she could shut the door, the dog leapt in after her and pressed herself to the floor. Cora did not have the strength to fight her. She did not have the time either and, looking at the injured animal, decided maybe it was for the best if she took the dog with her, so she steadied her hands enough to get the car key into the ignition. The engine caught despite the cold. The wheels spun for a sickening moment, but there was traction. She sobbed with relief when the car jolted forwards.

Snow-laden branches lashed the windshield as she drove down the narrow track. Half a mile later and she was on a back road where the snowploughs had passed through recently. It was easier to navigate. She drove with her eyes fixed on the rear-view mirror, on the road and the trees vanishing behind her, but he had not followed her. Her mind knew he couldn't – but her thudding heart, which had a different measure of things, did not.

Cora stopped a mile short of the highway. On a clear day it was possible to see the lake where the cabin was, but the weather had closed in and nothing was visible. She got out and opened the passenger door. 'I've got to leave you here, Trotsky,' she said, her voice ragged. The dog shrank back but because she had no choice, Cora reached in and grabbed her collar. Trotsky twisted her head this way and that in an attempt to escape. Cora held firm. Desperation gave her strength and she twisted the collar until the dog choked.

She had Trotsky half out of the car when fangs sliced into her wrist, but she could not let go: she could not risk being seen with his dog, so she yanked her out and, in the moment the animal was off-balance, jumped back in the vehicle and slammed the door shut. The dog threw her head back and howled and she heard it for the accusation of betrayal that it was. Cora swallowed the lump in her throat and drove off. The dog ran alongside the car, but the distance between them grew steadily until she could no longer see her.

She could only save one of them and, part wolf, part husky, Trotsky knew better than she did how to survive in this waste-land of ice. That was what she told herself as she drove through whirling snow, hers the only vehicle on the road. Half an hour later, she saw the sign for Dizzy's Diner & Gas, its forlorn neon flashing weakly. She turned in and pulled up behind the rest rooms. There was no sign of anyone except a lone waiter bent over his phone in the diner. He did not look up when she got out of the car.

She grabbed her bag, went into the bathroom, and stripped off her stained shirt. She closed her hand around the brass key hanging from a chain around her neck. The metal was warm from lying next to her skin. Its intricate teeth, hard against her palm, made it impossible to deny what had happened. Cora tightened her grip around the key. She had turned it in the lock, she was certain of that, but she was not sure that was enough to keep her safe from him. She couldn't be sure it was enough to protect her daughter. That doubt turned her stomach and she leaned over the sink, but she wasn't sick.

'Get a grip.' Cora spoke out loud and the sound of her own voice snapped her back into the present. She let the key go and, as she had done before, closed the door to her memory. The nausea receded, taking with it her fear and her rage, and when she turned on the tap her hands weren't shaking any more. She washed as best she could with the dribble of hot water in the hand basin. Face first and then her arms and throat where the fingertip-shaped bruises were starting to show. Nothing to be done about those except wait until they faded.

The blood on the white porcelain of the basin transfixed her because she felt no pain where the dog's teeth had lacerated the skin on her wrist. She fashioned a bandage from her scarf and stopped the bleeding. She pulled on a clean cashmere sweater and stuffed the stained clothes to the bottom of the holdall. She pinned her hair up, carefully avoiding the contusion at the back of her head, and patted concealer on the dark circles under her eyes and then hunted for her mascara. It was gone. That small loss made her cry, so that when she looked out of the window next to the basin, the empty undulating landscape blurred.

All she needed to do was to walk outside, lie down and accept the snow's cold embrace. It would be weeks or months before anyone found her . . . No. She could not abandon Freya. She turned resolutely away from the window, away from herself.

4

Her only daughter might have turned eighteen now, an adult in the eyes of the law, but for Cora, Freya was still the little girl that she had promised – crossing her heart and hoping to die – that no matter where she went, she would always return for her.

To return was a promise she had always kept and she would keep it this time too. She hunted in her bag for a tranquilliser. She slipped the pale yellow pill under her tongue, the dissolving bitterness giving her the strength she needed to go back into the freezing afternoon, to return to the car and drive on through the gathering darkness.

After a while, houses began to appear along the road, and lights and other cars and people, then signs indicating where she should turn off to reach the airport. She followed them, returned her hired car to a young man who wished her a pleasant flight. She smiled at him and walked through the brightly lit terminal to International Departures. At the security checkpoint she stripped off her boots, her jacket and the key round her neck. She put her bags into the trays to be X-rayed. Her belongings passed through unremarked on, but the metal detector went off when she stepped through it.

A security guard signalled her over for a body search, moving her hands along Cora's arms and along her clavicles, winnowing between her breasts, pausing at the wire under her bra and continuing down her belly, along the zip of her jeans, between her thighs to where the ache was. There had been no tenderness the last time she had sex, but maybe it had not been rape. She did not wince, however the guard was alert to the responses of strangers' bodies and she paused, her eyes on Cora's face, before her hands continued their journey down her jeans, brushing over Cora's feet, an index finger feeling under each instep – a neutral touch that felt for weapons and nothing else. Satisfied at last, she stood aside and let Cora pass. She was the last passenger to board.

The plane was buffeted by the rising wind when it took off, but the pilot steadied it. Cora watched the lights that illuminated the runway, roads and buildings shrink until they were nothing but streaks of white in the dark. After a time, the light of the city disappeared too and beneath her there was nothing but darkness. She waited for tears to come but they did not. She felt nothing at all. She had survived again. That was all.

TWO

The wind was up and it harried the snow this way and that when the hungry wolves and the abandoned half-breeds – half wolf, half blue-eyed husky with the wild in them, running too deep for them to be easy pets dozing by fires – emerged from their shelters. Watched Angel Lamar leave the wolf sanctuary's makeshift office. Howled in unison when she walked past their enclosure, an eerie harmony of welcome and supplication. Fell silent and loped up and down the enclosure when she went into the cold room.

Angel lifted the dead doe off the meat hook. Shouldering the animal, she carried it over to the cutting table and laid it out on the metal surface. The deer's leg had been shattered where the truck had collided with it. There was a small, merciful bullet hole in the forehead where the driver had placed his gun and ended the doe's agony. Sorrow for this waste of beauty and grace tightened her throat. She ran a gentle hand down the doe's neck – an acknowledgement and a farewell – before she switched on the meat cutter.

The blade emitted a high-pitched whine. She dismembered the carcass with a practised ease that she had learned at the Girls' Progressive Reform Institute, the part prison, part mental asylum, part summer camp, where she had been assigned to the kitchens. There, the butcher, a thickset and not unkind woman, who had heard what skinny, silent Angel had done with a knife, took her under her wing, demanding no favours in return – to Angel's surprise. She had said she was sure that Angel wouldn't mind the blood. Cutting meat for fancy delicatessens in the big cities, where people don't ask too many questions about the past was not a bad job, the butcher had said, if Angel wanted to learn. Angel had other plans, but she'd kept them – as she did all things – to herself. Still, by the time she left the Institute, she knew everything there was to learn about dismembering a carcass into joints of meat.

She turned off the machine when she saw the vehicle, a black SUV with tinted windows and city plates. It turned into the wolf sanctuary. Few visitors came this way: it was a distance from the village and not on the road to anywhere, which was how Angel preferred things. She moved warily to the door and watched a tall, fur-wrapped woman step out of the vehicle. Angel walked over to her.

'Is Tina Jackson here?' asked the woman, her voice as smooth and rich as coffee.

'She'll be in later,' said Angel. 'Can I help?'

The woman hesitated.

'I'm a volunteer,' Angel explained. 'Tina's my boss.'

A gust of icy wind seemed to decide the woman. 'I found a dog on the road,' she said.

'Where did you find her?' asked Angel. From the corner of her eye she could see the wolves pacing, wanting their dinner.

'On the crossroads near the lake,' said the city woman. 'I've got a cabin up by Devil's Peak. I thought she was a wolf at first. Blood on the snow from one of her paws. She ran at my car and I saw her collar. I couldn't leave her.'

'No,' Angel agreed. 'You couldn't.'

'She has a tag,' said the city woman, wrapping her arms around herself to ward off the wind. 'There's a phone number. I tried it, but the network just cut out and I was on my way. I thought whoever lost the dog would come here to find it.'

'Nobody's been yet,' said Angel.

'I looked up the name on the tag,' said the woman. 'Nothing in the phone book.'

'What's the name?'

'Trotsky.'

Angel looked sharply at her. 'Trotsky? Let me see her.'

The woman opened the boot. The dog growled, bewilderment and pain in her ice-blue eyes, but she thumped her tail when Angel held her hand out to be sniffed, before picking up the injured paw and spreading it out on her hand. The cut was deep, but the cold had staunched the bleeding and she didn't think it needed stitches.

'You'll be okay,' murmured Angel as she coaxed the dog out onto the snow.

'You'll be in touch with this Trotsky?' asked the city woman, looking at her watch.

'It's the dog's name that's Trotsky,' said Angel. 'Her owner is Yves Fournier.'

The woman's eyes widened a fraction. 'The art dealer?'

'That's him,' said Angel, her hand on the dog's neck. 'He has the cabin on the far side of the lake.'

'You know him?' asked the woman.

'There's a hide up behind his property. For watching the wolves. Mr Fournier gave permission to set it up there. I've met him a few times.'

'You do research?' The woman looked Angel over, not quite able to keep the disbelief out of her expression.

'I do,' said Angel.

'You're so . . .' She cast about for a word. 'Young' was what she came up with. Angel kept a comforting hand on the dog's head.

'Well,' said the city woman, 'the dog likes you. You've spent a lot of time with Mr Fournier?'

'No,' said Angel. 'I spend time in the hide. There were sightings of grey wolves in the woods behind Fournier's cabin. From the hide we can watch them come and go.'

'And he helped with that?' asked the woman.

'He's interested in conservation,' said Angel. 'Likes to watch the wolves. Tommy Jackson – Tina's husband – built the hide. I monitor the cameras.'

'Are you from round here?' asked the woman, looking closely at Angel.

Angel shook her head.

'You got family here?'

'No family,' she said. 'But Tina, she's been like family.' Trotsky whimpered and Angel was glad of the diversion. 'We should get her inside.'

'You think something's happened to Mr Fournier?' asked the woman.

'He was probably out skiing,' said Angel. 'There's no reception in some places. Dead battery maybe. I'll go up there and check.'

'I appreciate that.' The woman held out a hundred dollars. 'A donation. Food for the dog. For your trouble with Trotsky.'

Angel took the money. 'Thanks, ma'am.'

'I've got to get going now,' said the city woman, 'if I'm going to keep ahead of that storm.'

Angel watched the woman get into her car and turn onto the road that led south. She herself was meant to go that way this weekend, to check in with her benefactor; to demonstrate her progress, which so far had been good. Trotsky pushed her nose into Angel's hand. 'You hungry, girl?' she asked. The dog thumped her tail. 'Come with me then.' She walked back to the cool room with Trotsky at her heels. There she filled the large metal pans with the dismembered carcass and carried them outside to the cages.

It was two days since the wolves had last eaten but this feast or famine would give them a fighting chance. This was her mimicry of the wild into which she hoped to release them. She knew what it was to be caged and didn't buy it that the risk of dying in hostile terrain wasn't worth the stab at freedom. She had been put away when she was fifteen. *To help her make something of her life*, the judge had said to her benefactor, as if Angel had not been there in the court room.

The pack fell on the food as she pushed the pans in. As in any prison, the biggest creatures chose first, the smaller ones settled for what was left. But Angel had made sure that there was enough for all of them, and the animals ate in ordered camaraderie once the spoils were divided. She had saved the deer's liver and that she threw down for Trotsky. The dog fell on the meat. In a minute it was gone and the snow at Angel's feet was bloody, her friendship with the dog cemented.

She clicked her fingers and Fournier's dog fell into step behind her. She opened the door to the office and the dog followed her inside. Stoking the fire, she laid a blanket out in front of it for Trotsky, who curled up and licked her injured paw. There was a box of cereal on Angel's desk. She opened it and ate straight from the box, licking the sugar off her fingers and brushing the few grains off her chest, which no amount of starving herself ever got rid of. When she'd realised that, she'd started eating again, taken up weights, bulked up enough to be able to explain things with her fists rather than with words, which Angel found to be good for nothing. She grabbed another fistful of the sugary cereal and watched the exhausted dog sleep, thinking about where she had been found – five miles from Fournier's cabin if he was driving, three if he had skied across the lake.

She took out her phone and found Fournier's number. He had texted her last week to say he'd found a lone wolf's prints over on the other side of the lake and would she like to come take a look. He had said he could take her there on Monday, which was today, but he hadn't been in touch since. She called the number now but it went straight to voicemail. Out of battery or out of range. There was only one way to find out if Fournier intended to keep their rendezvous. If he didn't, she was going to find out why not.

Angel picked up the keys to the truck. She drove with the heat turned right up and the radio on – the news was full of talk of the polar vortex. The earth was gripped by an icy winter hand that had reached down from the Arctic. Fountains in Montreal frozen solid in mid-air. Roads blocked. Villages marooned. Communications cut. People lost. A family missing: four of them – the parents and their young children with them. This was a tough winter. *Coldest for sixty years*, the radio man said. Angel didn't need his statistics to know it was a killer.

THREE

Cora woke to find the cabin lights on and an air hostess offering her a breakfast tray and a hot towel. She wiped the sleep from her eyes, pushed up the blind and rested her forehead against the glass oval. Looking down at London now she felt as alone as she had been when she had first arrived in England. She had been in freefall then, as she was now. She had felt the same vertiginous loneliness then, too. It did not matter that now she was looking down at the city where at this hour, Freya – her only child, whom she loved and yet had harmed more than she could measure – was sleeping.

When Freya had been a baby, Cora would watch her while she slept, arms and legs flung out as if she had been caught in the middle of a star jump. The expression of tranquillity on Freya's small face had comforted Cora. There had been Leo, too, and she had found sanctuary in the unexpectedly pleasant weight of marriage, but it was around Freya that Cora had been able to create a new sense of home for the first time since she had left South Africa.

Freya had been her constant companion. First in her carrycot, then in a playpen, and from when she could walk, Cora – always utterly absorbed in her work – let Freya have free range of her studio. When she was older, Freya retreated to the window seat to read, draw, knit or doze. When she was about twelve, Freya had told Cora that she thought the paintings were where she put all the things she could not say. *A spoken silence*, Freya had called it. Her insight had startled Cora.

The pilot announced that they were in a holding pattern and he had not yet been given a landing slot: Heathrow was very busy. Cora looked up at the circling planes, their outstretched wings glinting in the dawn light like metal birds of prey. Her thoughts turned to the last time she had seen vultures drifting just like this. Not above the green southeast of England but above the bone-dry veld on Eden, the remote South African farm of her childhood, which was where Cora had, for the last time, watched vultures gyre in search of carrion.

She had been lying hidden in the long yellow grass alongside Dawid, her childhood companion and her only friend, both of them eleven during that last summer together. Their hands had not quite touched but she had reached across those unbridgeable six inches of red earth so that she could lace her

15

fingers into Dawid's, but he had the stone handaxe they'd found in his hand. She had been amazed at how perfectly that prehistoric weapon, that tool, had fitted into his hand. *This land belonged to my ancestors, not yours*, Dawid had told her. *Of course it fits my hand.* He'd smiled and raised the stone axe as high as his arm would reach and brought it down towards her head. Cora had not flinched and when he stopped the blow an inch from her face, she had grabbed the handaxe from him and kissed his hand, but she had never forgotten the look in her lost friend's eyes: it was as if Dawid had already known what was in store for both of them.

The feeling of a stone weapon lingered as the plane touched down on the wet runway. Cora unclenched her hands and looked at the cut in her right palm. She plunged her hands into her coat pockets, as if to banish the memory of where the injuries came from, and disembarked. She stood in line with hundreds of other dishevelled passengers, until a machine scanned her passport and a camera captured her image. There was nothing outwardly remarkable about her: a slender woman of fifty, green eyes, a fine-boned face, pale after a transatlantic flight. The metal gates opened and she walked through and went straight to the Underground. She found a seat and checked her phone. No messages except a voice note from Freya, but she could not listen to her daughter yet. She could not call her back. She could not lie to her, so right now there was nothing she could tell her. First, she had to put things to rights. Cora checked that the key was still around her neck. She had allowed the contagion in but she had closed the door on it and locked it. She had to believe that.

The stale air and the smell of other people made it hard for

Cora to breathe, but at each station more people crowded in. The train inched through a station closed for renovations and Cora stared out at the posters advertising last summer's hits – music, movies, fashion – still up behind the Perspex advertising boards. A time capsule of a season that already seemed so remote it could have been another century. She spotted an advertisement for a summer dress she had bought and never worn and then, just as she was thinking she should give it to Freya, she saw her own face at the end of the platform – the poster for *Forbidden Fruit*, her last exhibition – the word 'cunt' slashed in red across her face. Cora jerked back as if she had been slapped.

Her stop came at last. She escaped the train and was eddied towards the exit by the commuters and then she was on the pavement with the morning crowds, making her way to the Lucian Villiers gallery on Albemarle Street.

The imposing doors were made of bevelled glass that faceted her reflection; for a moment, it was as if she was seeing herself as she had been when she first stood here.

She had just sold Eden, her parents' farm, after they were killed in a car crash, and had left for a new start in London, arriving from Johannesburg with a portfolio of paintings and a letter of introduction to Lucian Villiers. Cora had assumed that distance would free her from the sins of the past – hers and theirs. She had been wrong. Leaving made no difference to unappeased ghosts; they had travelled with her, gliding unseen in her wake, haunting her. She had painted to keep them at bay, mixing the red soil she had collected on Eden before she left into the red paint she used on her canvases, painting the shimmering light of her abandoned home. The first time she had shown Lucian her work, his eyes had gleamed.

He'd said that the suppressed violence in her work was, *to be frank, erotic*. He had said he would take a chance on her. It had paid off for both of them.

Now she pushed open the door to the sleekly prosperous Villiers gallery and a spectrally thin young man behind the white reception desk stood up when she walked in. 'We weren't expecting you, Ms Berger,' he said, surprise rather than pleasure evident in his face. 'Things went well in Canada, I see. The press has been excellent. I was just linking it to our website. May I get you a coffee?'

'No, thanks.' She glanced past him into the gallery.

'Freya was here,' he said.

That stopped Cora. 'What was she doing here?'

'She came to collect copies of your work,' said the assistant. 'She said you'd be okay if we billed you for it. I hope that's fine.'

'Yes. Fine,' said Cora. She was willing to give her daughter anything except the truth. That, she did not yet know herself. 'Where are the *Forbidden Fruit* miniatures? Did you take them down as I asked you to?'

'We rehung them in the rear gallery,' he said nervously. 'They're safe there. Let's just wait for Mr Villiers. He can explain.'

She was already walking towards the private gallery at the back of the building, the gallery assistant trailing behind her. The doors were closed but not locked. She pushed them open and stepped into the clinical white space.

The walls were punctuated by oversized abstracted landscapes that evoked the cool murky light found deep inside a forest. When she'd painted them, Cora had been thinking of the fairytale forest where the huntsman took Snow White to cut out her heart. In Cora's version, the huntsman never changed course. There was no animal substitution. There was no rescue. Miniatures of girls, limbs lewdly tangled, hung from the branches of the trees in the landscapes. One had to walk right up to them to see what they were, and when one did, they made the vast room too small. They made her throat close up. She reached up and plucked the first one.

'Don't do that, please,' begged the gallery assistant.

She paid him no attention, simply moved methodically from canvas to canvas, plucking the obscene postcard-size portraits – the same green-eyed girl over and over – that she had created with such voyeuristic precision.

'Darling' – the familiar smoke-roughened voice – 'what a lovely surprise that you're here.'

'Hello, Lucian,' she said, turning round to look at Villiers: perfectly tailored suit; perfectly barbered hair; a face that would reflect any feeling that a client might require. He was at her side in an instant and he caught her wrist. She cried out.

'What happened?' he asked, seeing the blood on the scarf.

'Nothing. I cut myself, that's all,' she said.

His eyes widened.

'No, no, not what you're thinking, Lucian. Not that. It was an accident. I slipped.' She turned back to the painting in front of her, reached up and snatched the miniatures attached to it.

'What are you doing?

'I'm taking these home. Taking her home, me home.'

'Cora, why?'

'I don't want them looked at,' she said.

'You made them to disrupt how we – how men – look at things,' said Lucian. 'Don't give up now. Don't give in. We've all fought for them. For you.'

'No,' she said, grabbing another one. 'Don't even start with that nonsense. You know it's not true. You like them because they sell.'

'Cora, you're not yourself.'

'I have never been more myself.'

'Everything's been so awful, I know, but *Forbidden Fruit* is a success. You must hold on to that,' said Lucian. 'The collectors love it and the tabloids will soon find another target – there must be a stray Royal about to do something stupid – and anyway I'm doing private viewings only after all the fuss—'

'It's more than a fuss, Lucian. Look what happened to Freya. The police questioned her. The Child Abuse Investigation Team. Because of what I did. Her mother. Imagine that. They came to me, too.'

'And they left,' he said in his soothing voice. 'And the work is still up for private views, at least. Come on, Cora. You've had bishops in a lather before. You've made a career out of breaking taboos. No need to be coy about transgression now. I was worried – ours is a prudish age – but I am thrilled to say that all this scandal, this *notoriety*, means you can name your price.'

'There isn't one,' she shook her head.

'We have a contract,' he said, changing tack. His manicured hand was on her arm. She detached it.

'You have the landscapes,' she said. 'Sell them for whatever you like if you need more money.'

The tiny paintings in her right hand were almost weightless, but she held them as if she was holding a pistol and Lucian stepped aside. She stalked past him, past the assistant, and straight at the broad-shouldered security guard standing in the doorway. He stepped out of her way and she was outside, back on the pavement. She held out her free hand and a taxi pulled over for her.

At Euston Station, amidst a whirl of people with suitcases and crying children, she bought a ticket for the next train to Glasgow, boarded it and found a seat as the train pulled away from the platform and headed into the tunnel. She took out her phone and her earplugs and listened to Freya's voice note.

'Hi, Mum,' said her daughter. It was a balm to hear Freya's bright clear voice. Cora pressed the ear pieces closer so that her daughter's voice was all she could hear.

'So much to tell you. Missing you. Life. Life and work. All these things to discuss. I haven't spoken to Dad – don't know where he's been but that's okay. It's just that I haven't felt all that well – I don't know, a stomach bug or something. Where are you? I saw on Twitter that your thing in Montreal for those women students who were killed by that guy in 1989 went well. So many questions. But also mainly my work to discuss. I liked saying that – my work! I think I told you that my therapist suggested that I investigate – that was his word, not mine – your art so that I could explore my own feelings about it and all the stress of the last while, so I was doing that anyway and kind of getting nowhere, but then I spoke to the woman about my application for that art curating programme—'

Then there was an interruption to Freya's torrent of words. Cora could hear a muffled conversation and then her daughter saying 'bye' and 'see you later'. The boyfriend that Cora had not yet met.

'Sorry about that. Okay. I was telling you about the curation programme. I know it's really hard to get in, but the woman said they would be interested in me – because of you, I guess – I'd been talking to my therapist about an idea ... Self / (M)other, with the M in brackets so there's a play on mother/other – kind of which is which and *who is who . . . Anyway, I got copies of your work from Lucian's gallery. All the main things –* Stabat Mater *and* Paradise Lost *and those first lot of things you made about me –* Alien Self-Portrait. *I told them it would be okay if they billed you. Hope that's fine. I have less than no money.*

'I told Lucian why I wanted it, and you won't believe this, but he put his lizard-like hand on my arm and murmured in that creepy voice of his that the best thing, if I wanted to establish myself as a critic, would be to take advantage of all this outrage generated by your latest exhibition. I don't know how you stand him, but anyway, call me when you can because I wanted to ask you some stuff. Oh yes, I also found an old trunk in the storage space of the Hackney flat. It said "Eden" on it so I got it down and it's just full of photos. I am having a look at all of them too. Amazing. Like archaeology. Also I have to look at Forbidden Fruit *but . . .'*

Here Freya's voice stumbled and slowed.

'I find that really hard so . . . yes . . . maybe we should talk about all that . . . Okay, that's enough. Bye!'

Cora's finger hovered above Freya's number but she could not bring herself to call her daughter back yet. She needed more time to compose herself. She needed to get her story straight before she spoke to Freya, so she sent her a short text instead, switched off her phone and put it away. She looked about the peaceful carriage – a child dozed against her mother's plump body, a man straightened his *Financial Times*, a young couple with a single set of headphones between them watched a movie. It was safe. She covered herself with her coat and fell into a fitful sleep.

FOUR

ngel cut the engine. The wind had dropped momentarily and there was not a single sound: no deer slipping away, no birds in the leaf-stripped trees, no one in the weekend cabins that belonged to the rich people who came up from the city. Yves Fournier's was the last cabin on the edge of the forest that stretched hundreds of miles north. She scanned the landscape with her binoculars. The hide to watch the wolves from was set on the hill above Fournier's place, screened by the first line of trees. Inside it were the cameras she had set up to record the creatures' return to the forest – every now and then they caught snatches of footage of a lone wolf; once there had been a pack moving swiftly through the trees, persecuted predators in search of food. Fournier went up sometimes after a storm and checked the cameras. There was no movement there now. She turned her attention to his cabin. A curtain was half open in the front room but there was no smoke coming from the chimney. She would start there.

She jumped down from the truck. The wind was a knife through her clothes, coming from the north where the pale hills dissolved into the sky. Angel crossed the bridge over the frozen stream – twigs, plastic bags, and a dead rat caught in the ice – and walked towards Fournier's cabin. A windowless basement, wood stacked on one side, an empty birdfeeder hanging on the porch, the garage a shack at the top of the drive.

Angel went round to the back of the cabin. No tracks, either human or animal, in last night's snow. There was a rack of skis on the wall of the porch – children's sizes, long unused – the top bracket empty. Fournier's red and silver cross-country skis were not there. That made sense. He came out here to ski. A thousand miles a season was his target, she'd been told. She rang his number again but it went straight to voicemail. She knocked on the back door. No sound came from indoors.

Angel wanted to have a look in the cabin before she called in Tommy Jackson and set the official search in motion. Half an hour would make all the difference to her but, if Fournier was out there, where his dog had been found, little to him. She had never been inside the cabin before, but out here people didn't need to lock things up, so when she tried the door and found that it was open she was not surprised.

'Mr Fournier?' she called before she entered. Her voice disappeared into the silence, so she stepped into the cabin. She tried the switches but the power was out. She stood still, waiting for her eyes to adjust, and listened – there was just the ticking of a grandfather clock. Coats, gloves and scarves hung from the hooks, but Fournier's red skiing jacket was not there. There was a roughly made boot rack and on it was a jumble of old boots, leather straps, slippers. The trapdoor to the basement, next to the boot rack, was not quite shut and she opened it. A cord swayed on the exhalation of frozen air that rose to greet Angel, but when she gave it a tug the lights did not come on. She switched on her phone light and went down the rough wooden stairs with only her torch to hold the inky dark at bay.

'Mr Fournier?' she said again. There was no answer. Angel put aside her fear of confinement and went down a little further, the cold clawing at her gloveless hands. She repeated his name, but apart from the echo there was complete silence. She found the fuse box and flipped the switch; the lights did not come back on. The whole area was down. She scrambled back up the stairs and dropped the trapdoor, letting out the breath that she had not realised she'd been holding.

The main bedroom was ahead of her. The bed was unmade and Fournier's clothes were heaped on the chair in the corner. She opened the curtains. There was a gaslight on the window-sill, a couple of books, and a faded photograph of a handsome woman. Fournier's mother, by the looks of it. The same prominent nose and heavy brows.

There were two other doors to the left of the hallway. Angel opened the first one, revealing an icy room, the air stale and unused, the beds stripped. She checked the other bedroom. It had not been used for a long time. Angel flicked through the canvases stacked against the wall – paintings of trees, views of the lake, none of them breathing any life into the landscape. Yves Fournier's signature was scrawled in the corner.

The bathroom smelt of mildew. She opened the bathroom

cabinet. A jumble of toothbrushes, small bottles of shampoo from hotels, paracetamol, a packet of Viagra – two blue tablets left. When she closed the mirrored doors she caught a glimpse of herself. Hair cropped short as an army recruit's, shadows under her eyes, her body wiry, her eyes not the pretty hazel – *Tiger's Eyes*, her mother had called them – that Angel had hidden behind the dull brown contacts she ordered off the internet for five dollars a pack.

Angel turned her attention back to Fournier's bathroom. She ran her finger along the line of scum near the rim of the bath. It couldn't have been there that long because it came off easily. The towels were ragged. One had slipped to the floor. She picked it up. It was damp. So was the bathmat. There was a tube of mascara on the floor behind the toilet. Angel pocketed it and, thinking of the pillows on the unmade bed, she went back into the bedroom. The pillows lay side by side and both were dented in the middle. She bent over the bed. The pillow closest to the door smelled a little stale, that was all, but when she sniffed the pillow by the window, she detected a trace of perfume. She snapped upright. Fournier had not spent his last night in this bed alone. She turned the duvet back. There were no stains on the sheet, but that did not mean that there had been no sex.

Angel put her hands to her temples and massaged where the muscles of her scalp were knotting. It might suit him to disappear, but she was not going to let Fournier elude her. She had not known that a woman visited Fournier – she had missed that. Her mistake. She knew he was adept at hiding things from scrutiny. She knew how he could charm and manipulate. She dug her nails into her palms to make herself see what else she had missed. The kitchen was to the right of the small hallway. Two bags of dog food sat just inside the door. There were dirty dishes in the sink, a pan on the stove, knives in the block on the countertop – none of them missing. She took one out and ran it lightly against the inside of her forearm. It was razor sharp. She checked the cups. There was coffee sedimented at the bottom of both of them. The fridge was full of beer, but there wasn't much food – hunks of cheese, a red pepper, ham, a couple of apples. The milk was off. The bottle of white wine in the door was half empty.

There were sheepskins heaped on the window seat, a rug tossed aside, an empty wineglass on the sill – it had the perfect view of the lake. Angel opened the cupboards. Mismatched plates, chipped glasses. Remnants. Closing them again, she saw children's drawings tacked onto the front of the cupboards, newspaper clippings too. Articles about artists, men in airy studios. There was a photograph of a woman standing at the apex of a tall ladder, pointing towards the painting on the wall behind her. A landscape. A hostile blue sky above land bloodied by the sun, trees that stood like sentinels around an empty bench providing the only shade. Angel looked at the cartoon of Fournier next to it. The artist had captured his piercing eyes and beaked nose with precision.

She went through to the living room. A macabre menagerie of dead animals was suspended from the roof: a desiccated Komodo dragon, a spider monkey with one of its bright button eyes missing, a snakeskin, and a turtle. Perched on the rafters – a nail through each delicate claw – were dead canaries and an owl. On the walls were framed vintage comics, *Star Wars* and *Superman* posters, fading photographs of Fournier's blonde children. The room smelled of smoke, but when Angel stirred the grate, the ash was cold.

A Montreal newspaper lay on the dining table. It was folded open, revealing a striking painting of a woman in blue, her head bloodied, lying in the snow. 'ART FOR JUSTICE', read the headline above a large photograph of fourteen women, artists from across the world commemorating the murder of fourteen women, shot by a lone gunman at the École Polytechnique in Montreal in 1989. There were smaller photographs of the reception: a crowd of people, champagne glasses in hand, clustered around the arresting portraits of the dead women. A photograph of a smiling Yves Fournier caught her eye. Angel checked the date – Saturday – and put the paper down.

There was a pile of bills on the table, and Fournier's laptop. She opened it and ran her fingers over the keyboard. It had some battery left, but a passcode request barred her access – she snapped it shut and glanced about the rest of the room.

Objects littered every surface: African masks, puppets from Indonesia, a voodoo doll, tortoise shells of every size, peacock feathers, a baboon's skull, a wolf's forepaw. Angel picked the latter up – the cold fur was repellent to the touch. Fournier had told her he was a conservationist, that he loved the wolves, loved watching them return. She put the severed paw back. She had never known a man who wanted the things he said he loved to be free.

Angel slammed the cabin door behind her as she stepped outside, relieved to be where it was white and light and the air was clean. She walked over to the garage. His car was inside, the keys in the ignition – which was where everyone left their keys out here – a jumble of country music CDs scattered on the dashboard. An inch of black coffee in a takeaway Dizzy's cup beside the handbrake. There was a thumbed map and receipts from the gas station down the highway, and Fournier's wallet. She rifled through that: credit cards and six hundred dollars.

She climbed up the hill to the hide. In the autumn, she, Fournier and Tommy Jackson had stood in this exact place. Tommy had introduced her – Tina's new volunteer, he had called her.

Tommy had explained to Fournier that Angel would man the hide he would build on the hill behind his cabin. That she would install cameras to see how often the wolves returned. This would give them some statistics, facts. Tommy had added that it would give substance to the conservation work he and Tina were committed to. He had warned Fournier there would be a bit of an invasion of privacy, because they would be able to see him come and go. Yves had laughed and said all he ever did was leave in the morning, ski all day, return in the afternoon.

Then he had shown Angel a photograph on his phone of a wolf he'd seen up behind the house. He had looked closely at Angel, but all he'd said was that it was lonely up there with no one around in the week, and only him on the weekends. She had told him she was happiest alone. It wasn't the whole truth, not by a long shot, but it was enough. It gave her the time she needed to get everything to fall into place.

Angel kicked away the snow piled against the door of the hide and went in. Two of the monitors were working, the third was blank. She checked the cameras. Two were aimed towards the mountain and the woods, from which the wolves sometimes emerged. The third camera should have been pointing downhill towards the lake beyond Fournier's cabin, but the wind had torn it loose and its snow-filled eye was fixed blindly on the sky.

Angel went back inside and rewound the footage, the hours passing backwards in seconds until she was at the beginning. Saturday morning. She watched until she saw Fournier moving with skill and grace across the lake, his red skiing jacket vivid against the snow, his dog ranging ahead of him. They both disappeared from view and after that there was nothing to be seen of either. On the far side of the lake was a dark fringe of forest, the trees marching in narrow bands towards the hills where the city woman had found Trotsky.

She watched the pictures in fast-forward, the short day fading rapidly into an afternoon twilight, until a flash of light caught her attention. She stopped the recording and replayed it. Lights shining on the front of the house. The time stamp was 15.38 on Saturday. Angel played it again. A vehicle bumped through the trees, cutting its lights. It was a short cut, a track that led to the clearing where she had left her truck. She zoomed in. A dark sedan. The car was too far away for her to decipher its registration plates. A single figure got out of the vehicle, retrieved a bag from the boot and crossed the bridge that led to Fournier's house. Angel couldn't see the person's face and, although at that distance it was impossible to be sure, she had the feeling Fournier's visitor was a woman. Something in the gait.

Angel watched more of the footage, but the figure did not reappear. After a while, a wisp of wood smoke curled out of the chimney, but there was nothing else. She watched the empty white woods for what seemed like forever. It was past six when Fournier returned, moving swiftly across the snow gleaming in the rising moon's pale fire. He headed for the cabin and then he too disappeared from view.

She played the film again but saw nothing new. However,

when she fast-forwarded the images, on Sunday morning at 05.47 the footage did a dizzying loop, which must have been when the wind had knocked the third camera out. Angel checked it again – the camera on its back capturing the dark sky and then the snow falling, which covered the lens, rendering the screen blank. There was no evidence that Fournier's visitor had left the cabin; none that Fournier had either. All Angel knew for sure was that the car was gone, as was the driver and Fournier – there was no footage of him pushing off across the lake again. She played the footage of the car and the woman again, filming it on her phone this time. This, she decided, she needed to keep to herself. When she was sure she had what she needed, she wiped the footage from the camera back-up. Only once that was done did she call Tommy Jackson. She liked him, Tina too. They told her she was family. Treated her like that too. She had forgotten what to do when people were kind.

'I'm out at Yves Fournier's place,' Angel told Tommy when he picked up. 'A woman found his dog and brought her in to me. His car's here so he must have gone skiing because his skis are gone, but the dog was found miles away on the other side of the lake. His phone is going to voicemail. No sign of him.'

'Doesn't sound good,' said Tommy. 'Stay warm and wait there. We'll be up as soon as we can.'

'I'll wait.'

She was good at waiting. She had waited for years to get this close to Yves Fournier. She could wait a little longer. She'd learned way too young to bide her time, to trust that her patience would pay off, that opportunity would present itself.

FIVE

Freya woke to find that Johann's arm, thick as a python, lay across her body. Last night, when she had cried out in her sleep, Johann had mumbled and pulled her close to comfort her and she had gone back to sleep. Now she felt trapped but she didn't want to wake him, so she moved his arm and slipped out of bed. He turned over but did not wake up. She looked at him for a minute, trying to suppress the wave of nausea that had woken her. Asleep, he seemed like a stranger to her even though she had been sleeping with him since the scandal about *Forbidden Fruit* had blown up in the press. She had gone to a party that was full of people she didn't know, with the intention of getting drunk – an aim she'd achieved rather too quickly. Johann had found her crying in the kitchen and he'd told her jokes and made her laugh and taken care of her.

Because his South African accent had the same cadence that lingered in Cora's voice, it had drawn her to him. It had been a relief that he knew nothing about Cora and little about art. He had not read the story splashed all over the papers after it had blown up on social media. He didn't like the news, he said. It was always so terrible and what could anybody do about it anyway? So she had let him walk her home and, seeing as it was so late – past three – when they got to her flat, she'd invited him in and taken him to bed with her and he had stuck around. Now, however, she could not be sure if it was only fear of loneliness that kept her from ending things with him. It had been an easy pattern to fall into. He was uncomplicated company and handsome in a muscular blond way. Caring, too, but when he said he loved her she didn't know what to say. He remained as opaque to her as her own feelings.

Johann stirred again but she didn't want him waking up and asking questions and frying bacon, which made her want to throw up these days, so she slipped out of the bedroom and went into the kitchen. She checked her phone while waiting for the kettle to boil, and was relieved to find a message from her mother. She opened it. *Hello darling. All is well. Will call soonest. xxxx C.* That was all. She must be okay, but there was nothing about where she was. No response to any of Freya's questions, which made her feel both anxious and silly – as if she was the mother, not Cora.

The kettle whistled and Freya took it off the gas and made a pot of ginger tea. The first cup settled her stomach but it did nothing to ease the anxiety that she had woken with – the familiar residue of a dream that had recurred since childhood. In this dream she searched for her mother but didn't find her. When she was a child it would wake her and she'd cry out, bringing her mother hurrying through to her if she was at home, her father if she was not. He would remind her that Cora would be back in one or two or three sleeps, however many it was.

She had told her therapist, a benevolent whiskery man whose consulting room made her feel vaguely claustrophobic, about this dream when she'd been referred to him after the press and the police had questioned her about Cora's paintings. Those questions had filled her mind and she had not been able to sleep. It was Dr Adler who had suggested that she investigate – his word – her mother's art in order, as he put it, *to explore your own feelings about a mother who is so devoted and yet so oblivious to the effect she might have on you.*

Her therapist had asked her what had driven Cora to leave places and people behind – to guillotine the past. Freya was sure that 'guillotine' had been the word he used, but when she'd asked him at her last session he'd said that wasn't his word – it was too freighted with violence – so it must be Freya's. It was not hers, she'd insisted. *Cora's perhaps?* – a quizzical eyebrow raised – which was *really very interesting.*

Freya went through to the living room. It was cold, so she picked up the red shawl hanging over the back of the sofa. She'd knitted it years earlier, sitting in Cora's studio, her needles flying while she kept vigil as her mother vanished into the worlds she created with her paints. Freya would wait for Cora to return, with that faraway look fading from her eyes, for her mother to say, *let's put the kettle on, Freya, and make ourselves some tea.*

She wrapped the shawl around her shoulders and surveyed the familiar room. This was where she had spent the first seven years of her life. She felt Cora's presence in this place. Leo's too, but less distinctly, because this had been her mother's studio: an old warehouse on a bedraggled street, where Cora had stayed when she had arrived in London from South Africa. She had bought it with the first money she made from Lucian Villiers. *Buying roots*, she'd said.

Freya felt at ease here – it had been her first home – but she wished more than anything that she was at Lawhead, their home on the west coast of Scotland, walking with Cora on the hill above the house, where the trees had taken the shape of the wind. Walking in the heather and the crags and alongside Loch Long – Leo used to say that those were the places Macbeth's witches were at home in, which her mother thought was a compliment.

The copies of Cora's early work that Lucian Villiers had given her were stacked on the dining table under the window, all of them in her mother's stark palette. The yellow grass, the oxblood red earth, the solid blue sky where vultures turned in lonely arcs were the colours of Eden. That place had inspired Cora's first show, *Paradise Lost,* which had made Cora's reputation. Freya hung up the prints of Cora's vivisection of her childhood on Eden. Cora had mixed handfuls of the farm's soil with a viscous paint that, when it set, looked as if the everyday violence of that time had been caught in bloody amber, according to a review in *The Times* that Freya had read.

Paradise Lost had been the beginning of her mother's career, but because her mother was Cora Berger whose life was her source material, she had, after Freya was born a few years later, made a whole show out of her baby-making: forty paintings, one for each week of Cora's pregnancy, that she had called *Alien Self-Portrait*. Those Cora had hung, scan after unsettling scan of Freya in utero, her face squashed up against the inside of Cora's drum of a belly. They were manageable in the book-sized images that Lucian had given Freya, but for the show itself they had filled the Villiers gallery from floor to ceiling. Cora had gone into labour during the opening so she and Leo had missed the speeches and had drunk the champagne later in hospital with Freya lying between them in the hospital bed.

The first in Cora's next series, called *Stabat Mater*, the standing mother – a reference to Mary's suffering as she stood at the base of the cross – was Cora's work about human sacrifice, sex and the bloodiness of motherhood. Except Cora had painted herself as both the naked Christ on the cross and as the Mother standing at the foot of the cross and looking up at her crucified self. A bishop had written to *The Times* saying that a woman on the cross was deeply offensive. That had caused a stir in the hothouse of the art world but it was nothing like the explosion that *Forbidden Fruit*, Cora's most recent collection, had set off.

This was the public record of her mother that Freya had sequenced, but she wanted to read it against the private images she had found in Cora's battered trunk at the back of the storage garage, which Johann had lugged upstairs for her.

Freya felt like an archaeologist, digging around in the long-buried past and finding tantalising artefacts that revealed the gaps in her knowledge of her mother's life. There were stacks of old photographs and she lingered over a photograph of Cora, aged about seven, with a crayon in her hand, and Cora's mother – Eva – on a whitewashed verandah. Freya examined the carefully made-up face of her dead grandmother, searching for signs of happiness, but her eyes were as cold and hard as green glass. The same colour as her own eyes, the same green as Cora's too, but, unlike her mother's, Eva's were expressionless.

My mother, Cora had told her years earlier as Freya sat by the fire in her mother's studio and watched her work, *would sit for hours flicking through magazines, looking at photographs of smiling women with immaculate hair. She dreamed of a world without dust, a world of shining kitchens and canapé recipes, a world that wasn't the farm. I sat at her feet waiting for her.*

Cora had told Freya this when she was ten, maybe eleven. Just as she was starting to think of her mother as a person separate from herself, a person with a childhood of her own.

She was unreachable, Cora had said, looking at her canvas, not at Freya. *I wanted to make her happy.*

Cora had looked so sad when she spoke that Freya had gone over to her mother and put her arms around her. Cora had held her tight. *That's when I started drawing*, she said. *I made drawings of Eden because it was the only world I knew. It was my attempt to comfort her, because my father, well . . .* Her voice had trailed off. *My father was out on the farm.*

Freya had asked if Eva had liked her pictures.

No, Cora had said, brushing Freya's hair off her forehead and smiling a smile that did not reach her eyes. *She preferred her canapé ladies. And I loved Eden, so I went to find Dawid and we roamed free in the veld.*

Did she mind? Freya asked.

My mother never forgave me. Cora had looked at Freya for a long time and then she'd said, *I felt trapped in that house. Out there in the veld I could breathe and, for a time, freedom seemed possible.*

Freya fanned out the other old photographs. A picture of her grandfather in khaki with a rifle in his hand, a dusty road snaking across the veld behind him where the russet cattle grazed on Eden. One torn photograph of an unsmiling Cora in school uniform – maroon skirt and crisp white blouse, walking down a shadowy colonnade with a group of boys and girls. Freya turned it over but there was no annotation on the back. She could not remember her mother ever mentioning a school other thàn Queenwood – there were class photos from each year that Cora had attended the private all-girls school in Johannesburg, which Cora had loathed. *It was a prison*, she'd told Freya. *It smelled of cabbage and despair*.

Freya opened an envelope. Inside it were several photographs of Cora and Dawid as young children. In one picture – they could not have been more than two – they were sitting on the kitchen step, dipping biscuits into a shared tin mug, their wiry little bodies perfectly aligned. Lydia, Dawid's mother and Cora's nanny, sat behind them.

Freya turned that one over to check the back for a date. There was a smaller photograph stuck to it and she worked it loose. That photo was also of Cora and Dawid, but they were on the cusp of adolescence. Cora was mid cartwheel – upside down with her hands planted on the grass, a necklace dangling in front of her, gleeful, her legs pale against the solid blue of the sky, a grinning Dawid holding her ankles. Freya looked up at an early painting of Cora's, *Paradise Serpent*, that depicted her mother at about the same age as she was in this photograph.

She stuck the photograph next to the deceptively simple painting – six gum trees with trunks a ghostly white, a bench in the circle of shade they made. Cora, on the cusp of puberty, stood in the gap in the scrub and stared past the empty bench out at the viewer. Her gaze – afraid, defiant, filled with shame – caught Freya's attention as much as her nakedness did. At her feet lay what looked like a coiled serpent but when Freya looked at it closely, she saw that it was a whip. The scene pulsed with the feeling that something terrible had just happened. Even though her mother only ever spoke obliquely of violence and sex, even though they were not visible, Freya felt their pull. Freya sensed her mother's damage in the fluid worlds she painted, where beauty and cruelty were hard to distinguish.

The fear, the shame, the jeopardy so palpable in that painting of Cora on Eden, was present again in *Forbidden Fruit*, the miniatures of herself as a girl that Cora had painted for her last show. They were so unsettling to look at that Freya was glad there were no copies of the originals. Cora had insisted: no reproductions. No passing around of her pictures as if they were dirty postcards. But anyone could take a photograph, which was what Freya had done, printing all twelve of them and pasting them on the wall.

'Obscene,' said the *Telegraph*. 'Berger crosses the line of decency,' wrote *The Times*, and Freya had been door-stopped by the tabloids outside this flat after an awful *Daily Mail* article that said she was a 'survivor'. When she had insisted she wasn't, the journalist had insisted that Freya was 'in denial – survivors often are'.

Freya had said in response to the accusations that the word 'survivor' was not hers. Her life had been easy, she'd said, the tremor in her voice caught on video by the journalist who had shoved a microphone into her face and asked her questions. If anyone had survived the hard place she'd grown up in, it was Freya's mother. You only needed to look at her paintings to see it was Cora who carried the hurt.

But nobody had listened. 'EVIL', the *Sun* had headlined. The story, which stated that Cora's 'decadent' paintings were 'abuse, not art, plain and simple', had unleashed an army of internet trolls and self-appointed paedophile-hunters. The Villiers gallery, where Cora's work was on display, had been picketed and then attacked. A brick was thrown through the window and skimmed Lucian Villiers' head.

Freya tacked up the newspaper clippings of the attack on the gallery – the smashed glass on the pavement, a baying crowd with homemade placards, a picture of Lucian with blood on his forehead. A picture that gave her a disconcerting amount of satisfaction. Then she felt another wave of nausea coming on and ran into the kitchen, where she leaned over the sink with last night's dishes still in it and threw up.

SIX

T he hide in the woods behind Fournier's cabin was cold. It was a light structure – wood and Perspex – but Angel was out of the wind, which was something. She scanned the vast area between here and where the dog had been found. If Fournier was still out there, and had been caught in the storm, they might find him alive. If they didn't, Angel would be disappointed, but she couldn't say she would be sorry.

A robin alighted on the sill of the hide. It tapped out a Morse code of hunger on the window. Angel found the remnants of a biscuit in her pocket, opened the window slowly and held out her hand. The bird, its bright black eyes expectant, hopped closer. Hunger overcame fear and it pecked at the crumbled biscuit, its breast thudding against her palm. It flew off, a flash of red against the sullen sky, when the black four-by-four emerged from the snow-covered forest, 'Search and Rescue' emblazoned in red on the doors.

Two men got out. Tommy Jackson, in his park ranger uniform. Lean, not much taller than Angel, his face weathered by a lifetime spent outdoors. Angel didn't know his passenger.

'Hey, Angel,' said Tommy. 'This is Jeb.' Jeb looked about thirty, the same age as Tommy, but with hard lines on either side of his mouth.

'How you doing?' Jeb held out his hand. As Angel reached for it, her sleeve caught on the zip of her pocket, exposing her wrist. Jeb saw the fresh red line, the white feathering. Years of healed scars.

Angel plunged her hand back in her pocket. 'You're new here,' she said, to mask her discomfort.

'Visiting,' said Jeb, looking her straight in the eye. He knew what he had seen.

'Jeb's an old friend from my police days in the city,' said Tommy. 'He got sent out to the backwoods for some fresh air after some trouble at home, but with all the shit that's going down it's good to have an extra pair of hands.'

'I guess,' said Angel.

'I've spoken to Fournier's sons and they've heard nothing,' Tommy said. 'Control is working a location on his phone, but a couple of phone towers were knocked out, so it looks like we're going to have to search like we did in the old days. You got an idea which way Fournier went?'

'His dog was found on that side of the lake.' As Angel

pointed, the sun broke through the cloud for a moment, the light catching the ice, turning the lake into a glittering wilderness. 'The camera picked up that he left Saturday morning and never came back. One camera broke, though. The wind, I think.'

'What cameras you talking about?' asked Jeb.

'Research I'm doing,' Angel replied. 'I've got cameras up behind Fournier's cabin and in two other places where wolves have been spotted.'

'Angel works at the wolf sanctuary,' explained Tommy.

'I'd shoot the motherfuckers if I saw one,' said Jeb.

'What for?' asked Angel.

'Don't mind Jeb,' said Tommy. 'He likes to piss people off. You show us what you got.'

Angel opened the door to the hide. It was crowded, with the three of them in there. Jeb ran a hand over the expensive equipment. 'This guy knows about you filming his house?' he asked.

'Fournier saw a wolf on the lake,' said Tommy. 'That's why the camera pointed that way. It was all approved. Show us the footage.'

Angel pressed play and Fournier appeared, pushing out across the lake, receding until he was just a moving shadow. He disappeared between the trees on the other side of the lake. After that there was nothing but the day passing. At 15.07 the tape cut.

'That's when the camera blew over,' Angel said.

'Can you play it again?' asked Jeb. Angel did so and they watched the footage again. 'We have no idea if he's even out there in that wilderness.'

'He's out there,' Tommy said. 'Where else would he be?'

'It's a good question, that,' Jeb replied. 'And if I were a cop still, it's the one I'd be asking.'

'This is not a crime scene. This is the winter. Happens every year. No matter how experienced people are, the weather's been around longer. Fournier went out Saturday morning – like Angel said – and he never came back.'

'You don't know that, Tommy. He could have gone out again this morning, for all we know.'

'Okay, okay. Like I said, the sons have heard nothing. I just need to check the house before we call the chopper, so let's go do that.' Tommy stepped out of the hide; Jeb and Angel followed him.

'That accent of yours . . .' began Jeb.

Angel stopped to reset the toppled camera. She wiped the snow off the lens and reattached it to its support, aware all the time of Jeb's eyes on her.

'You're not from here, are you?' he asked.

'No,' she replied, walking on. The two men fell into step with her.

'What you doing out here in the middle of nowhere, then?' Jeb eyed her. 'Getting away from family trouble?'

'Is that the trouble you're avoiding?' Angel shot back.

'Touché.' Tommy gave her a wry smile. 'His girlfriend left him again.'

'Why did she leave?' asked Angel.

'We could all go to that new bar downtown when we've found this dude,' said Jeb, 'and I could tell you about it.'

'I tried that a couple of nights ago. Got the worst hangover I've had in years. I'd keep my distance if I were you,' warned Tommy.

'That's my intention,' said Angel. She walked just a little

faster so that Jeb, lungs tight from too many cigarettes and too little exercise, had to concentrate on keeping up with her. She led them to the back of the cabin.

They kicked the snow off their boots on Fournier's back porch. Tommy knocked, but there was no response. He opened the door and he and Jeb went inside. Angel followed them as they checked the rooms she had searched earlier. They went through to the living room.

Tommy rifled through the pile of bills on the dining table. 'Expensive plumbing trouble. Looks like Fournier tried to fix it himself,' he said. 'You go down to the basement, Angel?'

'I had a quick look,' she said. 'Didn't see much.'

'I'll go check again.' Tommy hooked back the trapdoor and clattered down the wooden ladder.

'You spend much time in here?' asked Jeb.

'Today's the first time I was ever inside,' said Angel. Jeb twisted the button-eyed monkey hanging from the rafters. When he let it go, it spun round and it seemed to Angel that it was reaching its macabre little paws to her for rescue. When Jeb wound the little monkey up a second time, she turned around so that she didn't have to see it spin.

The trapdoor slammed shut and Tommy reappeared in the doorway.

'You find anything down there?' asked Angel.

'Nothing down there but a mess.'

'Weird place, this,' said Jeb. 'It's like a museum. What's he do, this Fournier?'

'He's an art dealer,' Tommy replied. 'Made some money out of it too, or so I heard.'

'You know him?' asked Jeb.

'A little. He spent six months here last winter. I came past a few times because his land borders the park, but he mostly kept himself to himself.'

'Wife?' asked Jeb.

'What is this?' asked Tommy. 'Twenty questions?'

'Cop habit. Just getting the lay of the land.'

'Divorced,' Tommy replied. 'Not that long ago, if I'm remembering right. Nina. A nice woman. She grew up in these parts and she has a cottage in a village about an hour away from here. That's where she lives now, her son told me.'

'She spent time out here?' asked Jeb.

'Not much,' said Tommy. 'This was always Yves' place.'

'Girlfriends?'

'Not that I ever saw.' Tommy turned to Angel. 'You ever see a woman out here with him?'

Angel shook her head. 'Only ever Mr Fournier and the dog.'

'Doesn't mean there wasn't a girlfriend.'

Tommy took out his phone. 'What we need is that chopper. On Saturday, Fournier posted a selfie with a backdrop of snow and some fir trees, asking if people could guess where he was. That's not unusual either – there's a group of solo skiers who do that. A competitive riddle about who knows the terrain the best.'

'You got a location on that?' Angel asked.

'Not yet,' Tommy replied. 'Control want me to check with his ex-wife too – makes sense to eliminate all possibilities in a risky search like this. I couldn't get hold of her earlier, though, had to leave a message.'

'Why her?'

'It seems she's still listed as his next of kin,' said Tommy. 'So we have to check with her.'

'So many rules,' Angel said.

'Blame Canada,' muttered Jeb.

'The weather forecast is only getting worse. I could go see her now. See if she knows anything,' offered Angel. 'If she does, you can turn the chopper back, but tell Control you've sent someone to speak to her while you start the search. If we wait and he's out there, he won't make it.'

Tommy weighed this up for a moment. 'You do that. Radio in if there's anything. I'll call the chopper now.'

'Impressive!' Jeb put his hand out to touch Angel's back, but she stepped neatly out of the way so that he missed her. Tommy did not see the flash of rage that this tiny humiliation brought to Jeb's eyes, but Angel did. She would have to be careful with him.

Tommy called the control room and updated them. He told them Angel's plan. The chopper would be on its way, they said, as soon as they reached the pilot.

'It's a pity for Fournier that you're not going to join us,' Jeb looked Angel up and down. 'You must have sharp eyes from watching out for the wolves.'

'Give her a break, for fuck's sake, Jeb,' warned Tommy. 'She's trying to help.'

'Just kidding,' Jeb grinned. 'You and Tina coming to watch the match tonight?'

While the two men discussed ice hockey, Angel walked over to the window and looked across the frozen lake. Tommy would find Fournier for her if he was out there. He was alive, Angel felt it in her bones. She was less certain that he was out in the gathering storm. There was a chance that he had left with the woman who had visited: her touch had been so light it was as if it was deliberate that almost all trace of her had been erased. The pieces of the puzzle did not align. There was something that Angel couldn't yet see.

'I'm going to need something to keep me going,' said Jeb. 'You want a coffee, Angel?'

She shook her head. It was a relief when the two men left the room. She listened absently to the sound of them making coffee for themselves in the kitchen, talking about disappearances in the city, and of other rescues in the vast emptiness that Angel was staring at as she rearranged what she knew this way and that in her mind.

Her thoughts were interrupted by the sound of the helicopter that appeared over the treetops, its blades whirling the snow as it touched down.

Angel walked down the hill with the two men and watched them climb into the helicopter.

'We'll let you know when we find him, Angel,' Tommy shouted above the noise. 'He'll have you to thank.' The pilot took off and headed towards the pale hills that lay beyond the frozen lake. When the helicopter disappeared from view, Angel climbed into her truck, taking the same private road that Fournier's visitor had used. She needed time to find him again and that was what the search – and their absence – would buy her. She was in a hurry now that Tommy and Jeb were gone, and she was driving too fast when a deer ran in front of her. She slammed her foot on the brake and the truck skidded, coming to a stop inches from the animal. For a split second they stared at each other.

The animal's eyes were huge, as huge and as trusting as Angel's mother's eyes had been. The doe ran off, but the shock of almost having killed the beautiful creature made it impossible for Angel to move. It had been a speeding car, the lodger had told Angel when she was twelve, that had killed her mother when she ran across the road. The driver – the killer – was the old man who had lived next door to them at 342 Lawn Street. The lodger said the old man couldn't have avoided Charly, because she had appeared so suddenly.

Why her mother had been running, wearing only her robe, like a woman possessed, he never explained to Angel. Why Charly was clutching a notebook – or so the only remaining neighbour who had known her mother told her – Angel never found out, because it had been years before she returned to the white clapboard house where she and her mother had lived so peacefully before the lodger had arrived and Charly had married him.

Angel rested her head on the steering wheel and tried to steady the thud-thud-thud of her heart. *Charly*. That's what Angel called her mother, because that was her name. *Charly, pronounced Sharly, short for Charleen.*

That's what Angel's mother always said when they met a new person. Sometimes she would say, *Every Charly needs an Angel*, and she would smile and ruffle Angel's hair and say, *I've got one*. Those were the evenings when they sat beside each other on the swing on the sagging porch.

Good evenings, spent watching people come and go on the quiet street. Pretending that with their big hazel eyes they had in common, those eyes flecked with gold – *our Tiger's Eyes*, Charly would exclaim – they could, like tigers, see in the dark. They needed to see in the dark in those days, when there was no one else in the world, just the two of them in that white clapboard house in Ramsdale, with its porch and the roses that drooped their pink heads in the midsummer heat. That had been enough for Angel, but it wasn't enough for Charly because she had no money, which was why she had taken a lodger. Later that lodger became Charly's husband, and then her mother was killed and the lodger was, as he liked to call himself, Angel's stepfather. One thing Angel was sure of, no matter what people said, Charly had not abandoned her.

A car came over the rise and the driver's lights on bright snow blinded Angel for a moment, snapping her back to where she was: in her stalled truck, slewed halfway across this narrow forest track in the fast-falling snow. The driver pulled up next to her but Angel waved him on – she was fine. She got her truck started and drove on towards the village where Nina Fournier lived.

SEVEN

Cora, asleep in the train, dreamed of Yves – the beaked nose, pale blue eyes, the lined skin on his high cheekbones. She had traced his face so often that the memory of it was printed into the tips of her fingers. She did not know how to fill the hole he had left in her heart. He was standing over her, holding an impossibly tangled ball of wool out to her. She had to untangle it, he was saying, and then she would be free. But her hands had been severed. She held the bloody stumps up to show him; he gave a mocking laugh and placed the tangled skein in her lap. She pleaded with him: she could feel her mouth moving, yet she was unable to make a sound.

'Madam, excuse me.' She started awake, her hands crossed in front of her, defending her face. She looked up to see not

Yves, but the conductor standing by her seat. The man with the newspaper was staring at her.

'I'm sorry I frightened you,' said the conductor. 'May I check your ticket, please?'

'Of course.' She found her ticket and handed it to him. He clipped the ticket and gave it back to her.

'Your hand's bleeding, love,' he said with concern.

'I'm sorry,' she said, looking down. The gash on her wrist had bloomed. She pressed a napkin against it.

'You'd better get that seen to,' said the conductor as he moved down the carriage. When the sliding doors closed behind him it was quiet again. Warm. Safe. False – this sense of security. She had allowed herself to be lulled into it before. She hadn't meant to sleep. She might have escaped Yves' cold embrace but there were fissures in time, gaps in her memory that she needed to fill. She was not safe. She couldn't trust herself. Not yet.

She looked out of the window. The ragged outskirts of London had been replaced by the wintry English countryside – the white-black-brown quilting of fields, lanes and hedgerows, the flurries of rooks. The fields glittered with frost. It was a landscape she knew, gentle despite the cold, and the sight of it restored her heartbeat to its natural rhythm until she glimpsed a woman crossing a field with a large Alsatian loping alongside her. The dog made Cora think of Trotsky, the dog that had leapt to her defence, the dog that she had left to fend for itself in the snow. That was a sacrifice that she had had to make, Cora reminded herself, so that she could be here, safe on this train, able to listen to her daughter's lovely voice note.

She checked her phone instinctively, but there were no new messages from Freya. There were none from Yves either. In the past, Yves had used silence as a weapon against her and wielded it to devastating effect. In order to survive, it was a language Cora had learned to interpret. But this time she knew what his silence meant. The impulse to talk to him persisted, though, a phantom limb that refused to be severed. *There is still a way*, her recalcitrant heart urged, as it had so often before, *to undo what you've done*.

She stared, unseeing, at the landscape sliding by on the other side of the rain-streaked window. One call was all it would take. One more suspension of disbelief. There was one person who might understand the help she needed. Nina Fournier, Yves' ex-wife.

One call would make Nina, who had left Yves, responsible for him again. When Yves had first drawn Cora into his orbit he had given her the impression that he had been separated for years, but it had only been a few months. She could not say he had lied outright, but it had jarred because he had told her other details. Nina had left abruptly, he had said. He had found out when he'd received a call from a real estate agent, who had got their phone numbers confused, to say the owners had accepted her offer. That was, Yves had said with an aggrieved look, the first he'd known that Nina was leaving.

A widower's pain, he'd said when Cora had asked if that had not hurt. *It hurt for a month and then it was gone*. Cora thought about how much her divorce had hurt – how much it still hurt – as she adjusted the settings on her phone so that her own number would not appear on the screen when she dialled Nina Fournier's number, which she had once harvested off Yves' phone in a fit of desperation. She dialled and waited, her mouth dry, as the network took its time to connect.

'Hello.' The voice was a shock. Warm and low. Gentle. Cora pictured an unadorned face and clear grey eyes for this woman she had never met – this woman who had excised Yves from her life. 'Yes?' Nina Fournier was wary. 'Who is this?'

There were so many things Cora wanted to ask of her, but she found herself unable to speak. There was no way of going back. She could not confess. She did not want absolution. She did not, she was shocked to find, want to undo what she had done. She dropped her hand with the phone into her lap.

'Can I help you?' Nina Fournier's voice was faint now, but still audible.

There was nothing Cora could say that would make things right. All she could do was to shield Freya, and to do that she must protect herself. There was nothing she could ask of Nina Fournier. There was nothing she wanted to ask, so she cut the call, switched off her phone and put it away. She folded her jacket up and leaned against the window and watched the Lake District slide past on the other side of the glass. Dry-stone walls sectioned the hillsides into manageable sizes. It felt so much safer, so much more ordered than where she had been.

On the other side of Oxenholme, the train slowed and then stopped. A signal light flashed red up ahead. A farmer in a Land Rover waited in the frozen field right by the train tracks. The set of his broad shoulders, the jut of his jaw was the same as Cora's dead father. Perhaps because she was so tired and had been drifting in the no-man's-land between wakefulness and sleep, instead of seeing the safe English landscape, she saw, in its place, heat-blasted Eden when the sky was white with heat in the last innocent summer of her childhood.

That year, the parched scrub had dissolved into a heat-whitened sky above the isolated farmhouse, the oak tree next to it dead, its blackened branches a claw against the cloudless sky. The drought had flayed the grass from the soil, and the sprinklers, where she and Dawid had once cartwheeled water diamonds into the air together, were dry. She and Dawid, that summer morning they went swimming in the reservoir by the house. The water was cold, pumped from deep within the earth by the silver windmill that clanked as it turned. Both of them in their old khaki shorts, diving in and out of the dam as sleek and swift as otters. Catching each other under the water, turning somersaults together in a tangle of wet limbs. They forgot to be silent and their shared laughter roused Cora's mother from her torpor. She left the verandah and marched over to where they were swimming. She ordered Dawid gone and he got out of the water and ran, bare feet flying down the path that led to the stables.

'Inside,' her mother snapped, and Cora followed her back into the shuttered house where she was meant to stay during the hot afternoons. Her mother took her shoulders and turned her, forcing her to face the mirror. She did not say a word, but her gaze was directed at Cora's brown chest where her nipples had begun to bud. Cora's hands crept up to cover them but she could not hide from the molten heat of her mother's gaze.

'Put this on.' In her hands was the yellow bikini top she had bought for Cora and which Cora had refused to wear. 'I am going to speak to your father. You're not a child any more. You are not to swim naked again like a savage. Not with that boy. Imagine how it makes him feel. Imagine what that does to him.'

Shame burrowed under Cora's skin on that hot afternoon and she did as she was told. That, she believed, would protect Dawid and her.

At lunch her parents discussed her as if she was not there. Her mother said that because Cora was a girl, it did her no good to roam about as if she were a boy. 'Just look,' her mother said, with one pale hand at her throat, 'what almost happened with Dawid.'

'Nothing happened with Dawid,' Cora protested, but her father told her to be quiet.

The boarding school in Vrededorp, the town closest to Eden, would take her at short notice, her mother said. She had spoken to them. The nuns would put her right. It was time. They knew, her mother claimed, what was best for her: she was a child, they were adults. 'No!' Cora objected, her voice thick with the tears she refused to shed, but it did no good. There were two of them and one of her. She stared down at her heaped plate, unable to eat, and she was sent to her room.

She waited for the afternoon silence to endure long enough to mean that her mother was napping, which meant she could leave her room undetected. She went out onto the verandah, but the dogs, her usual companions in those endlessly hot afternoons, were not there. Slipping around the house, she went down to the stables to find Dawid, taking the path behind the clipped acacia hedge that divided the garden from the veld. As she got closer to the stables she heard angry voices. Cora crept up to the gap in the thorny scrub; her stomach had knotted.

Dawid was tied onto the bench in the shade of the ghost gums, his arms and legs spread-eagled. His mother, Lydia, was pleading with Cora's father, but her father's eyes were on the boy's quivering back as he ran the whip between his hands; it was as limber and slick as a cobra. Her father raised the whip and brought it down on Dawid's back. Dawid's head jerked up but he did not make a sound. Her father raised his whip hand again and this time, Cora stepped out from behind the hedge. Dawid's eyes locked onto hers, but Cora's presence had no effect on her father. He brought the whip down on Dawid's back again and again. Dawid's white shirt split open under the blows and turned red.

Cora was transfixed in horror and Dawid made no sound, but his eyes held hers until her father stopped and walked off. Lydia untied her son and tried to cradle him but he struck her in the face. Cora gasped, as if the blow had been to her own cheek. Dawid was silent, even though his thin body shook with pain and anger. It was Lydia who cried, a high-pitched keening that Cora had only heard women make when someone died. Only then could Cora move again. She turned and fled.

By the time she had to go to the boarding school, she did not resist. It was the only way she could get away from Eden. When Lydia came to the house she did not say a single word more than what was absolutely necessary to Cora. Dawid, Cora never saw again. He had, she was told, been sent away to relatives, but nobody would tell her where. After a year at Vrededorp, she went to boarding school in Johannesburg. She never went back to the farm after finishing school except for the hot, lonely afternoon when she collected her parents' ashes from the undertaker in Vrededorp. She set the urn on the seat beside her and took the lonely dust road to Eden, where she had not been for years. When she got there, she let the ashes drift through her fingers and settle on the veld. As she emptied out the upended urn, it was as if she was emptying out herself.

Then she sold the farm, thinking the money would free her of her origins and buy her a year or two to prove herself as an artist and make it in London. She went through the old farmhouse one last time, but the only mementos she took were a few handfuls of Eden's red soil, some old photographs and home movies, and a knapped flint handaxe that she tucked into her purse for luck.

Cora had never returned to Eden, but she never entirely left it or its violence behind either. She had simply buried what happened there, fixing the past in the frames of her paintings. That was how she split off the things that hurt. She would have to do the same again – bury what she could not bear. It would be the same with Yves, when she found a way into the malevolent beauty in his wilderness of ice. She would paint snow, she decided. The earth would be covered with it. That way she could hide everything she could not bear in plain sight.

The train moved again, gaining speed rapidly. Cora opened her sketchbook. There was a ragged edge where she had ripped a page out.

She had finally found the words to tell Yves what he had done to her, and she had written them down. She ran her fingertips over the page which carried the imprint of her last letter to him, the letter that she had written in one fluid rush during the final sleepless night she had spent in his cabin. She wanted a clean slate, so she tore that page out too and selected a pen. Then, with a quick and practised hand, she sketched the dimensions of the new painting that had formed in her mind's eye. When she had it worked out, she phoned the hardware store and ordered everything she needed to make things new again. It would all be delivered tomorrow. Her pristine canvas would be a monumental shroud that would bury Yves' sins – and hers. That thought eased the pressure in her head as the train stopped in Glasgow and she joined the stream of disembarking passengers.

EIGHT

Nina Fournier's house was at the end of a pretty street: a simple, single-storey bungalow with a view of a gentle bend in the river. Angel parked up. She had not told Tommy the whole truth about Nina Fournier. It was true she had never met her, but Angel had seen her, late in the summer. She'd only been up here a week when a car like the one she'd seen and then erased from the tape had arrived, bumping down the same track. A woman had got out then, too, and Angel had recognised Yves Fournier's ex-wife from a newspaper photograph she had clipped and kept. In that picture, Mrs Fournier was giving the fixed smile that wives, standing by disgraced husbands, offer the press, cameras pointed at them like rifles.

Up at the empty cabin when the leaves were just beginning to turn, Nina Fournier had looked different to the way she had in the newspaper clipping – less polished – as she had walked up the hill and disappeared inside. Half an hour later she had re-emerged, an open box of crockery and another of children's toys in her arms. She'd carried them to her car and driven away without looking back.

As Angel walked up the path she thought about the wives and the girlfriends. About what they saw and about what they chose not to see. About what they knew and what they chose not to know. She rang the doorbell. A woman, her body distorted for a moment by the opaque glass of the door, opened it. She wore a pair of faded red corduroys and an Icelandic sweater. She had short grey hair and a pleasant face. She looked expectantly at Angel. 'May I help you?'

'Tommy Jackson sent me on behalf of Search and Rescue. He tried to call you about Mr Fournier—'

'Yves. Is it bad? Is that why you're here? I was out in the yard, I must have missed the call from Search and Rescue. My sons called just now, though. They're on their way up from the city. It's for them to deal with, really.'

'I understand, but Tommy went with the chopper and he asked me to check if you'd heard from Mr Fournier. Maybe you could give us an idea about where he might have gone?'

'I haven't heard from Yves, but he knows how to survive. There are forestry huts and he knows them all. He'll find one. He'll make it,' Nina said. 'He always does.'

'Anything that narrows down the search area will help save time. His life, maybe.'

'Of course. I'm not thinking properly.' The wind gusted and Nina shivered. 'It's too cold to talk here. Come inside.'

Angel stepped into a warm hallway filled with carefully tended ferns.

'What is your name, my dear?'

'I'm Angel Lamar.'

Nina took her coat and hung it up. 'Follow me, then.' She led Angel into her living room. A fire crackled. There were plants on the windowsills. A tortoiseshell cat was curled up on a chair. A book was open on the table, a tea tray alongside it.

'How did you know to look for him?'

'A woman with a cabin over near Devil's Peak found Mr Fournier's dog - Trotsky was injured,' Angel told her. 'So the woman brought her to me at the wolf sanctuary.'

'The dog will make it?' asked Nina.

'She'll get better - but I thought it best to leave her at the sanctuary with Tina,' Angel explained. 'I came here straight from Mr Fournier's cabin. He's good with his dog, so something is badly wrong if she left his side.'

'I suppose that's something.' There was uncertainty in Nina Fournier's clear grey eyes. 'How do you know he's good with his dog?'

'I volunteer at the wolf sanctuary, so I go to the hide, which is above his cabin.'

'Now I understand.' There was a flicker of a smile in Nina's eyes. 'You're the girl who watches for the wolves. My sons told me.'

Angel smiled back. 'That's me.'

'You look like you need something to warm you up.' Nina became brisk and maternal. 'Have you had anything to eat since you went up there?'

'I haven't,' said Angel, realising suddenly that she was hungry, and thirsty too.

'I'll make some more tea. If you need the bathroom, it's down that way,' said Nina. 'I'm sure the one in the cabin was too dirty to use.'

It hadn't been, but Angel did not say so. She went down the corridor, past Nina's bedroom, and another room with bunk beds and a cot for grandchildren, then to the bathroom at the end. When she returned to the sitting room, Nina handed her a cup of tea and she stirred in three sugars. The tortoiseshell cat stalked across the room and rubbed itself against Angel's legs. She picked it up and stroked its ears, making it purr.

'That's a first,' said Nina. 'He never goes to anyone. You have a way with animals.'

'I find them easier than people,' Angel admitted.

'So do I.' Nina smiled at her and for a moment Angel glimpsed how pretty she must once have been.

'You been up to the cabin recently, Mrs Fournier?'

'Not since the fall. We're divorced. You heard why maybe – it's a small community, this.'

'I don't pay much attention to what people say.'

Nina looked closely at her, as if trying to read what could not be said.

'You know him best. Narrowing down the time would help,' said Angel. 'Knowing how long he's been gone. I have footage from the cameras in the hide. He set out just after nine on Saturday – one of the cameras set up for the wolves recorded that – but there's no record of him coming back.'

'Did anyone speak to Yves' mother?'

'Should we?' asked Angel.

'Yves called her most nights at nine o'clock. I can't imagine he stopped after I left.'

Angel remembered the photograph of Yves' mother in his bedroom in the cabin. 'They're very close?'

Nina's cup rattled in the saucer when she put it down. Angel noticed that there was a dent on the second finger on her left hand where her wedding band, now removed, had been. 'The only woman who never judged him: that's what he told me. I should have paid attention to that.'

'Can you ask her when he called her last?' asked Angel.

Nina nodded. She scrolled through her phone, dialled and said, 'Hello. It's Nina,' when old Mrs Fournier answered.

After that she spoke in rapid French, which Angel did not understand. Then Nina said goodbye and ended the call.

'She spoke to him on Friday evening,' said Nina. 'A few minutes after nine. He told her about the skiing. They spoke about the weather. He told her about an exhibition he went to in the city – she was a war photographer. She likes to keep up with things. That was it – he hasn't called since.'

'Could Mr Fournier have gone someplace else? Gone with someone else?'

'I doubt it,' said Nina. 'He goes up there for the entire season. Skis alone. Always has done. He's a man of habit.'

'Was he seeing someone?' asked Angel.

'Another woman?' asked Nina.

'Yes,' said Angel. 'A new girlfriend maybe.'

'For her sake, I hope not.' Nina stood up and Angel took her cue and stood up too.

'Thank you, Mrs Fournier,' she said. 'I'll let Tommy know, then.'

At the front door, Angel looked at the walls covered with photographs as she put on her coat. Photographs of Nina and her sons as children. Skiing trips. One of a grinning little boy on Fournier's shoulders beside a bonfire. The family at an art gallery. Then the sons were grown, and the photographs were of them with their pretty wives and pink-cheeked children. Christmas trees. Easter egg hunts. Swimming costumes. Celebratory meals around a refectory table that must have gone with the marriage.

'You were with him for a long time,' Angel said.

Nina looked at the framed collages of photographs as if seeing them for the first time in a long while. 'Feels sometimes as if I gave him my whole life.' She opened the front door and crossed her arms around her body, warding off the knife-sharp wind. 'He try anything with you?'

Nina spoke so quietly that Angel wasn't sure she had heard her right. But the look Nina gave her told her she had.

'No,' Angel replied slowly. 'He was going to show me where he saw some wolf tracks. Then he disappeared.'

Nina reached out and touched Angel's cheek. 'You were lucky, then.'

'Lucky.' Angel tested the word.

'Yves knew what you were interested in. He would have drawn you in. He can be so attentive.' Nina put her hands over her mouth as if to stop herself, but then she went on. 'He was so adept at it, you know, transfixing women with his attention.' Her words came out in a rush. 'I saw it so often. The shame of it. The pain.' It was as if the wind had freed her to tell the truth. 'I don't care that in the end they said there wasn't enough evidence. Not guilty is not the same as innocent.'

'That's true,' Angel agreed.

'You'll have seen in the papers. On TV,' Nina rushed on. 'Most of it was kept out – he knows people. He thanked me, you know, for standing by him. He thought he had won, that

I would continue to be his camouflage, do no more than that. I couldn't pretend any longer that I hadn't always felt the truth every time he touched me. I packed my things and I left.' The cold was piercing. Nina wrapped her arms around her body, but she wasn't finished yet. 'So if it turns out that the winter has taken him, then I'll have peace.'

Angel held her gaze for a moment. 'I'll keep the dog then, until things are sorted.' She climbed into her truck.

'You're a good girl to take care of her,' Nina called, as Angel climbed into her truck.

Angel turned the key and, as she waited for the freezing cabin to heat up a little, she watched Nina close the textured glass door. Nina stood absolutely still for a moment before she sank to the floor and dropped her head onto her knees. Angel waited, but Nina did not get up and Angel felt the scar tissue of her heart tear a little. She reached under her left sleeve. The razor blade was there, carefully wrapped, strapped to her forearm. Knowing it was there – delicate, lethal – returned her to her body.

Lucky was what Nina Fournier had called her. She had been offered that word before. Luck was something she had decided she could do without. *Lucky* was the word Angel's stepfather had tossed at her after her mother was killed. *Lucky* that she still had him. Angel's only luck was that the one photograph of the home she had shared with her mother had survived the bonfire her stepfather had made to burn all traces of Charly. *It is important*, he had said, *to forget the past. That is the only way one can move on.* Angel had watched that fire, the photograph she had salvaged and hidden under the new bra he had bought her. *To cheer you up*, he had said, after he had made her put it on in front of him.

She had that photo still, hidden in the box in the hidey-hole she had made in the wooden floor of her hut. In it, her mother was laughing. Angel preferred to remember the times her mother had been happy, as she had been when a man in cowboy boots had taken the picture of the two of them for one dollar. He had handed them the Polaroid, Angel loving the magic of it, how the image had bled slowly from the world into the cushioned square of glossy paper in her hand, revealing her and Charly. Her mother's eyes wide with laughter, her black hair long and loose over her bare, freckled shoulders; Angel standing beside her, her hair the same colour. There had been a funfair in the background, and she remembered the lovely lurch in her stomach when she and her mother went on the rollercoaster.

Angel flipped down the visor and looked at her face in the vanity mirror, tracing her features with her index finger - eyebrows, nose, cheekbone, lips - but even she could no longer recognise her face as the one belonging to the girl she had once been. That lost time before the lodger, before her mother had died.

Angel started the truck and headed back, needles of snow hitting her windscreen. Janis Joplin on the radio. She turned up the volume, filling the truck with Joplin singing in her smoky voice about freedom and having nothing left to lose. Her mother had loved that song. At the thought, Angel's eyes blurred and she jabbed the off button. She could remember what her mother sounded like - smoky like Janis - but her memory of what her mother looked like was getting hazy, even though she still feel her. Charly, whose skin was smoothest on the inside of her arms. She had let Angel stroke her there as long as she liked if she woke up in the night and was afraid.

Charly, who smelled of clean washing and sunshine. Charly. So pretty with her black hair and the widest hazel eyes, which Angel had inherited.

Charly, pronounced Sharly, short for Charleen. That's what Angel had heard her mother say to the man who had arrived about renting the spare room a few weeks before her eleventh birthday. Angel had been sunbathing, kneeling on a mat in a pool of sunshine. She had felt his eyes on her and she had turned around to look at him. He was handsome in a creepy movie-star way. Clouds had blocked the sun just then and Angel had wrapped her towel around herself and gone up to her bedroom. She could hear Charly saying that the shower in the shared bathroom wasn't the best. The lodger had said he could fix it.

After that, there were three in the house: Angel, her mother and the lodger. Charly was so easily taken in. Lonely, alone, left untouched for too long, she had not looked further than what she thought was on offer: someone to eat dinner with, someone to sit next to on the porch. Someone to sleep with. Angel had been happy too; the lodger had promised her a puppy.

He said he had a job as an art scholar, but he was always around. *A connoisseur of art*, Angel heard him say to her mother. He published articles. He spent a lot of time on the internet. Once he took Angel on his lap and showed her one of his written pieces, called 'The History of the Nude in Western Art'. She didn't like sitting there but she did not know how to get out of it without being rude. She didn't know what to say about so many women without their clothes on. She didn't tell Charly – however, the next time he wanted to show her something, Angel said no, she was busy. He never did get her a puppy.

Charly's bed was no longer the place Angel could flee to when the nightmares came. Her stepfather – that was what the lodger became after he married her mother – said of course she could come. There was room for three. But Angel knew it would not be the same and it wasn't. She tried it once, snaking her limbs around her mother's body as she had done for as long as she could remember, her mother's hand on her head, the sound of her voice coming through her chest into Angel's ear pressed there against the thrum of her heart. But behind her, Angel could hear the lodger's breath suspended in the warm night air. Angel got up, went to her own bed, and lay awake to stop the nightmares from coming.

When she heard the creak of the double bed and her mother whimpering, she got up. The door to her mother's bedroom was ajar and she stopped and looked in. The lodger was standing up. His lips were parted and his eyes were half closed and there was a strange fixed look on his face. Her mother was naked on her knees in front of him. Angel could see the narrow white stripe of her parting, because he had her long hair bunched in both fists as he banged her head against his body. He looked Angel straight in the eye.

'Oh, baby,' he breathed.

Angel stepped backwards soundlessly and ran back to bed. She lay still, her heart thumping, but nothing happened. She heard her mother's low voice. Her stepfather's too. Angel did not hear what they said but no one came to check on her.

Then she'd lain still on her bed imagining that she was alone at the centre of a terrifying centrifuge that flung her room, the white house, the town, the world, away from her.

Now Angel reached under her left sleeve and touched the lovingly wrapped blade strapped there. She pressed her fingertip against the corner of it until it pierced the skin. The sharp sting was enough to soothe her. She drew the finger out and placed the bead of blood onto her tongue. Love, solace and sanctuary were all things she had lost when her mother had died, but the need she'd had for them had made her weak. Loneliness had made her crawl and beg then, but not again. Never again.

The warning light flashed on the dashboard. She needed petrol but she was only a mile from Dizzy's Diner & Gas, the place Fournier got his coffee from when he drove up from the city to his cabin. Shortly, Angel pulled in by the petrol pumps and filled up her truck. The cashier was bent over his phone but he looked up when she went in to pay.

'Hey, Angel,' he greeted her, ringing up her purchase. 'How you doing?'

'Okay,' said Angel. 'Mr Fournier tells me you do good coffee here. You going to give me one?'

He picked up the pot and poured her a cup. 'You know he's missing.'

'I heard.'

'I saw on this' – he tapped his iPhone – 'that the chopper's out looking for him. The radio says they didn't find nothing yet. But they found those two hunters over at Saint-Luc – dead as fucking dodos in that avalanche. It's not looking good for him.'

'It's not,' she agreed.

'It's just weird, because he was in here like always a few days ago, buying beer and white wine, and now maybe we won't see him again. He bought a couple of fillets too. I hope he got to eat them.'

'Who was he here with?' Angel put the cash on the counter, not in his outstretched palm.

'By himself,' said the boy. 'Why'd you ask?'

'Just wondering,' she smiled. 'Fancy food for one.'

'Oh, yeah, maybe,' said the cashier. 'But he likes the fine things, Mr Fournier.'

She picked up her change.

'See you, Angel,' said the cashier, after her. 'Come by any time you want a game of pool. Beer's on me.'

'Soon,' she called as she walked out. Angel knew more about Yves Fournier than most people and she knew that he never drank white wine: red on occasion, but never white. He must have bought it because he was expecting someone who did – the woman whose mascara was left in the cabin's bathroom. That explained the half empty bottle of Chablis she'd seen in his fridge. Angel wanted to know who she was. She wanted to know where she and Fournier had gone.

NINE

The results of Freya's investigation covered three of the stripped brick walls. By the time that Freya turned to the cuttings of the most recent work her mother had done for Art for Justice – holding art workshops with women who had survived the war in Bosnia – only the windows remained uncovered with prints of Cora's work. She pasted the photographs Cora had taken of the delicate sculpture of wire and women's shoes – a kind of mobile – onto the back of the kitchen door. She knew how much this work meant to Cora. Her mother believed that making art helped broken people fix themselves. Cora always said that it did not alter the harms done, but it did help a woman if she brought something new, something beautiful into the world.

Freya considered, not for the first time, that Cora's attempts to fix the world were because it was she herself who was damaged; that much was hiding in plain sight in Cora's paintings of her childhood on Eden. Suffused with sunlight, red dust and violence, that place had shaped her mother as surely as wind and water shape rock. It held her in thrall to this day.

'Wow, babe!' Freya jumped. 'This is wild!'

'What?' She hadn't heard Johann come in. She hadn't heard him at all; in fact she had forgotten about him.

He came to stand right behind her. 'It looks like an incident room from some Scandi crime drama in here.' His hands went under her top, sought and found her tender, painful breasts. Irritation at the interruption, at his uninvited touch, surged through her, but she found it hard not to please, so she did not move.

'You find the evidence you need yet?' he asked.

'I'm not looking for evidence.'

'Hey,' Johann turned her around to face him. 'You've been crying.' He wiped her cheek with his large hand.

'I'm just tired.'

'You're up so early again.'

'I couldn't sleep.'

'It's all this stress with your mom. They're all fucked up – that last apartheid generation. You should see my folks. Fucked. My dad – he was in the army. It's like no one told him it's been over since 1994 with Mandela.' He let her go and buttoned up his work shirt. 'You want breakfast?'

'No, thanks.'

'You feeling okay?' he asked.

'I'm fine,' she lied.

Johann went through to the kitchen. Freya could hear him clattering about as if he'd lived there since time began, filling the kettle, putting it on the stove, opening cupboards, banging them closed. Frying bacon. The smell made her queasy again.

'Babe,' he called above the sound of the water coming to the boil. 'Did you speak to your mom?'

'I didn't.'

'I heard you talking,' he said.

'She didn't pick up. I left her a message.'

Johann appeared in the doorway with a cup of coffee in one hand, a piece of toast with the bacon on it in the other. 'Your mom's not seeing someone, is she?'

Freya frowned. 'She would've told me if she was.'

Johann took a bite of his toast. 'Would she?'

'Of course she would.'

'Have you told her about me?' he asked.

'It's not the same,' she snapped.

'Seems the same to me,' he shrugged, speaking with his mouth full.

Freya turned away so that she didn't have to witness that. 'It's just that she hasn't been herself for a while . . .'

'Jesus Christ, Freya. "Not herself" is putting it mildly. Look at what she made.' Johann jabbed a forefinger at the pictures of the girl in the yellow bikini. 'It's sick.' One of the miniatures fluttered to the floor.

Freya flushed with irritation as she picked it up and replaced it. 'Her work has always been controversial, right from the early feminist stuff she made about motherhood. It's not sick.'

'Baby, look at what she did to you.'

'Don't call me baby' – anger made her voice sharp – 'and she didn't *do* anything to me.'

'Those portraits,' said Johann with exaggerated patience. 'What was she thinking? How could any mother do that to her own daughter?'

'You know nothing about what Cora does. You've never even met her.'

'Exactly my point. What are you ashamed of?'

'I'm not ashamed. It's just . . .'

'Just what?'

'I want to keep you private, Johann. Keep you to myself for a bit.'

'You see,' he replied. 'She consumes you.'

'No, you don't understand—'

'Maybe not,' Johann interrupted her. 'But I care about you, Freya, and things aren't normal between your mom and you. You're so close that you can't see it.'

'You know nothing about her.'

'Fuck, man.' Johann pointed to the walls. 'With all of this up here in the lounge I know too much about her. I can't escape her and neither can you. The difference between us, though, is that I want to escape and you don't.'

'She's my mother,' Freya's voice rose.

'I'm not interested in her. I'm interested in *you*.' He saw the tears in her eyes, so he put his mug down and put his arms around her. 'I want to take care of you.'

Freya leaned against him, her ear pressed to his chest. Johann held her tighter, his upper arm blocking her view. It felt so restful not to see anything. 'Come to Cape Town with me. Take a proper gap year. Learn to surf. There's more to South Africa than your mother's paintings.'

'I can't yet.' She pulled away from him and the pendant she always wore caught one of his buttons. It fell to the ground.

She picked up the necklace, a silver butterfly on a delicate chain that Cora had given her when she was twelve – telling her it would bring her light and luck. Freya had never taken it off since.

'It's broken,' she cried.

'Give it to me.' Johann held out his hand and she placed it on his open palm. He examined it closely. 'It's only the catch,' he said, bending the clasp back into shape. 'Turn around.'

She obeyed and he fastened the necklace and kissed the nape of her neck. 'Why don't you come with me?' he asked. 'You're meant to be taking a gap year. All you've done is move into your mother's old studio.'

'I can't do it,' said Freya. 'Not till I've fixed this thing with Cora.'

'You need to choose your own life, Freya. It's not right, this spell she has over you.'

'It's not a spell,' she frowned. 'We're just close.'

'Call your dad. Maybe he knows where she is.'

'He won't.'

'Try him. They were married for twenty years. He'll know stuff you won't.' Johann picked up the photographs she'd been looking at. 'Who's this?' he asked.

Freya looked at the picture he held out to her. 'That's Dawid. My mother's only friend on the farm – they used to play together because his mother, Lydia, was the cook and Cora's nanny.'

'That's how it was.' He handed the picture back to Freya.

'She told me that she and Dawid built their own world together in a cave on a hill behind the farmhouse' – Freya pointed to a photograph of the whitewashed house – 'and hid from both their mothers.'

'I can't imagine that was allowed to go on for long.' Johann put the photo back. 'You know what happened to him?'

'No,' Freya admitted. 'I don't.'

'It's not a friendship that could've lasted long – not in the seventies in apartheid South Africa,' said Johann. 'Where your mother grew up was a rough place. It still is now. Little white girls were not meant to play with a black kid – son of a farm worker. Everyone on those farms: you ask the white kids – my parents' generation – they say they were best friends until you were seven, eight, nine years old. Then bang. The iron curtain came down. A shock if you were white, not if you weren't. There is no way those games would have continued. It changed a bit after Mandela but that's how things were. Ask your mother what it was like.'

'I have,' said Freya.

'What did she say?' asked Johann.

'Pretty much what you've said, I suppose.'

'Maybe you want to ask her about this bikini too.' Johann picked up a photograph of Cora. 'It's the same yellow as the one in that picture of you on the windowsill. That one taken in Greece, you said. Crete.'

'Come on,' said Freya.

'And here.' He held the picture of Cora cartwheeling right in front of her face. 'It's upside down, but it's the same as the butterfly necklace that you're wearing.'

'It's not the same.' Freya put her hand to her throat where the silver butterfly with its delicately articulated wings hung. 'My mother had this made for my twelfth birthday.'

'You told me that,' Johann said. 'You told that journalist whose video of you was all over YouTube that too, but it *is* the same necklace as in the *Forbidden Fruit* pictures.'

'So what?' Freya snatched the picture from him. 'She had one too.'

'Where is it?' demanded Johann. 'Does she wear it?'

'No. She lost it. I asked her. She said she didn't know where, but she wanted me to have one to protect me in a way she wasn't protected.'

'And what does that mean?'

'I don't know!'

'I don't mean to upset you, Freya. But it's weird – is that you in the pictures or is that her?'

'It's my mother. Just leave it now.'

'I don't know what's going on and like you've said, I know fuck all about art, but your mom has blurred the lines and you've got to learn to look at things how they are. Not how you want them to be.'

'Stop mansplaining to me,' snapped Freya.

'I'm not,' said Johann. 'I'm trying to get you to see things another way.'

Freya turned away. She didn't want him to see her tears. She did not want *him*, she reminded herself.

'I'm sorry, baby.' Johann put his hands tentatively on her shoulders. She didn't shrug him off. 'Leave all this, Freya. Come with me. Live your own life.'

He kissed her goodbye and, as soon as he left the flat, she went over to the window and picked up the framed photograph on the sill. She had been eleven when Cora had bought her her first bikini. She remembered the lovely tingle of those two butter-yellow triangles adrift on her flat chest, the third one over her crotch. She had felt special and conspicuous all at once when she had turned to pose reluctantly for her mother's camera, but she could not help but wonder, now that Johann had pointed it out to her, at the fact her first bikini was exactly the same shade of yellow as Cora's original.

Just then Johann appeared outside the window, as he stopped to light a cigarette and then walked down the road. He looked back when he reached the corner and Freya waved. He couldn't have seen her because he didn't wave back, but she felt sad at the distance between them as she carried the photograph of herself over to the table.

Freya compared it with the old photos of Cora, her yellow bikini askew, her green eyes slits of anger as she stared defiantly at the camera. Those photographs had inspired *Forbidden Fruit*, the origin of all the stupid tabloids' witch hunt and the police visits. She dismissed doubt's twist of the knife. Cora had been distracted and absent, but Johann was wrong. The police were, too. Her mother loved her and no matter what people said she had done, Cora – who had explained that she was trying to heal something in herself – had not done anything to harm her.

She had been watching Cora warily, long before the paintings of her mother as a child, the response to which had caused both of them so much distress. She felt that her mother was hiding from her and it gave her a persistent feeling of dread. Even when they were together, it was as if her mother was on the other side of a wall of glass. She feared the wilderness she sensed was on the other side of Cora's love for her. She knew Cora's despair intimately, even though her mother thought she kept it secret. It was the most dangerous thing about her. Daughter had kept watch over mother for as long as she could remember: waiting for her to come home, sitting in the studio with her, creeping into her bed at night to keep her safe from the demons that haunted her.

When Freya had been a child, her mother would announce to her and Leo that she was going away. Freya would put her hand in her father's and watch Cora drive down the road and then they would go back inside, Toby – and the dog before him – slinking in behind them, into the silence Cora left in her wake. When Cora returned, instead of gifts she would bring them tales that illuminated the places where she'd been for an instant:

I had fermented shark fin for dinner, she'd said once, her nose wrinkling.

I saw a heron in a river in the centre of a city. She caught a fish. I saw the lump move down her grey throat.

A glacier sounds like the earth weeping.

The rest Cora left obscured. Where she stayed, what she did, who she saw, why she went, when she was coming back.

In the last year, Cora had disappeared repeatedly for days at a time. Freya would try – and fail – to get hold of her, and when her mother returned, she'd just say she'd been away and the time zones were out of kilter. There was a jealous part of Freya that would have condemned her mother to a life of loneliness if it meant she could keep her to herself. Like Johann, Freya had wondered if Cora was seeing a man, because in the beginning Cora had glowed, but she could not quite bring herself to ask. And then, even though Cora continued her restless, secretive travelling, that lightness in her had gone as swiftly as it had arrived.

TEN

T he short winter day was over by the time Angel got back to the wolf sanctuary, but there was so much snow that the night gleamed with an eerie pewter light. She parked next to Tina Jackson's car – the back seat littered with kid-size skis and a toboggan. The penned wolves and half-breeds yipped a greeting to Angel as she walked over to the makeshift office. The woodstove was blazing and Tina was at her desk – pizza boxes and paperwork spread out in front of her. Trotsky thumped her tail when Angel came in, but she could not move because Tina's four-year-old son was curled up against her back, his hands in the ruff of fur around the dog's neck.

'Do you know who I am, Angel?' asked Damian, flicking his red cape at her. 'Can you guess?'

'I don't need to guess. I know – Superman.'

'Mom, Mom!' he shouted. 'I told you she was smart. Dad told you too!'

'The men in my family think you're a genius,' Tina said. 'Not me – I thought he was Spiderman.'

'Never.' There was horror in his voice. 'Can you cover us up, Angel?'

'I sure can,' she smiled as she tucked the Superman cloak over Damian and Trotsky. The dog licked her hand.

'You got no colour in your face, girl,' Tina said. 'You eaten today?'

'I ate.'

'Eat again. I kept you a piece.' Tina pushed the pizza box over and Angel nibbled at the slice. Tina eyed her. 'Where the hell have you been, Angel?'

'Out,' said Angel, hanging up her jacket.

'Don't try that bullshit on me. I've got enough people to worry about without worrying about you too. Where were you?'

'I went to see Nina, Yves Fournier's ex-wife.'

Tina looked sharply at Angel. 'Why?'

'Tommy didn't get to talk to her before the chopper left for the search, but he'd told Search and Rescue I'd do it for him so they let him fly.'

'That's nice of you – covering his ass. That drive in this weather is above and beyond the call of duty, though.'

'Tommy wanted to check if she'd heard from Fournier. That's all.'

'And?' asked Tina. 'She know anything?'

'Nothing. He hasn't been in touch with anyone. Not even his mother, who he apparently phones every day.'

'His mother?' Tina raised an eyebrow. 'I didn't have him for a mommy's boy.'

'Me neither,' Angel said. 'But what would I know.'

'I'm a mommy's boy,' Damian piped up. 'I'm your boy.'

'Course you are,' his mother said.

'I'm a Superman mommy's boy.'

'That you are.'

'Are you a mommy's girl, Angel?' he asked sleepily.

'I used to be.' Angel knelt down beside him and tucked his cape even more snugly around him. She stroked his hair and the little boy closed his eyes again. After a while the only sound was the crackle of the fire and the child's even breathing. 'Superman's out like a light,' said Angel softly.

'You've got the magic touch with him,' said Tina, looking at her sleeping son and then at Angel. 'I don't like the thought of Tommy out in this weather.'

'Tommy'll be okay.' Angel stood up. 'Mrs Fournier thinks Yves will be okay too. She says he'll have gone to one of those forestry huts. I'm sure that's one of the places they will be looking.'

The wind surged, lashing snow against the windows.

'I sure am going to be glad when Tommy's out of that,' Tina muttered.

Angel fetched the tracking equipment that needed a service. 'Best to keep busy. Not think about it.' They set to work companionably.

'She's a good woman, Nina Fournier,' Tina said after a while. 'She was a special needs teacher.'

'I liked her,' said Angel.

'Well, now, that's a compliment. First time I ever heard you say you like anyone without being asked.'

'There's a first time for everything.' Angel kept her eyes on the radio collar she was checking, her fingers deft.

'You still going to visit your benefactor?' asked Tina.

'I guess.'

'I signed the forms.' Tina pushed an envelope over to Angel. 'Read them if you like. All of them saying that you're a wolf whisperer and that we couldn't do without you.'

'I'd rather stay. With all this going on.' She could not elude Tina's sharp gaze.

'It's okay,' Tina nodded. 'I've got eyes. I was where you were once myself. You've got to go check in, get checked up. You signed up to that.'

'I did,' said Angel, 'but I don't like the questions.'

'She just wishes you well.' Tina placed her hand on Angel's forearm. Angel willed herself not to shrug it off. The hand was Tina's. Tina's hand was safe.

'It's part of the Reform Institute deal,' Tina continued.

'I've got Trotsky now. I can't put her in with the others. The pack just got sorted out in the enclosure. Big dog like this will turn it all upside down.'

'I'll keep an eye on her for you,' said Tina. 'If you do it, we can keep you on with us.'

'Did Fournier have a girlfriend?' Angel picked the envelope up and tucked it reluctantly into the back pocket of her jeans.

'Not that I know of.' Tina stopped what she was doing. 'Did Nina say something to you?'

'She said she didn't know.'

'Why did you ask?'

Angel shrugged. 'He was married for a long time. He must've been used to having a woman around.'

Tina sighed. 'Don't remind me. I've got to get home soon and make Tommy and Jeb something to eat for when they get back.'

'You like him?'

'I love him.' Tina zipped up her anorak. 'Although I could kill him sometimes.'

'I meant Jeb.'

'You don't like him?' asked Tina.

'Not my favourite.'

Tina shrugged. 'Mine neither, but him and Tommy go back so long that I can put up with him for a couple of days.'

'Let me help you with Damian.' Angel wrapped the child in a blanket and carried him to Tina's vehicle, settling him on the back seat. Damian opened his eyes for a moment then closed them again, his lashes sooty butterfly wings on his cheeks. Angel kissed his forehead and closed the car door. 'See you tomorrow.' She waved and walked back to the office.

Tina wound down her window and called, 'Angel?'

'What is it?' She turned around, her hands in her pockets to protect them against the wind.

'I just remembered. I did see Fournier with a woman once, but it was back in the late spring.'

Angel walked back to the car. 'Here?' she asked.

'No,' Tina replied. 'It was at Dizzy's. I was driving into the city to buy a dress for my sister's wedding and I stopped because Damian needed the bathroom. That's where I saw him. He was in the diner, but he had his back to me so he didn't see us come in. I saw her, though – this striking woman across the table from him. Black hair, green eyes. Thin like you.'

'Did you know her?'

'No, and I didn't get to meet her. I was going to say hello, but Damian was desperate to go and when I came through again they were gone. It didn't seem like anything until now because you asked, I guess.'

'Was she young?' asked Angel.

'Not particularly,' said Tina. 'Why?'

'Just asking.'

'You never just ask things,' said Tina, 'but okay, she wasn't young. Forty-five, maybe fifty. And thinking about it now, maybe he didn't even know her. The diner was busy like it can get sometimes. Maybe he just sat at her table. Now get yourself back inside. It's fucking freezing.'

Tina drove off, her tail lights splashing red on the snow.

ELEVEN

Freya stepped into the flat, hung up her coat, switched on the lights and put away her shopping. Johann was working a late shift at the restaurant he managed and she was glad to be alone. She made herself miso soup that she carried through to the living room. She looked around at the walls plastered with Cora's work. Johann had been right; it did look like a TV show's portrayal of a murder room. Except there was no murder, just a half missing person. Standing in front of the poster for *Forbidden Fruit*, her mother's face staring out at her, she had so many questions.

She tried Cora's number again but the phone went straight to voicemail and she could not bring herself to leave another message. Her sense of dread at not being able to get hold of her mother grew stronger. Cora had been so shocked at the public reaction to her paintings of the girl – it wasn't her daughter, it was herself, she had protested, so she had a right to paint herself in any way she chose. But then, just recently, she had called to tell Freya that she had withdrawn the offending paintings from public view. She had said to Freya that she was sorry, so sorry that she'd been dragged into this mess. She had said she had been trying to retrieve something that had once been part of her that was now broken. Something that had been stolen from her – but that whatever it was – hope maybe, or joy – it had been buried before it could flower.

That was all she would say and Freya was not sure it was enough. Not sure it explained enough, and that doubt, which she kept to herself, made her feel at sea. The *Forbidden Fruit* poster slipped a little and as Freya secured it to the wall her thought turned to the questions neither she nor Cora could answer. Questions that had plagued her since two plainclothes officers had knocked on the door.

Their names were Sharon Roberts and Tulip Kahn, they had told her. They were from the Child Abuse Investigation Team, CAIT, they said and handed Freya their cards.

'I'm eighteen,' Freya had told them, 'so not a child.'

They'd said that they were there to ask her some questions about her mother, Cora Berger. DS Roberts said Cora's paintings depicted a child of about twelve, so that meant they were investigating for historical abuse and could Freya tell them if she had ever had to pose for her mother.

'No,' she'd insisted, her heart beating fast as if she had been running. 'Those pictures at the Villiers gallery are not of me. They are of my mother. We look very alike, that's all. And it's that resemblance that's caused this furore. Ask her.' Freya saw the disbelief in their eyes, but she really didn't have anything else to tell them: she was not worried about herself, she was worried about Cora.

'You never posed for her or anyone else?' they asked.

'Never,' she said. 'My childhood was safe. Always.' DS Roberts kept her kind grey eyes on her all the time. As if Cora had done something, even though Freya didn't know what it was. DS Roberts said to keep their cards and to call if there was anything else she wished to tell them. The cards were still propped up on the mantelpiece where they had left them the day of their visit.

Freya thought now, as she pivoted slowly around the living room, looking at Cora's paintings that filled the walls from floor to ceiling, that she had not been entirely truthful. Once when she was a child – ten, maybe eleven – and she and her mother had been sketching together beside the loch, Cora had said she needed Freya to sit on a rock so that she could provide some sense of proportion – some human scale – to the grandeur of the landscape. And she had done so, sitting there smiling with her legs tucked under her.

Cora had a natural way with landscape. You could see it in her paintings of Eden, but there were certain scenes to which her mother returned – the primal freedom of childhood, its claustrophobia and banal brutality. Cora's ambivalence about her many departures was there if you knew what to look for. She had never returned to the place she had grown up in, but she never seemed to leave it either, despite the steady rhythm of the home she made in Scotland with Freya and Leo. Freya wondered if Cora missed Leo's quiet, reliable presence in the way she herself did. He had kept an eye out for Freya when her mother's attention, usually so undivided, was distracted when Cora was in public.

One exhibition opening was etched in Freya's mind. She could only have been four or five and, as the only child at the Villiers gallery, she'd got lost among the milling, kissing, drinking, shouting adults orbiting around her mother. The paintings hadn't disturbed her at all – her mother's studio was her nursery, so she knew them all – but the people had frightened her. Caught up in a forest of adult legs, she had realised that her mother belonged not to her, but to other people – and that they distracted Cora, made her mother forget her. Leo had rescued her, picking her up and taking her to a back room where she had sobbed until she had fallen asleep against his chest.

She felt a pang of longing for him now, and for home – warm and open – for childhood. Toby asleep next to the Aga; wildflowers, picked on a walk, placed in a jar on the scrubbed table; her father watching for her from his study; Cora absorbed in her studio until she heard the gate bang behind Freya as she came home from school. That was the sound that summoned her mother, who would come down and make tea and toast for her and ask how her day had been and what she had done at school. Afterwards, they would go back to Cora's studio together. Cora would work and Freya would sit in the window seat and do her homework until it was time to take the dog for a walk with her father.

Fuck it, she thought, maybe Johann was right. Maybe she should try him. She dialled his number and he answered immediately.

'Freya, darling.' The delight in her father's voice made her feel guilty. 'How nice to hear your voice. Is everything okay?'

'Everything's fine,' Freya reassured him. 'I just . . . I have some things I wanted to know about Cora. She messaged me but she's not answering her phone.'

'You know your mother, Freya. If she doesn't want to talk, she won't. Is it important?'

'It's the research I'm doing about her.'

'What's that for?' asked Leo warily.

'It started out as something my therapist suggested I could do, as a way of exploring where Cora ended and I began.'

'I see,' he replied, but in a tone that conveyed that, as with many things to do with Cora, he did not see at all.

'It's turning into a kind of visual biography. *Self / (M)Other* is what I'm calling it.'

'*Trouble in Paradise* might be a better title if it's your mum,' Leo sighed. 'She's given you more than your fair share of trouble.'

Freya thought about the last time she had been home, when her mother had driven over the stray cat. That had been both their faults, though. Neither of them paying attention, because of the questions that Freya had asked about the girl in the yellow bikini and what her mother was doing with those images, that were obscene, just like the newspapers said they were. And they did look like her – because Freya looked so like Cora. That was nobody's fault, but everything had become so confused.

'The more Mum tells me, the less I feel I know.'

'That's Cora for you,' said Leo.

'Did she ever tell you why she never went back to South Africa?'

'She left after her parents were killed and she sold the farm,' he said. 'But she didn't speak of it much so I didn't bring it up.'

'You're not the best person at asking questions that might have difficult answers, Dad,' said Freya.

'There you have me.'

'When you met her, what was she like?'

Leo was quiet. Freya was used to her father's silences. There was no mystery to them; he was just a man who gathered his thoughts methodically. It took time.

'She was mesmerising,' said Leo at last, his voice filled with nostalgia. 'I went to a party at Lucian Villiers' gallery on a whim. Lucian had been telling everyone how he had discovered this savage little waif, living and painting in an abandoned warehouse – the same place as you're staying in now. There was such a crowd and she looked so lost. She asked me to walk her home, so I did. We walked for an hour or more through the empty London streets. It was beautiful – stars out. The moon. Your mother telling amusing stories. I felt like the luckiest man alive.' He sighed, then added, 'She can make you feel like that, can't she?'

'Yes,' said Freya. 'She can. She does. I think it's because she's the centre of her own universe.'

'Your shrink told you that?' asked Leo.

'Not exactly those words,' said Freya, turning slowly so that the images around her turned like a kaleidoscope. 'But something like that.'

'When we got there, Cora asked me to put her to bed. Then she asked if I would lie next to her and tell her a story. So I did, and she rested her head on my chest and said she felt less alone in the shelter of my arms. She didn't move all night and I didn't either, even though my arm went numb, because I didn't want to lose her.'

'Was she lonely?' Freya thought of her mother's fierce independence – how hard she could be, yet how fragile she was.

'I don't know,' Leo replied. 'I think she always wanted to have someone close – but she couldn't really stand being close to anyone, except for you.'

He fell silent. Freya could hear the crash of the waves on the shingle of the loch: the sound of home. 'Dad?' she prompted. 'Are you still there?'

'Sorry, Freya. Of course I am.'

'I miss us.' Freya thought of all the times she and Leo had waved goodbye to Cora as she got into a taxi or a car or on a ferry or a plane. Remembering how he would make them both toasties with extra cheese when they got home. How cosy it had been, just the two of them; how lonely she had been without her mother.

'I do too, and I'm sorry about everything. I meant it to be—' he broke off. 'I thought it would be different.'

'It's okay, Dad.'

'I miss you, Freya. I miss it all.' A dog barked at Leo's end of the line – three quick yips.

'Toby! Give him a pat for me.' There was a catch in her voice. He was her dog too – he had arrived on her fifteenth birthday.

'When I take him home – to Cora's, I mean,' Leo corrected himself, 'I'll see her then. Tell her to call you.'

'When will that be?'

'Toby's with us till Thursday.'

Us. Freya absorbed that. 'Don't worry,' she cut in. 'I'm sure I'll have spoken to Mum by then. I've got to go, Dad.' She ended the call. Her father was lost to her. His 'us' no longer meant her and Cora.

Freya's father's relationship with Kayla had made Cora incandescent with rage. Freya had heard them argue about it, lying under the apple tree outside the kitchen at Lawhead. Leo had heard Cora's anger, but Freya had sensed her mother's humiliation. Her shock. It did not seem to matter to Cora that the relationship had started after she had left Leo. It was the age gap that she could not stand. Freya had never heard her so distressed, but there had been nothing that she could say to her mother to comfort her. She had been shocked, too. It was true that there was no law that Leo had broken, but it disturbed Freya to think about her father and Kayla together being an 'us'. Kayla was only five years older than she was, and they had overlapped for a year at school. Freya had seen her in the same uniform she'd worn every day.

Freya's chest burned, but no tears came. She walked over to the bookshelf and ran her finger down the uncracked spine of her father's last book. He had self-published it years ago. No one had reviewed it. No one had read it. The attic at home was filled with unsold copies: her father eclipsed by her mother's brilliance, neither of them happy.

TWELVE

Angel finished up long after dark. She switched off the computers, rinsed the cups and locked up. When she clicked her fingers, Fournier's dog came to heel, falling into step behind her as she walked across the empty lot at the back of the wolf sanctuary. It was dark already and very cold – the temperature had plummeted that afternoon as the wind had risen. Both she and Trotsky slitted their eyes against the wind. She was glad of the dog's company as she walked into the trees behind the sanctuary that sheltered a tiny cottage. She unlocked the door and the dog slipped inside.

Trotsky was Angel's very first visitor. No other living creature had crossed the threshold into her little house before, but the dog sat down, perfectly at ease. Angel dropped her keys onto the table in the centre of the room that – thanks to her benefactor – she could call her own.

She did her habitual visual inventory. Everything was in its place: the pot-bellied stove, the rug between it and the bed. The ragged teddy bear propped up on the pillow, which was the only object she had brought with her from her previous life. The kitchen – just a kettle and a microwave oven next to the sink where she brushed her teeth. The table and chair in the centre of the room. Only when she was satisfied that nothing had been disturbed, did she take off her jacket and hang it on the hook behind the door.

Home was well insulated and warm, but most importantly, when she locked the door behind her, it was impenetrable. There were no pictures on the walls. No television set, no screens, no mirrors – and Angel always kept the curtains closed. It was a habit that had endured even though there was no one watching her any more, no slot in the door for a guard to pull back and check on her every hour, no cameras with their cold fisheyes recording her every move. As they had in the Girls' Progressive Reform Institute, the juvenile prison where she had been sent because the judge, who had kind eyes, had felt sorry for her. He had ruled that Angel should get a second chance even though she had stabbed the man in the belly, in the neck, in both eyes and in the back. That whiskery judge, as hunched over and hairy as a squirrel, had looked at Angel and said that even though he believed what she said, it was still murder. He had said that Angel was only fifteen and he was not surprised she'd turned out the way she had, considering her history. So he had sentenced Angel to three years' protective custody. Everyone – including Angel – had agreed it was the best she could have hoped for. *Lucky*, really.

Angel had not been an easy prisoner; despite being such a little thing she was prone to violence, so she spent most of her time in Solitary. It was the oldest and grimmest part of the facility, but it was quiet there and she didn't care about things like strip lighting or steel doors or the fact that in her room the radiator moaned and spat but, like old men without Viagra, produced no heat. No one interfered with her in Solitary and that was good enough for Angel.

The same could be said for this wolf sanctuary hut. It was a haven – warm, dry and impenetrable – and she had her benefactor to thank for it. Angel had met her on the day of her sentencing: a dark-haired woman with sunglasses and a suit so tailored it was like armour. Angel's lawyer had introduced them. 'This is Ms Hunter, Angel,' the lawyer said. 'She's your benefactor.'

Angel had not been familiar with that word.

'It's a person who gives money or help to someone else,' her lawyer explained. 'It means she pays my fees. It means she's got your back.'

Angel's lawyer had left her alone with Ms Hunter, who had skin so pale she could have been dead, but at least she did not have the look of a social worker or a cop or a shrink. She smiled when she sat down.

'You're not on your own any more, Angel,' she said. 'I want you to know that.'

'Thank you, ma'am,' Angel said, as her mother had taught her.

'I know what happened to you, Angel,' said Ms Hunter.

'I killed a man,' Angel replied, eyeing her.

'I know what you did. And I know why.' Ms Hunter took off her sunglasses. Her eyes were black and alive and focused on Angel, who saw herself mirrored in those dark eyes, and in that gaze everything that could not be said was spoken. No one had looked at Angel in that way since her mother had cupped her face in her hands and seen everything that was in her heart. 'I'm offering you a chance.'

'What's in it for you?' Angel asked.

'Nothing. I was like you once, and someone helped me, and I promised that, when I could, I would do the same.'

'What do you want?' Angel asked, disbelieving. No one did things for her unless they wanted something in return.

'I want you to be free,' came the reply.

'Three years,' said Angel. 'And I will be. The judge said so.'

'You'll be out of prison,' Ms Hunter said. 'But it will be a long time before you're free.'

Angel folded her arms. She had taught herself never to think into the future, because it held nothing for her. Ms Hunter seemed to know that.

'When you're released,' she told her, 'there will be a passport, money and a vehicle waiting for you. My foundation will help you find work and a room of your own. You take this.' Ms Hunter gave Angel a card with her name and a phone number embossed on one side. 'If you need help, you come to me. But I trust that you will find your own way in the world.'

To Angel's surprise, Ms Hunter had been true to her word. When she'd reached the end of her time at the Institute there had been a car, a new passport and a bankcard for an account that had enough money for what Ms Hunter termed 'emergencies'. There had also been a letter from Tina confirming the position Angel had asked for as a volunteer at the wolf sanctuary. All Angel needed to do was to check in with her benefactor at the prescribed intervals.

She lit a fire in the wood-burning stove and soon the flames were licking at the little glass window. She put a blanket on the floor and Trotsky curled up on it. Only then did she shift her bed and lift the loose floorboard. She reached in and took out the box she kept hidden there. She opened it and removed the photograph of herself as a child, curled like a cat on her mother's lap. The two of them sprawled on the loveseat on the verandah of their house in Ramsdale.

She propped the photo up on the bedside table so that her mother could watch over her as she removed the folder that lay beneath it. Inside the folder were the notifications that the police had sent through about her case. She opened the file where she kept the information she had gleaned about what had been done to her. She had a list of names. Yves Fournier's name was on top. She turned the page. Next was a news clipping of a photograph of him, his face that of a man who took from people what he wanted, discarded what he did not. She reread the statement Fournier's lawyer had presented to the court, even though she could have recited it.

He'd lost himself. That's what he had said. It wasn't an excuse, but it was understandable, perhaps, after what he'd gone through – the loss of the company he'd built up with his eye for talent. An investor who'd turned hostile had sidelined him. It did things to a man – not an excuse, of course – and what was it, after all? A picture of a clothed person. A drawing – art, really – and what was permissible shifted through the ages. A crisis in his life and he had made an error that many innocent men make. An error for which he was truly sorry. For the pain it had caused and the upset and the effect on his loyal wife and his beloved children, his grandchildren. To whom he was devoted, of course. A family man, and they had stood by him. Look how they had stood by him. That was what the judge had believed. He had believed because he had wanted to. Perhaps he had looked at Fournier and seen himself. Angel knew the truth.

She thrust the papers aside and watched the fire. Tracking was a science. She had a method and a sequence that required precision and focus. It was what she was good at. It kept her alive. She had to hold on to the task she'd set herself of tracking down Yves Fournier, and she was certain she had missed something. She had watched Fournier push out onto the snow so many times. She had paid such close attention to detail. What was it that she was not seeing?

Angel thought about the vehicle she had seen on the monitor. The woman getting out of it. A woman who was not Nina Fournier. Angel had business to settle with Fournier before she could leave this cold place. She ordered her thoughts by running through the day as if it were a film. She slowed it down and speeded it up, but could not rid herself of the feeling that something crucial remained out of focus. She thought about how few traces the woman had left. What should she look for? It was not always easy to find a woman who was not trying to hide; to find a woman who had reason to hide could be impossible. This shadow woman occupied Angel's thoughts. She had been so focused on her list of men that she had not considered a woman. The men, Angel knew. The men she understood; the women she did not.

She could not think about what the women knew and what they chose not to know because that brought her to the brink of questions about her dead mother – Charly-pronounced-Sharly. Those were questions for which Angel had no answers. There must have been things Charly had not seen because she had not known she was looking at them. Angel knew too well that most things were hidden in plain sight. Once, she had been one of those things.

She must have made a sound because Trotsky lifted her head and fixed her pale blue eyes on Angel's face and whined softly. She put an arm around the dog, burying her fingers in the thick ruff of fur around her neck. She rubbed behind her ears, along the back of her neck where her fur was shorter . . .

Angel's fingers stopped in their tracks. Trotsky's harness. She always had it on when Fournier took her skiing, but it wasn't on her now and it hadn't been when the city woman had brought her in. That city woman, her fur-wrapped arms tight around her body, would have said if she'd had it. The harness. Angel had seen it. She was sure she had. She just could not place the memory, but it had to be in Fournier's cabin. Before it was light, she would go up there again and see what else she had overlooked. She lay down next to the dog and pulled her quilt over both of them, listening to the wind howl through the trees. The wolves answered its call. The half-breeds in their kennels joined in, and Trotsky, asleep against her body, stirred, and was still again. It was a long while before Angel slept.

THIRTEEN

Daylight was fading when Cora caught the ferry across the Clyde. She took shelter in the cabin, watching the familiar shoreline advance. The village of Kilcreggan came into view: the stone houses where the lights were starting to come on, the pub, the school which Freya had attended when they had all moved up here from London like a family from a storybook. The mother, the father, the child, the dog. It seemed so long ago now that she, Freya and Leo had come up to Scotland for that holiday. It had been as if they were trying to escape themselves, but Cora had fallen in love with the austere embrace of this rocky peninsula on the west of Scotland the first time she had seen it.

'Let's come and live here,' she'd said. 'Start anew.'

Leo had said it would be a good idea to get away from London. He'd thought that it would be a good place for him to write and, in the beginning, Cora had held on to that hope. It had taken her a long time to think of the contours of lochs and mountains – seabirds circling above the rippling grey water flecked with silver, the sailing boats with their white sails like butterfly wings on the dark water – as home.

Leo's book had not sold and he stopped writing new ones. When he stopped writing, he seemed to stop altogether – he certainly did not look for a new way of earning money. When she brought it up with him his gaze would shift so he wasn't quite looking her in the eye, and he would say there were 'projects' in the pipeline. There weren't of course, but because she was successful and Leo seemed to have the best intentions, she never knew how to hold him to account, not then, when she still loved him, when she still believed in him. So her family's survival had depended on what she made as an artist, and that had felt too precarious a way to keep putting food on the table. The burden of providing for all of them, always. The pretence that she wasn't doing it all, that Leo was part of the marital effort, that he held up his half of the sky, was hard to bear. The fear that they would lose the house gnawed at her happiness until it was gone. Cora, so unable to ask for help, so unpractised at vulnerability, had asked Leo to help her by earning money, but he had stared straight through her and done nothing.

She'd had no idea what to do in the face of Leo's paralysis, but it had dissolved her faith in him. The tender cord she had called love and that had tethered her to him snapped; without it there to hold her steady, Cora was adrift. Despite that, the end of her marriage had seemed to come without warning. It had been a sunny spring morning and she had been packing for another trip. Her nightdress lay across the unmade bed and when she picked it up, she noticed that there were two worn patches on the bed sheet. One where Leo's body had lain night after night, one where hers had. When she saw that white abyss between them, she could no longer bear the loneliness of this silent marriage. She went down to Leo's study to tell him.

He was sitting at his desk, the objects on it arranged in a facsimile of activity. The line of his shoulders caught at her heart and she wavered, putting her hands on those stooping shoulders and drawing them straight, bringing his body into hers. She leaned over him and rested her chin on the top of his head and breathed in, but she could no longer stand the smell of him.

'I can't go on, Leo,' she said. Those words spoken aloud shocked her as much as they did Leo. 'What we had . . . it's gone.'

'You're here,' he said, quietly. 'I'm here.' He put his hands onto hers.

'You're not,' she shook her head. 'I have felt so alone.'

'What do you want me to do?' His voice was hollow, as if he were speaking to her from the bottom of a well.

Find work, she wanted to say. *Take care of me. Write. Come back to life. Finish your stories. Fight for me. Know my secrets without me having to find the words for them.* But it was too late to say any of that.

'It's too late, I think,' is what she said instead.

'I've loved you,' he said. 'I've done my best.'

As if that was enough. As if that was anything, Cora thought. Their faces were reflected together in the window above Leo's desk, tenderness and incomprehension in equal measure in his eyes. She waited for him to stop her, to say he would bear the burden of being alive with her, but he said nothing. The moment was gone and she felt momentarily relieved of a great weight. As if he was a drowning man whose arms she had just prised from around her neck, she felt herself shooting towards the surface – away from him and back towards life.

'I'm going to be away for a week,' she said. 'It'll be best if you're gone when I get back.' She had not planned to say that, but once the words were out of her mouth she could not call them back. He did not argue with her. He did not fight for her, either. Instead, he asked, 'Have you told Freya?'

'No,' she responded. Freya, the thread that had woven their family together. She could not bear the thought of delivering that blow to her daughter. 'We made her; we love her. That won't change.'

There were tears in Leo's eyes then. There had also been, she reflected now, looking out at the choppy grey water, a look of relief on his face. Whatever it was, he had let her hands go and she had slipped from the airless embrace of their marriage.

The divorce was quickly done. 'A new start,' the silver-haired lawyer had told her when she signed the papers. It had not felt that way to Cora; she had felt as if she was at the funeral of something that she had killed. 'You'll soon meet someone new. An attractive woman like you. Still in your prime. And you have your career. Quite stellar, by all accounts.'

The ferry bumped up against the stone jetty, tossed by the waves. She scrambled off the boat, queasy from the crossing. It was dark already and only the Costcutter was open. There would be nothing to eat at home so she rifled through its meagre offerings.

'Have you just come off the ferry?' Fiona, the girl behind the cash register smiled when Cora placed the basket on the counter.

'Hi, Fiona.' Cora smiled. The girl had been at school with Freya. 'I have.'

'Welcome back, then. Leo was in this afternoon with Toby.' Fiona scanned Cora's items. 'We were saying how we remembered him as a puppy at your house. That party when he ate Freya's birthday cake – that beautiful chocolate one.'

'Oh, God, I had forgotten that. It took me an hour to ice. One minute for him to wolf down.'

'Tell Freya not to be such a stranger next time she's here,' Fiona said as Cora picked up her bag. 'I saw her get off the ferry a while ago but she never came in to say hello.'

'I'll tell her. It was a bit rushed the last time.' Cora hurried out of the shop, her thoughts filled with the last time Freya had been home. Freya had stepped off the ferry and into Cora's open arms, as she always did on her return. Cora had held her tight: her firm young body a comfort – as it always had been – the familiar smell of her child, there beneath the perfume and the smoke. But Freya had pulled away abruptly and said that the police had been to interview her.

That drive home had been difficult. Freya's incomprehension at what the tabloids said Cora had done to her with her paintings was unbearable. Cora had tried to explain herself, but she had failed. She knew what she had done. That she had not intended harm made no difference, because she could no longer convince herself of her own innocence.

It had been a relief to turn into the driveway and to see Toby running towards the car, yipping in delight at Freya's return as if nothing had changed.

They'd only heard the mewling, high-pitched as an infant's, when Cora had switched off the engine. Freya, who had climbed out to open the gate, dropped down on her belly to check. The kitten was trapped under the wheel, but she still managed to slash Freya's face with desperate claws. Undeterred, Freya had put both hands on the little animal, its heart rapid-firing against her palms as Cora inched the car back and set it free.

Freya had held out the tiny creature while Cora checked it, the two of them crouched side by side. Its back leg was dislocated, but Cora had deftly returned the bone to its socket. 'She'll be fine,' Cora had said. 'Just hold her against your heart.'

Freya had wrapped the kitten in her scarf, lifted up her top and placed it on her skin. They had gone inside. The kitten had struggled, but its terror was fading and after a while it burrowed deeper under Freya's jersey and was still. Cora had wiped the bloody scratches on her daughter's wrists. 'This little cat we can save,' she had said.

'Will you keep her for me?' Freya had asked, tears in her eyes.

'That I can do,' Cora had promised. She had broken so many things, but this kitten was one thing she could fix for her daughter. Freya had named her Kit-Kat and she had been their unspoken truce. Later, when they had gone up to the studio as was their habit, Freya had settled herself and the wounded kitten by the fire, far away from the jealous Toby whining on the other side of the door.

Cora's was the only vehicle left in the small parking lot. She got it started after a couple of tries and drove along the road that hugged the contour of the hills. She took the sharp bend in the road and there was Lawhead. Her house built from golden stone. It had generous sash windows and a forest of chimneys on the roof. It had been a farmhouse once, and there were outbuildings behind it.

The curtains were all open and it made the house look naked, open to any gaze. She tried to shake that thought – she had always loved that she could move from room to room and look out onto her garden and then the loch beyond. She scanned the illuminated triangle cast by her headlights. There was no evidence that anyone had been here since she left.

She got out, opened the gate, and drove up to the house and switched off the engine. Opening the car door, she listened to the night. Wind. The roar of the harried waves on the shingle. The eerie cry of a fox. Nothing human. Only then did she grab her bags and hurry towards the dark house.

She opened the kitchen door and reached for the switch. Warm light flooded her kitchen. Everything was as she had left it: the glasses and plates in the sink, the tea towel over the draining board. She was home. The danger was behind her. Here, she should have felt safe, yet the skin between her shoulder blades twitched. She put her bags down on the floor, locked the door behind her and closed the blinds. She went to check that the front door was locked, then she switched on all the lights and began to close all the curtains.

In Freya's room, the dark window mirrored Cora's face back at her. The sharp features, the green eyes – it could have been her daughter's face. Yves had called Freya Cora's mirror, the first time she'd shown him a picture of her. He had asked her if she thought of Freya as a younger version of herself, with a shot at a life she had not led. His question had made her uneasy and she had said no, absolutely not, that she saw Freya as her own person. Now she wasn't sure if that had been the truth.

She unhooked the thick velvet curtains from the tiebacks and hid her daughter's bedroom from view, dislodging a picture from the pin board that was next to them as she did so. Cora picked it up. It was a shot of Freya – eleven years old, honey-skinned, perched on a rock on a Greek beach, the sea deep blue behind her. She looked so delicate – a fledgling perched on the cusp of adolescence – wearing the bikini Cora had bought for her in the market. It was canary yellow, like Cora's first bikini had been – the costume she had used for the paintings she had taken from the gallery. Culpability pierced her as surely as if it were a blade. She let the picture of her daughter drop from her fingers.

Back in the kitchen, she lit the Aga, opened her bag and pulled out the stained clothes she had taken off in the gas station bathroom. She shoved them into the machine and watched the water in the drum blush pink before it ran clear. Now that she was home, she felt the pain in her body – the abrasions, already healing, on her skin. The bruises purpling. The ache in her bones to do with loss as well as blows.

Supper, she needed supper, even though she had no appetite, because meals were the rhythm of normal life: coffee in the morning, wine at night, food in between. This was how days were anchored, how madness was held at bay, so she made toast and scrambled eggs, which she could not eat. She poured herself a glass of wine instead. That, she managed to drink, sitting with her back to the stove with Toby's empty basket beside her. Divorce had split everything – teaspoons, motor vehicles, money – between her and Leo, with scalpel precision. Even the dog was divided, which meant that Leo arrived every second week to fetch Toby.

Cora longed for Toby, but she was too proud to phone Leo

and tell him she needed the dog now. She could not bear to hear him say again that it was her fault that the house was empty. She could not bear that Kayla might answer Leo's phone. She took another gulp of wine. The fact that Leo's new girlfriend was practically Freya's age made her feel sick, as did the memory of their fight about it.

'She's so young, this girl,' she had hissed, knowing that Freya was somewhere in the house and not wanting her to hear this.

'Kayla's a grown woman—' Leo had protested.

'She's hardly five years older than Freya. They were at the same school. It makes me sick.'

'Why do you warp everything, Cora? You make out that I'm a monster. You make men into monsters. What's wrong with you?'

'You erase the woman I became by being involved with this' – her voice had been ice, but it had broken nonetheless –'with this spectre of a girl. That's all you wanted in me. It's all you want in her, this poor little Kayla.'

'These things happen all the time—'

'That never made anything bearable.' She had pushed him out of the kitchen and slammed the door on him. 'It's all men want, the ghost of girls.'

She had looked out of the window when she finally heard the crunch of the gravel and his car starting. That was when she had seen Freya lying under the apple tree, her eyes fixed on her closed book.

Cora finished her wine, hugged her knees to her chest and wished again for Toby's warm, shaggy presence as she listened to the familiar sounds of the old house settling itself around her. Mentally, she checked off the sounds. The pipes ticked because the plumbing was old; the boiler hummed as it refilled. An owl called, and in the distance, its mate answered. A loose gutter cracked against the house – it always did that when the wind blew from the west. She scanned for other noises, but the silence beyond those familiar sounds was as taut as skin and she was afraid. She put her glass in the sink, ran upstairs and locked herself into her bedroom. She stripped off her clothes and, leaving only the key round her neck, scrubbed herself in the hot shower. After that, she fell into bed and sleep took her without warning.

FOURTEEN

I t was eerily quiet when Angel woke. The wind had dropped. The dog was warm, curled up against her back, but the fire was out and the smell of cold ash filled the room. The same smell as there had been in Fournier's cabin. With the smell, the feeling she'd had yesterday of looking at something that she couldn't quite see returned. Angel got up and dressed. When she opened the door, the cold hit her like a cleaver. A pair of headlights sliced through the darkness on the other side of the fence, then vanished. She waited, but they did not return and then, with Trotsky at her heels, she got into her truck. It was four-thirty when she reached Fournier's cabin.

There were no lights on inside and no vehicles visible, although the porch had been cleared of snow and a shovel leaned against the wall next to the back door. She tried the door, and it was still unlocked so she pushed it open. Trotsky ran past her. As soon as she was in the hallway, the dog let out a long, lupine call. After that there was silence. Angel stood still, getting her bearings. There was a faint whiff of blocked drains. She listened. The grandfather clock ticked. Apart from that, there was no sound. The house felt different, however – no one in it and yet it did not feel empty. It smelled of the men who had been in it and of the cigarettes they had smoked.

Trotsky sat down on the trapdoor to the basement. She made a low pleading sound in the back of her throat. Angel leaned over her to get to the hooks filled with outdoor gear. She lifted off the jackets, searching for the dog's harness. No sign of it.

She looked through the rack of boots and shoes. No sign there either, but when she shone her torch underneath, she saw a tongue of leather. Angel tugged at it and the harness emerged in her hands. She held it out to Trotsky. The dog cocked her head to one side and gave it a lick.

'He didn't take you with him, did he, girl?' she said to the dog. 'Did he just throw you out of the car and leave you to fend for yourself?'

Trotsky looked guilty, as if she had done something. 'It's not your fault.' Angel patted her head and the dog whined and turned round and round on the floor. 'And it's not your fault you can't tell me where they went.'

They.

Angel stood up. The woman, whoever she was, she was part of it. She had to be. She went through the house again, checking each room in the order in which she had searched the first time. The bedroom was the same as before, except the bed had been made. She searched the other bedrooms again. In one she found a hairgrip under the bed, but there was no way to know how long it had lain there.

She checked the bathroom cupboards again – the same as before. When she closed them, she looked at her reflection in the cracked mirror above the basin. Putting her hand into her pocket, she pulled out the mascara she had found the first time. She applied the mascara, then stared at herself in the mirror. Bambi lashes. Hers was a girl's face, with the mole on her cheekbone that her mother had always kissed and called her *beauty spot*. The mouth, the eyes, the fucking heart-shaped face that made men grip her chin in their hands. The memory of it took her breath away, but she stopped herself from punching the glass that had her face in it. She rinsed off the mascara and watched the water drain slowly away. The primitive plumbing in the basement gurgled in protest.

She went through to the living room. It was unchanged. The bowl of sugar was still on the table. So were the newspapers and the bills and the laptop. The DVD player in the bookshelf winked its red eye at her. Angel ducked the desperate monkey hanging from the ceiling and pressed eject. *Annie Hall* popped out. Angel pushed it back in again and, as she did so, she toppled a stack of novels listing on the shelf. A girl's eyes, half hidden by a book, stopped Angel in her tracks. It was a tiny painting and it compelled Angel to go up close to look at the girl in it. She removed the books to reveal a painting. A child. A girl in a yellow bikini. The rage shuttered behind the girl's painted green eyes made the fine hairs on the back of Angel's neck stand on end. She knew her. She had *been* her.

Revealing her like this made Angel into a voyeur. She was looking at things that should not be looked at.

The girl was sitting cross-legged on a vivid green lawn. Her top was askew, revealing one swollen pink nipple on a flat brown chest, and she was twisting a silver butterfly on a chain tight as a garrotte around her neck. The light was a blade in her eyes. The heat of that distant sun blistered Angel's skin, while she shivered as if she had a fever. The eyes of the girl in the yellow bikini had questions in them that Angel could not answer. The need to escape, to get away from her mute entreaty was overwhelming, and she stacked the books in front of the girl's face again. She felt as if she were burying her. And then the vertigo started. Her mind spinning her away, removing her from where she was, lifting her out of her own body. It had been a survival strategy, but she could not allow it now – the girl in this picture was not her.

Breathe, breathe. She had to remember to breathe. In and out. *Be mindful of the breath and the fear will pass. If the fear goes, so will the rage.* She had been taught this in the quiet therapy room with the barred windows that squared the sky. Breathe in and out. Hold the past at bay. Don't let time collapse. In and out. In and out. Stay with yourself. Stay here. Fight. But it was only when she dug her nails deep enough into the skin on the inside of her wrist to draw blood that it stopped.

The pain halted the spin and brought her back to Fournier's cabin. Back to herself. She removed the books and lifted the little painting off the shelf. The tense thighs, between them, the narrow waist, the triangle of yellow fabric stretched over the pink-skinned nipple showing that puberty was coming at her like a train. The artist had to have seen it, to know it too. Angel picked it up. The signature was indecipherable, a sinewy scrawl that could have said anything. Angel turned it around. The writing on the back was a fluid crimson scrawl. *THE GIRL, for Yves, a private view.* ♥ *Cora*

The silence in the cabin was absolute, except for Trotsky circling the floor in the hallway, her claws making metronymic clicks that made it impossible for Angel to think. She had to get out, but she had to take this girl, this familiar girl, with her, and get them both out of this place.

She slipped the small painting inside her jacket and opened the door. The dog refused to follow her out. There was a bag of dog food in the kitchen and Angel gave Trotsky some. When she picked up the bag, the reluctant dog padded after her. She locked the door and returned the key and walked down the hill, the painting hard-edged against her ribs as she walked. She moved with care, as if it were an explosive she carried. It was hard to breathe, even though she was now out of the cabin, which made it hard to think. But she had to think, not to feel. So much was at stake. So much careful planning had come undone. Angel opened the truck, tossed the dog food in. Trotsky jumped after it and she closed the door behind them both.

The day had started with a sullen gash of grey, low in the eastern sky. She started the truck, but the wheels spun in the snow. She thought she heard a chopper in the distance, but it was hard to tell because the wind was up. It was time to get out of here. She tried once more, and this time she got the vehicle clear of the drift and her mind clear of panic. As she drove down the track, she touched the St Christopher medallion on the dashboard. His mission, as a patron saint, was to look out for travellers. Hers was to track down Fournier, a man with reasons to disappear, wherever he had gone.

FIFTEEN

Cora spread her hands out as if to brace herself against a fall, but her fingers found velvet instead of the ice of which she had been dreaming. Her heart was pounding as if she were still running through the blinding snow, but when she opened her eyes she saw that it was her green dressing gown clutched in her hands. She sat up, disorientated, but filled with relief. This was her bed. Then she noticed streaks of blood on the sheets. The gash on her wrist had bled in the night. The injury was proof that it was not a nightmare - Yves and his cold and dark and ice - that she had escaped. Cora shivered and pulled the blanket closer. This wound, caused by the terrified dog, the only evidence of how hard she had fought at the end. She adjusted the bandage and wrapped the green velvet dressing gown around herself. If this injury marked the end of things, then she had to settle on a beginning: that hotel room in a small town east of Belgrade, where the scars left by war were hidden by sunlight the colour of honey.

Cora had been invited there because there was to be an Art for Justice fundraising auction for the women who had asked Cora to work with them to make a monument – something beautiful – in that place where they had suffered so much. She had been so lonely there. Her divorce from Leo had left her so hollowed out that she felt weightless. Such easy prey, in that Eastern European hotel room where she had gone after she had lost the thread of meaning and purpose that had stitched her life together. She had not known how to go on any more, and she had felt so alone with the sharp new razor lying next to the bath, the sleeping pills in her toiletry bag. She had counted the pills. There were enough, but however much she wanted a way out, she could not break the promise she had made to Freya that no matter how often she went away, she would always return.

That was a promise Cora could not break and so, instead of swallowing the pills, she had reached for her phone. *Hotel rooms*, she'd tweeted into the insomniac internet, *make everybody feel welcome and no one feel at home.*

Why are you awake? Yves Fournier's reply had come as quick as a dart, as poisonous as one too, but she had mistaken it for a lifeline so she had grabbed at it because she was going under. He had liked a few of her posts before, but the unexpectedness of this man, with his reputation as a discerning curator, contacting her, was flattering.

Can't sleep, she had written.

Why not? This came as a direct message and so it was just for her. *I've been watching your tweets,* he wrote. *Reading between those short lines and you seem . . . undefended.*

Cora had felt exposed by this disconcerting intimacy, but she was comforted. He had seen her and the idea of his gaze on her was an unexpected solace. *It's the work I do,* she wrote. She couldn't tell him the truth.

Send me your number, he messaged. *I can text you then. More old-fashioned. More . . . intimate?*

She hesitated only for a moment. She knew him – not that well, but they were part of the same professional world. She had met him at a dinner Lucian Villiers had given. Yves Fournier, well respected collector and curator, had shown a keen interest in her work. In her. He had a reputation for power and influence in parts of the world where she was a stranger. That fleeting desire she had felt that evening and then forgotten, returned.

She sent him her mobile number. A minute later and there was a text.

You spoke in London about Scheherazade. You said you painted for the same reason that Scheherazade told stories to that murderous sultan she married. To stay alive. That stayed with me. You're messaging me, so you must be alive – so you must be painting.

I am alive, wrote Cora. *And I'm painting.*

I'm on my way to the Art for Justice auction in Serbia.

Cora was surprised. *I didn't know you were that involved.*

Behind the scenes, Yves typed back. *Donations from wealthy clients. I saw you would be there and I thought, as I was in Europe, why not. More tomorrow, but I'll see you there.*

Yes. She was a moth to a flame. *You will.*

Sleep now x Y.

Cora had been happy to obey. She felt that Yves Fournier had caught her falling. It was such a wonder to be held that she slept after he had told her to, for the first time in months.

In the morning, she checked her phone before she was properly awake and she was rewarded.

I didn't sleep, thinking of you, Yves had texted.

It was so unguarded that it disconcerted Cora. *I must be less sensitive than you then . . . I slept well.*

On instruction?

Yes.

What will you do today?

There was a massacre here, she responded. *A group of survivors invited me to come and help them find a way to memorialise it.*

Making things of violence, breath and memory, he wrote. *You're so good at it. You'll do it perfectly.*

His attention, his presence even before she was awake, had given her a buoyancy that got her up and dressed and into the postcard-pretty square. The cobbles were covered with delicate blossoms. Blackbirds called. An onion-domed church. There were tables outside cafes, and red geraniums in the sunshine. A carpet of blossom. New leaves luminous in the sunlight. There was no trace of the carnage that had taken place here.

An interpreter took Cora to meet the women. There were ten of them. They told Cora their names and one by one they recounted what had happened. The jagged words of their story were ill-suited to the pretty interpreter's mouth.

'The men and the boys were taken from us.'

'The soldiers held the girls down.'

'One little girl would not stop screaming. They shot her.'

'They made us dig a grave. The soil was soft, so it was easy.'

119

'She was my daughter. They made me throw her in there.'

'But we survived.'

'There is a break in my heart. I want to knit it together again.'

'When it happened, we could hide nothing, not even our bodies.'

'The soldiers made us take off our shoes so we could not run.'

'We kept the shoes of those who were killed that night. This was all that remained in the square, these shoes were our witnesses.'

The women set out the shoes. Brown and black and white. In the centre, a child's single black shoe conjured the ghost of a plump infant leg.

The sun was warm on their backs as Cora and the women set to work together to make a mobile, as finely balanced as any by Alexander Calder. Removing one shoe would have meant that the whole structure would unhinge. The woman who had buried her daughter began to sing softly and the others joined her, their requiem for what had died in them during that long, violent night; their voices filling the fine, sunny room where they hung the installation.

Cora switched her phone on when they were finished and the message she received from Yves felt like a caress. *How did it go? Thought of you today.*

She sent him a picture.

It's beautiful, what you do.

It was moving, replied Cora. *Their faith in a process I don't believe in any more.*

He replied at once. *Why don't you believe?*

When I started I believed that if I spent enough time in the presence of evil, I could absorb it, disperse it, stop the pain by making beauty out of the shattered remnants. I was wrong. There is no healing; there is no end to the pain. It just has to be endured.

You think too much, wrote Yves. *Be careful. Tomorrow. I'll find you. I'll make you laugh.* The flippancy of the message jarred a little, but she was tired and unmoored and she had mistaken her unease for anticipation.

A driver had picked her up and driven her to the Art for Justice auction. Cora's sleekly suited host was waiting for her in the crowded reception room. He hoped she liked the way her paintings had been hung with the mobile the women had made. He was honoured that she was in attendance. It meant the world that she was here. He introduced her to the men with the money, to their young mistresses in short dresses and the vigilant wives in longer ones. He held her hand and told her how hard it was to make a return on investment in art, how hard it was to sell anything at the moment – but that this would sell. This would make sure that the terrible events were commemorated. They all wanted that so that they could move on and live for the future. He talked until Cora's head ached. It was a relief to be ushered onto the platform.

Cora spoke of the courage of the women she had worked with that past week. About what had been done to them by the men with guns who'd come here in the night and separated them from their families. She spoke of how the soldiers had ranked the women by age – the youngest a little girl of three, the oldest ninety – and had done to them what men have done throughout history to women in order to prove to themselves that they have power.

She said that the women had also done what women throughout history had done – they had survived. Some of them had been able to love again; all of them had had to find ways to live with memory and forgetting: one of the ways being to make beauty out of what had been broken. She paused, and there was no sound in the warm room except for the repetitive metallic click that the mobile made as it swayed in the breeze. Her audience looked up at the shoes – a ballet slipper, boots, high-heeled yellow sandals.

'Art,' said Cora, and they turned to look at her once more, 'is like the legendary mirror that Perseus used so that he could look at the Gorgon and survive it. Art – making things – is a way to look at horror and survive. That's what artists do. We make things that can be viewed, when looking at the original would turn us to stone. That original is all around us – the violent get away with things because they are prepared to hurt and kill. People who do the damage are almost always free and they live amongst us. But art reminds us – and warns them – that some of us do live to tell the tale. Art can be a form of revenge because it says to the perpetrators: *You did not destroy beauty: that thing in me, in all of us, that makes us human.*'

There was a brief silence when she finished speaking, but then her host clapped and so did everyone else, and the waiters brought trays with champagne and the auctioneer opened the bidding, the buyers clustered and she was free to move away.

'There you are.' She turned to see Yves Fournier coming towards her, a look of pure delight on his face. 'You were wonderful. Art as a way of slaying the Medusa – that was so well put.'

'A bit short, perhaps,' said Cora. In his presence she felt unsure of herself. It was not a feeling to which she was accustomed. She picked up another glass of champagne to give herself confidence.

'These people are here to drink, not to think,' he said. 'Your job is to tell the story of violence and living to tell the tale. To convert art into money.'

'No,' protested Cora. 'That was never my intention.'

'And yet you did that perfectly – making a living from what you create.' Yves took her arm and steered her towards the balcony. 'Now look what I've laid on for you.' The stars were pale, but the lights along the river glittered in the somnolent water.

'How wonderful to be outside.' Cora breathed out. 'I felt like my head would explode in there.'

'I could see.' Yves pointed inside and said, looking at her questioningly, 'That painting of yours.'

The six trees, the bench in their circle of shade, the green-eyed girl wearing khaki shorts and nothing else, her feet dirty and her knees scuffed, standing in the gap in the scrub, staring past the bench at the viewer. At her: Cora, looking back at herself aged eleven. The beginning of the things that had turned her into the woman she now was.

'One of my earliest. It's from *Paradise Lost*.'

'Wonderful. How old is the girl in the painting?'

'Eleven.'

'Savage,' Yves murmured. 'Vulnerable.'

'Neither,' Cora replied. 'Angry.'

'With whom?'

'Everything.'

'You caught the fire in her, Cora.'

'That's not fire you're looking at.' Cora turned away from the painting and looked at the starlit river. 'That's shame.'

'Shame.' He leaned so close to her when he asked the next question that she felt the heat of him. 'What does it do to a girl?'

'It makes her want to cross those lines which she had not known were there until the moment of her shaming,' she said quietly. 'It fills her with a helpless rage at her own body. That it is her body that draws a gaze, she never imagined until that moment. And then it's all she can imagine. She sees herself through the devouring eyes of another and she is lost to herself.'

'That's how it happened to you?'

'I think it's what happens to all girls.'

There was a flicker of desire in his eyes when he looked at her. 'You're interested in crossing the line?'

'I suppose I am,' she replied. He had a way of getting to the heart of her – as if he knew her better than she knew herself. She found herself saying things she'd rather not. 'But I know what my limits are.'

'Knowing where the limit is makes it tempting to try to break it,' said Yves. 'Trust me.'

'I'm not sure I trust you at all.'

Yves seemed to look through her and for a moment Cora felt naked before him, but she could not find in herself the desire to move out of sight, out of danger. Her dress was too light, too summery. The jacket he placed on her shoulders was thin, but she was less exposed.

'You're coming for dinner with me.' It was not a question.

They took a taxi back to the town square. They sat close. Cora's skin was alive, her hands restless, but she did not know how to reach across the divide of the seat between them and break the tension between them by touching him. Instead, she tucked her hands into the inner pockets of Yves' jacket. Her fingers brushed against a key on a chain. She drew it out, swinging it in the space between them. 'Is this the key to your heart?' she asked.

He took it from her abruptly and put it around his neck. The hostility was so fleeting that Cora thought she must have imagined it, because then he smiled and said, 'To the innermost gate in my mind, where no sensible woman would want to go. Pull over here,' he ordered the taxi driver.

They were back in the square with the cherry blossoms, where Yves led her to a cafe and ordered for both of them. Steak, bloody and rare.

She was famished, but she could not eat. She drank too much, instead, and he asked her questions and she told stories of the farm where she grew up. The indolence, the servants, the horses. He listened. Told her it was exotic. That she was exotic. He had no idea of the heat and the tedium and the bursts of violence that drove her away, but he was adept at listening. There was an unfamiliar warmth between her legs and she had no desire at all to turn away from the beam of his attention.

'You need to be taken care of,' said Yves.

'Will you do that for me, just for a while?'

'Of course.' He said it with such sincerity that Cora believed him. She felt light with the relief of putting the weight of responsibility for herself into the hands of another, and she mistook this unmooring for falling in love.

Yves talked of people he knew who would buy her art. He talked of collectors he knew who would be interested in what she did. The portraits. The intelligence of her work. Her acute perception. Cora let herself believe him. She was so tired of fighting, of doing everything on her own that she inclined her body towards his. She had seen other women do it just enough to make it clear what was on offer. It seemed so easy that Cora thought the terms would be hers.

It was past one when he paid, pushing her offered credit card back across the table. She put it in her bag and as she did so, she felt the small, perfectly knapped handaxe that she had taken from Eden the last time she was there. It was her last physical link to the land that had made her, her last piece of home. She took it out and weighed it in her hand for a moment. She did not need it any more. The warmth she felt with this man, the ease – she did not want to give it another word – wasn't that a kind of home?

'Take this instead,' she said, placing the handaxe in his palm.

It fitted his hand as if it had been made for him. He examined it carefully. 'This is something fine.'

'I've carried it with me since childhood,' said Cora.

'It's from the farm where you grew up?'

'Yes,' said Cora.

'How special,' said Yves, with a smile. 'I have a piece of the flinty girl you once were.' He closed his fist on it. 'Come,' he said. 'Let's walk.'

They bought cheap cigarettes from a kiosk just before it closed and walked through the empty streets. She did not notice the car coming too fast round the corner. Yves grabbed her and pulled her out of the way. It was the first time he'd touched her and he did not let go of her until they reached the hotel. They hesitated in the lobby, but Cora did not ask him to her room – she had not done this in so many years – and he did not follow her when she kissed him on the cheek and went upstairs.

Her phone vibrated as soon as she was back in her room. She texted back. He replied, she responded and he replied again. He was spinning a thread, ensnaring her, but he was funnier in a text than he was in person, less overwhelming, and he made her laugh. The messages were intimate, haiku-length compositions. None of them false, none of them true either. The seduction she could not pull off in his presence was accomplished, but it was she who was seduced.

At four he wrote, *You must sleep. I must sleep.* And he stopped texting. Cora was suspended. The sky was as black and as smooth as obsidian but she did not sleep. And then her taxi came. There was a flurry of messages on her phone when she reached the airport, photographs that faded from her phone seconds after she looked at them. There were more when her plane landed. More on the train that carried her back to her empty house. Less intimate in the daylight – clever things about politics and art and people they both knew.

Yves' intelligence matched hers, and his admiration of her creativity and intellectual vision – so different to Leo, who had turned away from her and then inwards – drew her in. He was a born curator. His critical eye was astute and practised. He understood her work. He knew what needed to be built up, what needed to be cut away. He had a sense for what would sell, just as a shark senses blood. *I will set you up here. It would be a scandal if someone else got you. I'll make it happen.*

When she got home after that trip, she stood naked in front of the mirror in the bathroom. The skin on her arm where he had pulled her out of the taxi's way was marked with four symmetrical fingertip bruises and a thumbprint. The ache when she placed her fingertips where his had been spread up her arm and through her body, taking possession of her.

Pain and love, for her, were so close as to be the same thing. That is what made the pain feel like release. Yves felt like home.

He conjured in her the desire to be moulded, to be bound, to capitulate, to step off the high wire of loneliness where her failed marriage had stranded her, and be absolved. To be contained. To be taken in. And she was. She read the hiero-glyphs printed on her skin as containment – Yves had arrested her fall. It felt like sanctuary and Cora had no desire to free herself from the voluptuous thrall. *At last*, was what her perverse skin whispered.

A thrush called outside Cora's bedroom just then, and she got up. The chill air nipped at her bare feet as she stood at the window and looked out at the dusting of snow on the leafless oak tree. The mountains on the far shore of the loch were etched against the sky and the near shore beckoned. If Toby were with her, she would take him for a walk on the shingle.

Just then, she saw a solitary man walking beside the loch. He was tall and spare, his red anorak the same colour as the skiing jacket Yves wore. For a dizzying moment she took it to be him. But it could not be. It could not be Yves. He would not come here, even if he could. She reached for the key hanging around her neck.

She had not worn anything around her neck since she had lost her butterfly pendant, an heirloom her mother had given her, when she was twelve. Her hawk-eyed mother had asked where the necklace was, but Cora had not been able to explain the circumstances of its loss even to herself, so she had said she did not know. If she closed her eyes, she would be back in the past. She would see it falling again, the sun catching the silver filigree wings so that it became, for a moment, a living thing vanishing down that deep dark well, but she kept her eyes wide open so as not to short-circuit the march of time.

No good came of being unable to distinguish what had happened this week from what had happened decades ago, this blur between the past and the present.

Cora only let the key go when the man in the red jacket disappeared into the trees at the end of the shingle. The key was for a door she would not be opening again, even though to free herself, she needed to inventory the secrets hidden behind it. After that, she searched through the drawers in her dressing table, collecting the detritus that was left after the end of an affair. Love tokens turned memento mori.

She felt lighter, cleaner, as she placed each thing, each tawdry thing, into a box. She put the bundle of miniature paintings she had taken from the gallery in last, then she dressed as if for an expedition and walked up to her studio.

SIXTEEN

Angel arrived back at the wolf sanctuary as the sun crept upwards on its low arc over the horizon. Tina's truck wasn't there, so she could go straight to her house. Trotsky slipped in after her and lay down on the mat, keeping her eyes fixed on Angel as if she sensed her distress. Angel locked and bolted the door behind her. She leaned the painting she had taken from Fournier's cabin against the cereal box on the kitchen table and sat down in front of it.

Angel took out her phone and photographed the painting. The girl's gaze filled her with impotent anger; she recognised that look in her painted green eyes. It was the same expression Angel saw in her own eyes when she looked in a mirror.

She had learned to hide it, but she felt a sisterhood of shame beneath the defiance. Angel put her phone down, her hands shaking.

Shame and defiance. Angel burned with those feelings now as she had done when she was twelve and the lodger, whom her mother had loved so blindly, had watched all the time – without her mother noticing, but Angel had felt it. His eyes on her had made her shiver as if he were brushing his fingertips over her skin. He had watched her, photographed her and sketched her because he was an artist, or so he said. It had been a relief when Charly had decided to send her to summer camp.

Angel had loved the road trip up there in Charly's battered old car, the two of them laughing and listening to the radio and watching the country roll past the windows of the car. They had stopped at a gas station in the middle of nowhere. That was where her mother had bought the bear with the tacky satin heart stitched onto its chest. Angel fetched it from her bed now and held it close. How could she have known then that this bear – who would be her companion and her only witness – would be her mother's last gift to her? How could she have known that its little satin heart – so pleasant to stroke – would be her last connection with her mother?

At that summer camp there had been no TV and no mobile phones. There had been swimming and singing and a boy Angel had liked. He had kissed her, putting the tip of his tongue into her mouth. The sensation had made her want to throw up, but at the same time it rippled electricity across her skin. Angel – so used to being her mother's keeper, the two of them always each other's only company – could stop worrying about Charly, because her mother wasn't alone now.

She was like the other mothers in the small town now, with its white church and elms and everyone doing things in twos at the weekends.

Her mother sent her a letter every few days, giving her snippets of news – the neighbours had a new ginger kitten, for example, or she had baked a new kind of chocolate cake and would bake another for when Angel came home because it was so delicious. Or she had gone to the movies for the first time since forever. She was enclosing – she wrote, in what would turn out to be the last letter – a sketch of Angel. *You look so pretty!* wrote Charly. When Angel unfolded it, she saw that it was of her in a swimsuit on a scarlet towel. The lodger had drawn it. She didn't like the thought that he had been watching her sunbathe. She tore it up and threw it in the rubbish.

Two days later the lodger arrived. *I've come to collect Angel,* he told the camp organisers. *Charly, her mother and my wife, is ill and she wanted to see her daughter. Our daughter.* He smiled his movie-star smile.

The camp people said, *of course*. They hugged Angel and said they hoped she would write when she got home. Angel promised she would and the lodger drove them out onto the highway. She asked to use his phone to speak to Charly but he told her to wait. That it was best to do that in person. It was dark by the time they stopped at a house at the end of a quiet, dirty street in a city that Angel did not know. She followed him inside.

'Here we are,' the lodger announced. 'Home.'

'This isn't home,' Angel whispered, because she was afraid and her voice would not work properly. 'Home is where my mother is and I want her.'

'Tomorrow, Angel. Now it's time to sleep. There's your room.'

Tomorrow came and tomorrow and tomorrow. The days crept past, filled with television and takeout and still no mother. Angel ventured out onto the porch but there was no one in the street and the curtains in the houses opposite were closed. She went back inside.

'Take me to my mother,' she said, her hands on her hips, the last of her defiance flashing in her eyes.

'Not possible, Angel, baby.' The lodger pressed the remote, killing the sound. The images from the television kept flickering silently on his face.

'Why not?'

'I was waiting for the right moment to tell you, Angel,' said the lodger. 'I hate to be the one to tell you this, but your mom's dead, honey.'

'You're lying to me!' shouted Angel. 'What have you done with her?'

'I'm not lying, Angel-baby. Charly was careless, she was running – fuck knows why – across the road, and the old man from over the road was driving and he hit her. She flew up over the windscreen and her head hit the pavement.'

Angel stared at him.

'Don't look like that, honey.' The lodger tucked a strand of her hair behind her ear, his finger lingering on her earlobe. 'You've got me.' He pressed the remote again and the sound filled the dingy room.

She went to lie down on the narrow bed with its iron headboard. Terror and grief a vice around her chest. Three days and three nights she held out, but the lodger understood children. He knew all he needed to do was wait.

On the fourth night, the ache was too much: she crept across the hallway to the lodger's bedroom and climbed into bed with him. And he opened his arms and opened her legs and that was the end of her childhood. Afterwards she lay on the bed, her legs pulled up into her chest, her arms tight around them.

The strawberry milkshake he bought for her the next day went untouched. So did the burger, so did the fries. There was no reaching her. There was no reasoning with her. She never went home and she never wrote to the people at camp. They needed to eat and the lodger's articles about art didn't earn enough, so she was put to work. No one could deny they needed the money.

Angel's hands were shaking when she reached into her sleeve and unstrapped the hidden razor blade and unwrapped it with care, winding up the piece of white silk as she did so. She pushed up her sleeve until there was enough new skin exposed. The slender scars were beautiful in the dim light – delicate as lace on the inside of her arm. It was a long time since she had done this. She selected the place carefully and pressed the blade down. A perfect bead of blood welled. She drew the blade down one inch, two, and three. For a moment, she felt nothing at all, so she went another inch – and then she felt it, that fire that spread from her arm into her shoulder down her torso and into her pelvis. The physical pain relieved the pressure in her head. This crimson inking on her skin calmed her enough to be able to breathe again. She rinsed the blade, then dried it and swaddled it tenderly once more, strapping it securely under her sleeve.

Her hands were steady when she started the image search. It took some time, but she had long since learned her way around the web – light and dark. She froze at the images that appeared on the screen – arms and bare legs. Other versions appeared on her screen. The same girl. Ten, eleven, maybe twelve. An angry child, wearing heart-shaped red sunglasses, draped across beds, bent over in the sun, standing on a verandah with one bobby-socked leg curled around the other.

Angel clicked on the link and a face appeared on her screen. A fine-featured woman, dark hair, green eyes – the photograph taken in a bright white room. There were paintings on the walls behind her. The work had been exhibited in a gallery in London. There had been outrage at the woman who had done this. There had been accusations that the artist, who had said that the pictures were hers, were of her – her as she had been as a child – had plundered the bodies of children, her own daughter, even. Windows had been smashed. The owner of the gallery was assaulted. The show was taken down. The police investigated.

Embedded in an article was a video of a girl being doorstopped, a reporter shoving his microphone into her face. *'Freya Finch, the artist's daughter'*, read the caption. Angel knew her name now and she said it out loud.

'Freya. Freya Finch.'

Saying a girl's real name wasn't much – but it was better than nothing. Nobody had ever known *her* name. No one ever said it. A person was nobody without a name – that Angel knew for sure. A girl was just a sweetie or a darling or a dirty little slut and there was no way for a girl without a name to hold anyone to account. She pressed play on the video.

'Freya!' shouted the journalist. 'Freya, look here, love. Don't you think where there's smoke, there's fire?'

Freya put her hands up as if fending off a blow.

'Looks just like you, love,' said the journalist. 'Is that why the police were asking?'

'Those are my mother's pictures.' Defiance and desperation in her voice. 'My mother is an artist. Those are self-portraits. Look at my mother's work. She's always done that.'

'Pretty necklace,' the journalist said. The camera zoomed in on the silver butterfly. Freya, caught off guard, reached for it. 'Same necklace as the girl in the pictures is wearing. Some pictures it's all you're wearing. How did that feel?'

Freya retreated back inside the door then and the video cut back to the journalist, who said that the police were investigating – but when Angel searched she did not find any report of that.

She played the video clip of Freya wearing her necklace. A silver butterfly. Angel looked at the girl in the painting. She was wearing the same silver butterfly as the girl in the video standing on a wet pavement. The girl in the video had the same eyes, the same sharp features, the same expression, and the same slender body as the girl in the paintings that had caused the outrage. Freya was the girl tucked behind the books in Fournier's cabin. Cora Berger, her own mother, had done this.

Art was not a thing Angel knew, but this woman, thought Angel, this Cora, she apparently did. She had done something for Yves Fournier – this painting was part of it – and they had both got away with it. Got away. Fournier was gone, so Angel would find this Cora and find out what she had done.

The sound of Tina's vehicle made her look up from her screen. She pocketed her phone and ran over to the office. 'Don't take your jacket off,' Tina instructed when Angel walked in. 'There's a roadkill deer in the back of my truck.'

'Good timing,' Angel said. 'The wolves will need to eat again in a few days.'

'Tommy hit it last night on the way home from the search for Fournier,' Tina replied. 'He was not a happy man. Her leg was broken. He had to shoot her to put her out of her misery and you know how he doesn't like hurting anything.'

'Did they see any trace of Mr Fournier yet?' asked Angel.

'Nothing yet,' said Tina. 'I parked right by the cutting room. You need help?'

'I'll manage.' Angel walked over to the truck. The dead animal was a white-tailed deer – not more than a hundred pounds – a delicate foreleg smashed. Angel manoeuvred the doe so that she could balance her across her shoulders and carried her into the cutting room.

SEVENTEEN

Cora's spirits lifted as soon as she stepped inside her studio. Here, she felt invincible. Here, she felt that she could do anything she set her mind to. It was her domain and in it she was free. The building itself was an old milking shed that she had converted for her own use. The roof was vaulted, the heavy oak trusses draped with spider webs, and the hay loft could only be reached by a vertiginously steep flight of metal stairs. It was filled with ancient hay bales that had once fed the cows who had been milked there for decades, tethered to the metal stakes in the centre.

Cora fetched wood and filled the stove with logs. They were dry and the fire took, the flames writhing when she opened the air vent a little. The half-grown cat –the one Freya had rescued when Cora had accidentally run over it – came down from the loft and she gave it a little milk. After lapping it up, the cat curled up on the sofa and went to sleep while Cora arranged her brushes, sorted her paints and cleared the trestle table – this restoration of external order bringing back into focus what she needed to put things to rights.

She opened her sketchbook. It was filled with her drawings of the lake and the mountains around Yves' cabin. The elegant curve of the lake, Yves skiing alone towards the mountains. The shabby cabin rendered with architectural precision: each brick, each wooden roof strut, each window inked into the blank pages, a fulcrum for the vast landscape that spread out from it.

Next she unpacked her sparse salvage and laid it out on the flagstone floor. A pale grey cashmere jersey. The box of thin, unsmokable cigarettes she'd bought in that quiet Balkan town where it had all started. The black handaxe she had given and then taken back from Yves. A crow's glossy black wing feather and a few dried wildflowers that Yves had given her. The treasures children collect.

There were the letters she had written and not sent. In them were the secrets she was unable to tell anyone because she could not believe them herself. The Polaroids she had taken in bathroom mirrors – her body marked after each encounter. Each time, each one, evidence that she had refused to countenance. The first one was of five fingerprints branded onto her arm. She had not questioned the ache when she pressed the indigo bruises – the pain had released her from the numbness she'd felt for as long as she could remember. She had been sorry when the bruises faded, but not sorry when his attention intensified.

Yves had begun by messaging her as he woke up, starting her day with his. It had removed her from where she was, cutting her off, filling every moment of her days and her nights. He had bound her to him effortlessly with that rarest of gifts – his attention, which was infinite in the beginning. When she had tried to set limits, he had swept them aside until it no longer occurred to Cora to resist any more. She had done everything he'd asked of her – insignificant things, at first. She had not hesitated long – just long enough to know what she was doing – before she'd stepped off the fragile jetty of reason and into the open sea. The recklessness had been intoxicating.

You brought me back to life, she wrote to him once.

That sounds like a line from a sentimental Hollywood movie.

Sorry, she wrote.

Don't be, he returned. *I like Hollywood movies. I'm sentimental.*

Cora was not sentimental, but in that moment it did not occur to her to say so, and after that it was too late. So she spoke of the scope of her life, her career, her Scottish home, her daughter, her friends, her politics. He would say, 'I am only interested in you. It's you I want. Only you.'

That diminished her. Cora countered him. 'These things are all part of me,' she would say. 'This is what I am, what I have become.'

'Come now, Cora. I'm not interested in the public woman, in the private mother, in the housewife who sees that the sheets are clean and there's food in the fridge,' he said, and she had sensed his quick irritation. 'I want your secret self. I am interested in *you*.'

Cora stood at the edge – there was a moment when she could have stepped back and walked away – but his desire to have her at the exclusion of all else was so compelling that she had overridden her instinct for separateness and let herself fall in love with him. The weightlessness of that fall was exhilarating, but once she fell, there was no stopping herself. She just had to pray that Yves would have his arms open, ready to catch her.

And he caught her and he did not let her go, transporting her instead to a hermetically sealed world of two, where he was fascinated by her stories of her childhood on Eden. He stripped away her womanhood and made her into a girl again, returning her to that time before the guillotining of her childhood. It was as if she was that feral child again – naïve enough to mistake being singled out for recognition and love. The girl she had been budded once more under the fierce sun of his interest and she found herself unable to think of anything but her past. That was why, when she came across the photograph of herself in that long-forgotten yellow bikini, she started work on a portrait. Painting filled her with an erotic fever that restored the fierceness and the freedom she had once felt in her own body. She had no reason to suspect that in his hands her desire would be a weapon that would be used against her.

Yves shaped her life around his. He was a nocturnal animal and so she became one too. He was awake after midnight and that was when he conducted his courtship – on into the night till two, three, four in the morning. He deprived her of sleep, but Cora found that she loved best in the dark and he led her to places that she had kept hidden even from herself. She had kept a close guard on her heart for as long as she could remember and Yves opened it with an expertise she had not then questioned.

I love you, he wrote to her.

She did not reply. Those words filled her with a delighted terror.

He persisted. *Say that you love me. You know you do.*

Love. That must be the word that described how she felt. She could not find another word for it, but she resisted. Her word was her bond. The thought of giving herself over to him filled her with fear. She told Yves this, but he insisted.

'You're in love too,' he said when he called her on Skype. 'Give in to it. Stop thinking. Trust me.'

'How can you know?' For her, the words *I love you* had an alchemical power – saying them made them true. She looked for ways out. 'You don't know me yet.'

Yves' condition was that she give in and believe she was loved. He told her that often enough over the days and weeks. He sent her music. Ballads. All of them tried and tested seductions, which worked their sentimental magic on her anyway. He sent images too, beautiful ones, giving her a private view of things he saw, his world carefully curated just for her. He left her no time to breathe and no space to think until he was certain that he had her. There was no respite and so she relinquished the desire for it. Her reward was dream-spun words that meshed her to him until all her resistance dissolved.

His attention, which transfused the deep vein of her loneliness, enthralled her, but it was Yves who controlled when they spoke and for how long. If she called him when she wanted to, he would be curt – he was busy, he would say – he would call her back. And then she would find herself unable to focus until he did so. Without her realising it, he taught her to wait:

that was the peculiar thrall of those days that were emptied out by waiting.

Cora came to understand that it was not the desire for cruelty or pain that lay at the heart of masochism. Rather it was the capacity to defer, to yearn, to anticipate without any idea of when this waiting would be brought to a close and she would be satisfied again with his voice, his touch, his attention. Cora stopped eating, she stopped sleeping, and she did not breathe – no more than was necessary for survival.

Yves' digital companionship shifted imperceptibly from novelty to necessity. He drew her closer and closer until she capitulated and said the words he insisted on hearing from her. *I love you*, she said, and when she had said it, seemingly of her own free will, it became the truth.

'There is nothing I don't know about you,' he informed her late one night on Skype. 'I've searched for every single thing about you. Read everything. Seen every image.'

'That's just the internet,' she had replied. 'It tells you nothing.'

'You haven't searched for me?' A wariness in his eyes that gave her a moment's pause.

'No. I want to know you as you are. I want to understand you myself, not through some algorithm.'

'You're so sweet,' he said. 'But there is something I must tell you.'

'Tell me now.'

'No, I need to be able to see you, to hold you in my arms, to touch you when I say it.'

Cora had not argued with him on that. She wanted his touch too. She felt trapped by the flickering world of video calls and text messages. It was his touch that had marked her.

It was his touch that she craved. She did not turn detective. It was she who had insisted on moving from the screen to skin and booking flights and flying west.

EIGHTEEN

The sound of the hardware van pulling up sent Kit-Kat scrabbling up the stairs into the roof. It was the deliveryman in yellow gumboots and a turban, offloading Cora's order – wooden slats, nails, canvas, metres of silk, acrylic paint, wood and the tallest ladder they had in store – and carrying it into the studio.

'Welcome home, Cora.' Hardi set everything down in the centre of the studio. 'New work?'

'Absolutely, Hardi.' The two of them were long-time collaborators. 'A fresh start.'

'You want some help putting the frame together?'

'Thank you,' said Cora, and the two of them assembled the frame, riveted the canvas onto it and got it vertical, though with some difficulty. When they were done, they stood side by side and got the measure of it.

'This will be your biggest yet.'

'By far,' Cora agreed.

Hardi opened the ladder and tested its slender giraffe legs. 'The floor's uneven,' he observed. 'So the ladder's not stable. It's a health and safety nightmare, this place.'

'It's my heaven. I'll be fine.'

'You'll use that harness I went to the trouble to put up for you?' he asked, pointing to the safety harness twisting from a beam, a gentle noose in the warming air.

'Of course I will.'

'No fibbing now, Cora.'

'Okay, okay,' she said. 'You caught me out there. It gets in my way when I'm working.'

'You're not a woman to take advice, are you?'

'Not my strong point.'

'You be careful now, Cora.'

And then he was gone. It felt good to be alone in her studio with just the hiss of the stove and her waiting canvas. *Be careful be careful be careful.* It was much too late for her to be careful. Careful had come to an end with Yves, but here she was, alive and at home. Beyond his reach.

You be careful now, Cora. Hardi's warning echoed in her head as she climbed the unsteady ladder in her studio. As she did so, the sun broke through the clouds and shone through the clerestory windows in the apex of the roof. She looked down as the light glanced off the metal spikes where the feeding troughs for the cows had once been affixed, when her studio had still been a milking shed. Freya had called those spikes dragon's teeth.

Be careful. Use a harness, Hardi had said. *You could hurt yourself on one of those.* It really was too late to worry about hurt, she thought in silent reply to Hardi's concern as she took the handaxe that she had retrieved from Yves' cabin from her pocket. She warmed the worked flint on her palm – this had been her first gift to him. To understand how she had got here, to record her history of original sin, to atone, she needed to return to the beginning. She placed the handaxe in the middle of the empty canvas. The bull's eye around which she would centre her story.

Careful was not something Cora thought of much. *Careful* was not what Cora had been thinking when she had stood naked in her bedroom deciding what to wear. *Careful* was not what she had been thinking as she had looked at her clothes spread out on the bed. *Careful* was not her intention when she had selected a close-fitting red dress to wear on the plane, knowing that Yves would be waiting for her at the airport.

There had been delight in his eyes at the sight of her walking towards him. 'You look marvellous, Cora,' he told her as he enfolded her against his chest, his cashmere sweater a caress on her cheek. Yves' arms were lean and hard, bands of steel around her. His embrace felt like coming home. She breathed him in. Smell was a thing Cora could read like an animal: the smell of the rain coming; the metallic tang of blood; the sourness of sickness; the sharp odour of adrenaline that told her if someone was lying. She tried to detect the scent of him, his essence – the traces of sweat that reveal a man, his desires, his secrets. There was nothing. She filled this gap with her own smell – smoke and musk and perfume – so she could read this absence as love. As affinity.

That first day passed in a blur. She met with collectors. Some of her work sold. There was a cocktail party: art people, drinks, and not enough food. Yves was pleased with her, proud. He seemed to like having her on his arm. He showed her off to everyone they met. She smiled and charmed. It exhausted her to the point of numbness. When it was done and they'd had dinner, she and Yves walked alone through the rain to her hotel. Inside the mirrored lift, Yves put his hand on her breast.

Her desire for him was a fire that burned as he unlocked the door to the room, but when they entered, he did not undress her. She couldn't think what the next step should be, so she opened her suitcase and took out the gift she had made for him. 'Here it is,' she said.

He studied the painting. 'Exquisite,' he said, and then he looked at her with an expression that she could not quite read. 'So this is what you've been working on?'

'It is,' she said. 'All your questions about my childhood returned me to this state – that cusp between child and woman. You've distracted me from my usual subjects.'

'It's sexy,' said Yves. 'People are tired of violence. No one ever gets tired of sex.'

'It's not about sex,' she protested. 'It's about a girl's awakening. That quiet before the storm, that moment just before men's eyes are daggers on her body.'

'Whatever, darling,' said Yves. 'She's a beautiful child and you have captured perfectly that elusive nymphet moment before bud turns to rose.'

'The painting is about innocence,' Cora insisted.

'There are connoisseurs of this kind of innocence,' said Yves. 'They'll make you a fortune. Trust me.'

'This is not for show.'

'You underestimate yourself,' he said. 'Your capacity to go to places most people won't.'

'This is only for you. This moment. I captured it for you. That moment a girl stands on the threshold. That moment she becomes visible to herself. It's the end of paradise.'

'But the beginning of life,' Yves said. 'Look at her eyes. Everything is in them. She's no innocent.'

'One cannot be if one is observed,' she explained. 'The meaning of everything one does becomes double-edged.'

'Sign it then,' he instructed. 'Make her mine.'

She turned the painting over and wrote: *THE GIRL, for Yves, a private view.* ♥ *Cora*. She handed it back to him.

'Perfect,' he said. He leaned the painting on the desk. She waited for him to embrace her but he did not. He did not undress her either. He simply stripped and got into the hotel bed and looked at her. Because she wanted him, she took off her own clothes.

'You have a shockingly young body,' he said, 'for a woman of almost fifty.' She supposed it was meant as a compliment, but it disconcerted her. The portrait's fierce painted eyes followed her as she crossed the room and climbed into bed with him. She switched off the light so that she did not have to see the girl any more.

He kissed her and then pinned her wrists down with one hand and put the other across her face. She put his lack of finesse down to too much desire and too little familiarity. The sex was abrupt, a slamming blue-pilled hardness that did not give either of them the pleasure she had imagined for this consummation.

Afterwards, when he was asleep, she put her hand between her legs and then held her fingers to her nose. No smell, no lingering of his skin on hers. He left no trace of himself on her. All she could smell was herself. Wide awake and wired, she shifted away from him, but he sensed her movement in his sleep and followed her across the bed and held her close. That made her so happy that she matched the rhythm of her breathing to his and fell asleep.

In the morning he pulled her into his arms and kissed her tenderly and it was as if she had imagined the strangeness of the night. 'What is the secret thing you wanted to tell me?' she asked.

'Wait just a little longer,' Yves murmured into her hair. 'It will take time to tell you. I want things to be right. Wait till we're up at the cabin.'

And because it gave her so much pleasure to please him, that is what she had done.

NINETEEN

Freya was happy to hear Johann's key in the lock. Her day had been lonely and she listened to him banging about in the living room, rustling papers, turning on the radio. 'Hey!' she called, over the presenter's voice. 'I'm in the bath.'

He opened the door.

'You smell of the Underground.' Freya wrinkled her nose when he leaned over to kiss her.

'Eau de London,' he said. 'The world's most expensive perfume.'

'Did you see them?'

'What?' she asked, sinking back under the bubbles.

'Those rolls of old film.'

'I don't know what you're talking about.' Freya sank lower so that the bubbles came up to her nose.

'In that trunk,' he said. 'At the bottom. I found some rolls of old film. Must have been your mother's from when she was a kid.'

'I didn't see those.' She frowned. 'I thought I'd taken everything out of it.'

'They were under the old Afrikaans newspapers,' said Johann. 'Made me think of home, so I picked one up to read and there they were.'

'Show me.' Freya got out of the bath and wrapped a towel around herself. She followed Johann into the living room.

'*Die Burger*. It was the main Afrikaans daily. Still is. Look.' He straightened out the yellowing pages that had been at the bottom of Cora's trunk of photographs. 'All from 1988. P.W. Botha and all of them. Seems like another planet now.'

'That's when she left,' said Freya. 'Straight after her parents were killed.'

'Your grandparents, were they murdered?'

'No,' Freya shook her head. 'It was a car accident.'

'That's okay then,' said Johann.

'Not really.' Freya stared at him.

'In South Africa, a car accident is better than a murder,' Johann assured her. 'So you never got the chance to meet them.'

'No. My mother's father – my grandfather – rolled their vehicle on a bend on the road between Eden and Vrededorp.'

'That really is the middle of nowhere,' Johann told her. 'Even the mines are shut round there now.'

'I asked Cora what happened, but she said no one could say if he was driving too fast or fell asleep at the wheel or swerved to avoid an animal on the road. Apparently it took my grandmother longer to die. That's what the undertaker told Cora when she collected their ashes,' Freya told him. 'They were in one urn – not to save money or anything, according to my mother – but because the undertaker said that they were joined in death as they had been in life.'

'That's fair enough.' Johann knelt beside the trunk. 'Look, here are the rolls of film.' Four 8mm film canisters fitted perfectly into the base.

Freya took them out, her fingers tingling. She was holding her mother's life in her hands. The dates were written on the curling labels: *Xmas 1979.*

'They are useless without a projector,' Johann pointed out.

'I know that.' Freya was irritated. 'I'll find one.' She put down the reels of film and checked her mother's old trunk to see if she had missed anything else, but apart from a few more photographs of cattle standing in the veld, it was empty.

'I was thinking that you're never going to leave this flat unless I drag you out. So here I am. Dragging you out. A couple of my friends are in town and they found this amazing pub. The Rose and Crown. They said it's not gentrified yet; there's beer you can afford and pool tables.'

'You go.'

'No, babe. I want you to come with me,' he pleaded. 'And check this out.' He held out his phone so she could see the photographs his friends had sent of the place. 'It's not that far. We don't even need to take the Tube.'

'Okay,' she smiled. 'I'll come.'

'That makes me happy, Freya, thank you.' There was affection in his eyes that made her smile again.

'Give me a minute to get dressed.' Freya pulled on her

jeans and a black polo neck and ran her fingers through her tangled black curls. Some lipstick and she was done. 'Let's go then,' she said, putting on her blue coat. Johann locked the door behind them. They bought a wrap each at the falafel stand and ate them as they walked hand in hand down the wet street.

Freya realised the minute they stepped into the pub that she had made a mistake. People were three deep around the bar and the music was deafening. Johann's friends – South Africans and a sprinkling of Australians – were already there and they joined them at a tiny, crowded table. They were drinking. Johann was drinking. She was not. The smell of alcohol, the stale smell of cigarettes when Johann and his friends returned from smoking out on the pavement, made her feel sick.

All of them were talking about how, in December, the weather in Cape Town and Sydney was *way* better than in London. 'And so is the surf,' said a blonde who seemed to resent Freya's presence, or Johann's attention to her.

'No one comes to London to surf,' said Freya.

'Yes, well, whatever,' said the girl. 'I just can't wait to get home for Christmas. How about you, Johann?'

'Totally,' he said. 'It's like, a couple of weeks. I've been trying to persuade Freya to come for Christmas, so she can see for herself. I keep teasing her that in the year she was meant to be travelling the world, she's got as far as her mother's old flat in the east of London.'

To escape them, Freya went to the bathroom. The queue went on forever, but she was desperate so she waited for her turn. When she got back Johann was playing pool. His cue was aligned, his eye on the ball. He drew his arm back and the ball shot home. Game over. He'd won. His defeated opponent bought more drinks. Someone else put coins on the side of the pool table and Johann started another game. The blonde girl giggled and patted Johann's arm and spoke to him in Afrikaans.

Freya was suddenly desperate not to be there. She went over to Johann and said that she was going home.

'Stay a bit longer, babe,' he urged, but his eyes were on the new player who was readying the table.

'I'm tired,' she said.

'You want to break?' Johann's opponent asked him.

'I'll break.' Johann dropped his arm. 'Wait one game,' he said, looking briefly at Freya and then back at the balls.

'I need my bed,' she said. 'You don't look like you want to leave.'

'Not now that I'm on a winning streak,' said Johann. She kissed his cheek. 'You'll be okay getting home?'

'Of course I will,' she said. 'I'll see you later, if you can still find your way.'

'I'll find my way.' Johann grinned at her as he picked up his pool cue. He tipped it with chalk, then took aim at the white ball, smashing it into the neatly arranged triangle, sinking two balls at once. She took a step back and then another and then she was outside. It was dark and this was an unfamiliar part of London. The wave of nausea finally broke and she threw up. Enough of this, she said to herself as a passer-by made a wide berth around her. When it was over, she walked to the late-night pharmacy near the Tube station and bought a pregnancy test. She hid it right at the back of the bathroom cabinet when she got home, fell straight into bed and was out like a light.

Freya woke up when Johann came in several hours later, but when he climbed into bed and laid a hopeful hand on the small of her back, she pretended to be asleep. After a while, he took his hand away and rolled over and fell asleep.

TWENTY

The sky had been a tender blue the afternoon Yves drove Cora to his cabin. The city soon fell away and then the last straggle of suburbs was behind them. As they drove north, Cora's gaze expanded to meet the vast landscape through which the road they were on unrolled – a black ribbon of tar in the snow that stretched from horizon to horizon.

'It has an echo of Eden to it – a landscape so big that you can see all the way to where the earth meets the sky and not see a building,' said Cora. 'I can breathe here.'

'Could you live here?' asked Yves.

'I could,' said Cora. She would, if he asked her. She would

move. He had filled her world so completely that all she could imagine now was inhabiting his. 'Shall I be DJ?'

'As long as you're happy to choose between country and western.'

Cora searched through the CDs scattered across the dashboard – amongst them Willie Nelson, Johnny Cash, Dolly Parton. She chose Patsy Cline. 'Crazy'. Her grief-sized voice filled the car and they sang along with her. *Crazy for loving you.*

'Tell me now,' Cora interrupted the song. 'This secret thing you have promised me for so long.' She had considered so many things. Beads of worry that she had turned over this way, that way – a wife not actually divorced, an illness, another woman closer to home, cancer. All the normal things.

'Wait till we go up into the woods. You'll love it there.' Yves had his hand on Cora's knee, pushing up the skirt to find the strip of naked skin at the top of her stockings. It was not possible then for her to imagine that his promised confession, for which Yves had made her wait so that he could tell her in person, could be anything other than a delight – a dangerous one, perhaps – but still a delight. So she put all her suspicions aside and trusted him and watched the wilderness open up.

Yves turned off the highway and into the forest at dusk. The road narrowed to a track, until the trees were brushing their dark green fingers on the car. Yves took the bends fast. The headlights glanced off the trees and the snow gleamed. They turned a corner and there, through a gap in the trees, was the dark water of the lake. They had reached the end of the road.

Yves stopped and got out to open the gate. He drove up the steep track to the little house in the clearing in the woods. 'Wait here,' he said and disappeared around the house.

The cabin was crisp Snow White colours – a black roof, red clapboard, white window frames. Yves reappeared inside it a few minutes later and she watched him light tea candles and place them on the windowsills, each one a bead of light holding the falling night at bay. Cora was charmed. He came back to fetch her.

'Welcome,' he said as he ushered her inside. He had already placed the painting of the girl on the bookshelf and so Cora had the odd experience of catching her own eye as she entered the living room. While he got the fire going, Cora walked through the rooms, touching the objects that had become familiar to her as she had seen them framing him during their endless video calls. The strange collection of animals and birds, some perched on the rafters and some suspended. Masks and fans from the places he had travelled to – Asia and South America. She ran her fingers along the spines of the books that she had wondered about when they spoke.

She unpacked her things in the spare room. It was cold, so she put on another sweater and returned to the fire. Yves poured wine for her. It was good but she was nervous, so she drank too much and chattered while he prepared the food. He had refused her help, telling her to curl up on the window seat. She was happy to oblige. While he made the salad and sautéed potatoes and fried the steak, Cora looked out over the lake gleaming in the moonlight and imagined that this moment of perfect contentment would last forever.

The fillet was as good as the wine and Yves ate quickly – more quickly than she did – and pushed away his plate. She knew he did not like to see people eating so, before she was full, she put her fork down too. The meal was over. The waiting was over. 'I'm telling you this,' Yves lit a cigarette, 'because you love me. Because I trust you.'

'What?' she'd asked, impatient now. Sick of this waiting. Wanting it done so that he could take her to the big bed in the bedroom that had a view of the lake.

'I have a criminal record.'

Cora laughed. 'What for?'

'Images. There were images.'

'What images?' she asked

'Just two. Nothing really.'

Cora wanted to see them. To see what they were. What he had looked at.

A girl. Girls.

'How old was she?' Cora asked

They were nothing. Just things that are everywhere on the internet. Nothing you couldn't buy if you went downtown to where such things were sold. But in this puritanical age . . . Yves lit another cigarette.

'But what?' demanded Cora.

'It was nothing,' he said, but then, 'That isn't everything, though.'

There was more. Cora could see it. There was more. How could that not be all? What else could there be? She pressed her hands together for something to hold on to because her grip on reality was slipping.

Yves told her. He told her that there had been reports of a girl. A girl of twelve. In a hotel. A hotel room. In a hotel room. A girl in a hotel room. A pornographic film made or a webcam. Cora could not make out which.

Yves said there was a man there. No, men. Men. Other men. Two men. Known offenders. Directing. A room. A chatroom.

A chatroom log. An IP. IP addresses. His address the third. His. No, but not him. Not his.

He was hacked.

How?

He did not know.

Were you there? she asked.

'How could you ask me that?' Yves accused. 'How?'

It did not tally, but she could not bear the hurt in his eyes when he asked, *You believed I could do that?*

No, she heard herself say, *no, no.* But it did not tally. It did not. 'The record,' she said. 'How did you get that if you did not do it?'

A fine was paid. Admission of guilt. His lawyer's advice. Not his wish, but to save his family. All done now. All gone. A mistake, perhaps, but over.

'You didn't fight the case to save your family?' she asked.

A trial would have been too much. The scandal. His whole search history – imagine that. And you didn't know?

She didn't know. She didn't think to look. Love is blind.

He said he looked up everything about her. *Every single thing.* The way he said it was an accusation.

Should she have known? She should have known. She could not let his secret be this. She had to make it different. She had to make her mind work, make herself work, find her voice . . . Speak.

'The girl,' she asked. 'What happened to her?'

'There is no girl.' Flint in his eyes.

'The girl,' said Cora. 'The girl in the hotel—'

'There was no girl. There is no girl. It was a chatroom. They made it up.'

'If you weren't there, how do you know that?'

'The police didn't find a hotel because there was no hotel. There was nothing. It was only words.'

'Your words?' she asked.

'Not my words. I told you, Cora.' There was anger in his voice. 'I was hacked. Now, let's put this aside.'

But Yves' words echoed in her head. They kept going, not letting her hear, not letting her think, getting louder and louder. He was explaining. Explaining, but making no sense.

Explaining and reeling her in with the threads of her love and trust that he had enmeshed her with during his long seduction.

Explaining that there was no evidence in the end. No charges – or rather, charges dropped. She could not make out which. It made no sense. She could make no sense. She saw the words. She knew them. English words. They were there in front of her. Those words of his. His words. Her mind refused them entry. Her mind shut down. Her mind said *no, no, no* to his bombardment of words.

No when he said that it was nothing. It came to nothing.

No when he said that it was hell. For him.

Her mind said *no* but her mouth said nothing because the present – and who she was – was slipping from her grasp. Cora thought of the girls in the pictures and the naked girl in the chatroom – twelve years old – and her own skin burned with the shame of what Yves had told her.

'I was that girl.' Cora wrapped her arms around her stomach. 'Once, I was that girl. That girl was me—'

'Don't do this.' Yves cut her off immediately. 'Don't make this about you. This thing, this train smash, happened to me and it's done. I've dealt with it. It's in the past. I'm telling you so that you know. I'm telling you because I am a considerate man and because I love you. So don't try to make it yours. Don't put yourself at the centre of a drama that is not yours. This nonsense almost destroyed my life. But it's over now. And I have you. Here. Don't I?'

'It's too late,' Cora said.

'No, darling. I love you.'

'You're telling me too late, Yves.'

'I wanted to be able to see you when I told you. To be able to touch you.'

But Yves did not hold her. He did not touch her. He did not try to staunch the wound he had opened up in her chest. The pain of it stopping her breath. It felt as if a huntsman had ripped out her heart and then pressed it back into the cavity, where it would never quite fit again. Cora rose from the table and went out on the balcony, looking for an escape.

The trees were hunched along the frozen lake. No lights in the distant shuttered houses. Across the lake, a car's lights raked the darkness, setting a shimmer on the ice – and then it was gone. The cold leached the sense out of the landscape, her breath suspended mist. The night made no sound, but the story Yves had told her roared in her ears and she could smell hot stagnant water, which was not possible because the snow-laden forest stretched north, south, east, west.

Below her was a track that led away from the cabin to a footbridge. Beyond that was a narrow road that vanished into the trees. That road – muddied, frozen – beckoned her to come. *Walk,* it seemed to promise, *and you will find shelter.* But she was afraid. She did not know where she was. For miles, there was nothing but trees and the wolves within them.

Instead of choosing the beckoning embrace of the snow, she turned and looked back. Inside was the fire. The bed that they had yet to sleep in, the wine. Him sitting there watching her. Waiting. She knew where the danger was. She knew where the darkness lay, but she turned her back on herself and walked into his waiting arms.

Yves took her into his embrace as if it was he who had to do the forgiving. He said, 'Let's leave the dishes and go to bed.' He fucked her with his fingers splayed over her face, a cage barring the light. She could not breathe, yet she did not protest. He twisted her face away so that she could not look at him when he came. As soon as he was finished, he pulled her into the crook of his arm and fell asleep.

The stars glittered throughout that cold night. Cora looked for herself, for her will, but she could find neither. All she could hear was her heart hammering in her chest. She was stunned as if by a blow – the feeling at once so alien and so familiar. In the dark it was hard for Cora to hold on to herself. It was hard to keep the tide of the past at bay. Cora was both with Yves in that deceptive bed and she was again the twelve-year-old in the empty art room at her new boarding school. Her drawing of a rose done *to perfection*, her art teacher had said the first time she handed in her homework. *Which is why you must stay after the others have left. You will be my muse.* And so she sat for him – moving only when he gave permission.

She had done exactly as he told her; he was her teacher and she had loved him because he had seen how she good she was. He had singled her out from the beginning, paid her special attention, taught her how to look at things properly so that she could draw them, paint. Shown her how to do things that would help wing her away from her parents and the farm and into the wider world where there was light and air and change.

Twelve-year-old Cora was checking the notice board: next week's assignments pinned up on it, when her teacher entered the room. He was behind her. Too close. Her body hummed. There was a suspension in his breathing. Fear rooted her to that polished square of blue linoleum in front of the notice board and in those minutes that stretched across the years his arms around her chest were bands of steel. Her breasts that were just buds pressed in against her ribs and his breath was hot in her ear. His beard on her neck, her face, everywhere. His knee parting hers as he pinned her to the wall. Fingers inside her, burning shame into recesses of her being she did not know existed. It happened too fast. Like falling. How could something that happened so fast mean anything at all? Who would believe her when she did not believe it herself?

In the quiet dark in Yves' cabin Cora knew herself to be like the girls in the pictures. She was twelve again and a pair of hard, smooth-skinned hands had her in their grip. And she was weaving and feinting and there was the smell of dank water and the long call of *CoraCoraCora* – and when it stopped she was running but after that everything was blank. She tried to make sense of it but, as always when she reached for the memory, it eluded her. And, as always when it did that, she fell away from consciousness, fell away from memory, fell asleep.

When Cora woke it was morning – sleep had interred the distant past again. Instead, she was caught in the nightmarish present, a caged bird entwined in the secret of the man lying beside her. Her heart refused to accept the facts as her mind understood them. She studied Yves' profile: the nose, hooked and hard as a hawk's beak, the lines fanned around his eyes that gave no indication of laughter. He made her think of a vampire wasp, a graceful lethal-looking creature, that her Dawid had shown her once in the garden on Eden.

'This wasp stings a particular kind of spider,' he had told her. 'Paralyses it and then lays its eggs in the spider's stomach. The spider is alive – it feels everything, but it can't move. When the eggs hatch, the baby wasps eat the spider from the inside out until it's hollow. When the wasps fly away, the spider dies.'

Cora got up to make coffee. She brought it to Yves. She told him to take her back to the city but he pulled her back into bed with him and kissed her, removing the words of departure she had gathered so painstakingly from her mouth. 'We can get through this,' he said, 'I just need to know that you love me.' And she had said that she did, because it was true – her heart had refused to take in what her mind knew. When he said, 'I need to know that I have you,' tears had welled in her eyes and slipped onto the crisp white pillowcase. He had seen that and smiled.

TWENTY-ONE

As the alarm went off, grey light seeped in though the gap where the curtains did not quite close. Johann dragged himself out of bed. Freya dozed off again and then he was back, standing next to the bed with a mug in each hand and a contrite look on his face.

'It's black. Sorry. The milk's off.'

'That's okay.' Freya found the smell of coffee nauseating. 'Just put it down. Why are you up so early?'

'I forgot I had the breakfast shift at the restaurant today. Do you have any painkillers? My head's killing me.'

'On the dressing table.'

He swallowed two and sat down on the edge of the bed.

'You're so pale.' Johann ruffled her hair. 'Have you got a hang-over too?'

'I didn't drink,' she replied.

'Wise.' Johann rested his big head in his hands. 'My brain is fucked today. You going to drink your coffee?'

'You have it.'

'Thanks, babe.'

'Don't call me babe.'

'You don't like it?' he asked.

'Not really.'

'Okay. Sorry.' He finished her coffee and put the mug down. 'I've got to go.' Johann tried to kiss her but she turned away.

'You getting your period?' he asked, a hurt look on his face.

'I hope so.'

'That explains things.'

'What things?'

'Your mood . . .'

'My mood is fine,' she responded warily.

'It wasn't so perfect last night.'

'I was tired,' she insisted. 'I just wanted to get home.'

'Okay, I believe you. I'll see you later.'

As soon as she heard the front door close she went to the bathroom, retrieved the pregnancy test, tore it open and read the instructions. *Place the absorbent tip in the stream of your urine. Wait.*

Freya urinated on the stick without making too much mess. While she waited for the chemicals to inform her of her fate, a dog barked in the street, an ambulance siren whooped in the distance, and a blackbird called. A second thin blue line appeared on the soaked strip in her hand. Positive. Desperation burned her throat. All it would take was a scrape, some cramp, some anguish and then there would be a return to her life, uninterrupted. She found the nausea unbearable; it was as if she was at sea in her own body. She wanted to stop this unintended cluster of cells from bedding down in her. She did not want Johann to be able to claim her just because the cells were half his. She wanted to take some sharp shiny instrument, insert it into herself and drag out this thing in her that made her sick.

Cora was the one person who would not flinch if Freya told her that. Life or death. That was a thing her mother knew how to judge. Cora could look at an injured animal and say *the kindest thing we can do is put it out of its misery*. Freya had seen her do it. There was a small cemetery behind her mother's studio above Loch Long where they had buried wounded creatures Cora had killed. Birds, mice – a broken-backed ferret, once. And she would do it herself – circle a small neck with her fingers and break it. Clean and sharp, that crack of a spine. Freya dialled her mother's number, willing her to pick up this time. And she did. Almost immediately.

'My darling,' said Cora.

'Where were you, Mum?'

'In Montreal,' said Cora, her voice calm and steady, as if all was normal. 'I told you. I'm home now.'

'You are.' Freya felt a flood of relief. 'Did I wake you?'

'I'm up,' said Cora. 'I'm jetlagged. How are you, sweetheart?'

She could not answer that.

'Freya,' Cora urged, 'what's wrong?'

She swallowed, but the lump in her throat did not move.

'Are you all right?' asked Cora. 'Has something happened?'

'I need to ask you something,' she finally managed to say. 'About me, this time.'

'What is it?' Cora asked.

Freya could not answer but her mother knew how to listen when Freya was quiet: Cora understood that like Leo, Freya gathered her thoughts first, spoke second. Impatient and quick as Cora was, she had learned to wait for Freya to find the words she needed. And she did find them.

'When you got pregnant with me,' Freya asked, 'what made you choose to keep me?'

'Freya—'

'Just answer my question, Mum,' she said, tears breaking through. 'Please.'

'It wasn't a choice,' said Cora. 'I just knew I wanted you. Why are you asking me this, Freya?'

'I'm pregnant, but I don't feel like that. I don't know what to do. It feels like the end of the world. I just think of it in me, growing. Growing like a parasite.'

'There are no rules about these things,' Cora said, carefully.

'You were never sorry you had me?' Her voice was lighter – the weight of her secret halved by the telling.

'Never. Not once, but that doesn't mean you have to be the same. It seems to be a thing that has its own logic,' said her mother. 'A body logic.'

Freya was quiet for a long time, then she asked, 'Wouldn't it have been easier if you hadn't?'

'It might well have been,' said Cora. 'But then it wouldn't have been my life. What does Johann say?'

'Nothing,' she said

'Have you told him?'

'Do I have to?'

'No,' said Cora. 'Not if you don't want to. It's yours to have or not to have.'

'I don't love him,' she said. 'I don't want him. He's going back to South Africa.'

'Those are not all the same thing,' said Cora.

'I can't think straight.' She rubbed her temples, overwhelmed by the impossibility of her decision. 'I can't feel straight. I don't have any ground under my feet.'

'I'm here,' Cora reassured her. 'We'll work this out. Believe me.'

'I do believe you,' said Freya. She thought of the cells within her body – their cells – endlessly doubling. By now they would look like a tadpole – bulbous head and the intricate knotting of an embryonic spine. Cora's practicality was what Freya needed.

'Maybe I'll come home for a bit,' Freya wondered aloud. 'Things are always simpler when we're in the same room.'

'Do that,' said Cora. 'This weekend. I'll be finished by then.'

'You're working again?'

'Yes,' said Cora. 'First time since—' She stopped short. Neither of them was quite ready to talk about *Forbidden Fruit* yet. She breathed out. 'We can start again at the beginning.'

'That sounds good.' For the first time in months, Freya felt that even though things could never be the same, perhaps they could be fine. 'I must tell you what I found in your old trunk from Eden.'

'Tell me.'

'Some film reels,' she replied. 'Old home movies.'

'I'd forgotten about them.' Cora sounded surprised. 'It was my father's camera. Only he used it, so endless cattle shows, plus birthdays, Christmases and whatever else he considered a special occasion. Have you looked at them yet?'

'I don't have a projector. I thought I would hire one here.'

'Bring them when you come,' Cora said. 'We'll watch them together. It will be quite something to see them after such a long time.'

'Don't you miss it ever?' asked Freya.

'I left it behind.' There was a catch in Cora's voice. 'I closed it all off.'

'That's not true,' Freya countered. 'You carry that place with you wherever you are. It's just that you never really talk about it – about what happened. About what you did there. About why you left. About leaving.'

'There's going to be no more leaving.' Cora took a deep breath. 'I love you. Get the train.'

'How about the day after tomorrow?'

'Perfect,' her mother replied. 'I'll come and pick you up and we'll sort everything out.'

Freya didn't feel so alone with her secret now that her mother knew. Full of energy and purpose again, she searched online for a film equipment company. She found one that hired out old 8mm projectors and called them. They had one available, if she could collect.

She went to the kitchen, hungry for the first time in a week. She put two pieces of bread in the toaster. When her toast popped up, she buttered it and added lashings of Marmite. As she was eating, the sun broke through the clouds and light splashed through the kitchen window. She tilted her face towards its wintry rays.

TWENTY-TWO

Kit-Kat purred in Cora's arms and she was glad she had something warm to hold in place of her daughter. She buried her face in the cat's soft fur. This baby of Freya's, if it was going to be a baby, felt to Cora as if a lifeline had been thrown to her. Freya had turned to her and there, in the bond that had always held them close, was her way back to her daughter across the gulf that had opened up between them. That gulf could be measured in unanswerable questions, questions that had been posed to Cora by the policewoman who had arrived at the Villiers gallery the day after the protests and the smashed windows.

A Detective Sergeant Roberts had informed Cora that she

wanted to ask her a few questions. '*Forbidden Fruit*, that's what you called your exhibition?'

'Yes,' Cora had replied. 'It's a Biblical reference to Eve and her transgressions – her fear and her desire to know.'

'I am aware of the religious reference. It is also the name of a number of illegal porn websites. Freya Finch is your daughter?'

'Her father's surname. Not mine,' Cora had clarified. 'I thought privacy would be good for her.'

The policewoman had raised an eyebrow. 'There's been so much upset about these pictures of your daughter in a bikini that barely covers her,' Roberts said as she scrutinised the miniatures. 'Here, she's in nothing at all. So perhaps you could help me understand, Ms Berger. Art is not my remit – although quite often photographers who have shot similar images to your paintings claim what they were doing was art, not pornography.'

'That's not my daughter.' Cora kept the anger out of her voice.

'I've looked at the paintings. I've met Freya. The likeness between the two of you is striking. A large part of my work these days involves looking at pornographic images of children, so I have to investigate complaints that seem to hold some validity.'

'It's me as a child,' Cora said, struggling to keep her frustration out of her voice. 'I used myself because images like this, pictures of young girls, are everywhere, but the obscenity comes via the eye of the beholder. It is nothing the girl does but all of us, me and you, we are implicated in these images. The only way I could legally depict this – understand this, bring it into the light – was to make the images of myself. To do these self-portraits. I was wrong. I was stupid not to think of the conflation of mother and daughter, but it shows that we carry the girls we were within us. I have said this over and over to the press and on social media, Detective Roberts. As has Freya.'

'She's very loyal, your daughter, and she obviously knows all about art – how could she not, with you as her mother – but she is distressed.'

'How could she be anything but distressed with what has happened?' Cora asked the detective. 'That I know is my fault. That is something I will have to undo, but because she's eighteen, the tabloids have hunted her as if she was prey and I could not protect her.'

'Then perhaps you have a complaint to make.' DS Roberts' expression was so kind, so expectant, that for a moment Cora felt such a strong urge to give in, to unburden herself by telling her about Yves and what he had done, because the secrets of others were dangerous things: Cora had known that since childhood. They bent their keepers to their own shape in the end, unless one found ways to tell of harms done. But she resisted and the urge passed. She was not sure enough where her secrets ended and Yves' began. The detective gave an almost imperceptible sigh. Cora was not sure that she had convinced DS Roberts of either her innocence or her guilt, but she left after that and Cora had not heard from her again.

The fire cracked and snapped, but the comforting sounds of Cora's studio did not muffle the questions that the detective, who had the eyes of someone who had looked at too many secret things, had asked. They had made Cora's head hurt then, and now she felt a sharp twist of pain behind her eyes. She put her hand to her neck and there was the key: cold, hard, certain. She flicked the key around so that it dangled down her back. Yves had warned her playfully – or so she'd imagined – when she had asked him what that key was for, that it was to the innermost gate in his mind. No sensible woman wanted to go there, he had told her, but like the wife in the fairytale, *Bluebeard*, she had been determined to enter that forbidden chamber whatever the price.

She would have to go back into the darkness one last time to bury forever what she had seen. She had been ignorant, yet she should have known. In the court of her own self, ignorance had never amounted to innocence. She could not face Freya with the contagion still within her. It would be there until she had interred every trace of it.

Cora fetched the portraits she'd plucked like the forbidden fruit they were from her large canvases on the walls of the Villiers' gallery, miniature obscenities that drew the viewer so close that they made all complicit, and laid them out in sequence – from oblivious child to bruised conquest. She would bury twelve of them in this canvas. The first one she had, in her panic-stricken dash, forgotten in the cabin. She thought of herself as the original, her tanned wet skin, the yellow bikini top pulled askew to expose her defiant girl's body. She had painted that for him to try and communicate how it felt for a girl to transition into something – no longer some*one* – that men look at. His acquisition – the girl lost to herself.

That had been the moment that had brought her here, reduced to this. She could never return to the origin and save herself from betrayal, but the rest she could erase so that she could release herself from Yves' cold embrace. That would close the wound he had opened again in her, she thought as she folded the miniature paintings into the shapes of the snow-laden fir trees around Yves' cabin.

She fixed the pictures of the girl to the vast canvas before covering every one of them with whitewash, vanishing them into the forest. Then she unrolled the bolt of silk across the studio floor. It snagged on one of the metal spikes in the floor. She unhooked the fabric and stitched together the small tear. Things were never going to be right, she thought as she stretched it, thin as skin, across her canvas. When she had fixed it in place, she ran her hand across it: her secret history, this buried confession, as yet incomplete, of the cabin and the pain, the dog and the blood. She closed her eyes so that she could see the snow again. See herself and the dog running, the lake, the ice, the serried ranks of trees, the jagged mountains. When she opened her eyes again, the canvas was in front of her and she knew what to paint.

Cora poured the white acrylic paint and selected as large a brush as she could find. It made no sound, each stroke receding the present as she applied wash after pale wash over the doubled canvas. The paint, which swirled and ridged over the things she had buried under the silk, ghosted what lay beneath, then she leaned back on the ladder, narrowed her eyes, and surveyed her huge canvas. White on white on white, as it had been on her first journey up to the cabin. An icy Eden.

Cora narrowed her eyes and looked at the lattice of ice on a branch that she had created with shades of white paint and texture. In her mind's eye she could see the frozen lake criss-crossed with tracks, Yves crossing the ice, returning to his cabin for the last time. That was what she wished to conjure. She rifled through the jumble of paints, replenishing her palette with whites, greys, greens and subtle blues, and climbed up the precarious ladder once more. She set to work again, scraping off some excess paint, revealing the bruises on the ice, the forest where the wolves were. The forest she should have escaped into on her first night in the cabin, when Yves had told her what he had done.

ngel showered for a long time when she got back from the cutting room. She needed to warm up but she also needed to wash the smell of blood off her hands and out of her hair. So she stood under the hot water until it began to run cold. Only then did she turn off the taps and towel herself dry. She dressed, opened a bag of crisps for dinner and sat down at the table to eat. There was a lot to think about. She did not like to change plans, but she'd had to because of Cora Berger.

The woman had thrown Angel, because she had never let herself consider what her own mother had seen or chosen not to see. That, Angel could not think about, but she could think about Cora Berger and about what she had done to her daughter, for Fournier and why. She needed to find Fournier and as long as he was absent, she had only one person to ask. The only way to ask the kinds of questions she needed answers to was in person.

Angel knew Cora Berger lived in Scotland. A profile in the *Scotsman* had a photograph of her in front of her house, its roof pitched as sharply as a witch's hat. And there was a photograph of Cora standing in the garden. She seemed so close that Angel could imagine putting her hand out, touching her. That was what she needed to do. Touch her. Angel would find a way to make her say where Fournier was.

She searched for a flight. There was one seat left on a flight via Reykjavik the following morning. She checked her bank balance. Two thousand, four hundred and thirty-three dollars. More than enough to cover the cost. She wanted answers and this was a gamble she felt compelled to take.

Trotsky growled as she paid for the ticket. Angel patted her. 'I won't be long,' she told the dog, but Trotsky's hackles were up and she was staring at the front door. Angel looked that way too, sensing with Trotsky that someone was there, but no knock came and no one said her name.

Whoever was out there was circling the cabin. Angel knew this, because Trotsky followed the movement with her eyes. For a moment, the dog fixed on the window. Then she swivelled her head slowly towards the door.

Angel waited for the knock. It did not come, but the door handle moved down and then up. She felt as if a steel band was tightening around her chest. She put her eye to the peephole. Jeb's face was fish-eyed on the other side, looking blindly into hers. She pushed the door open and he stumbled backwards. 'Hey, Angel,' he said.

'What are you doing here?' she asked.

'It's dinner time. I thought I'd come get you. We could go to Dizzy's Diner. Get dinner.'

'Very funny,' she said. 'Where's Tommy?'

'He went home with Tina,' said Jeb. 'Let's go. I'm starved.'

'No.'

'Why don't you come out?' he pleaded.

'I ate,' said Angel.

'What?'

'Dinner.'

'You can come with me and tell me a bit about it,' he said.

'I said no.'

'You could have a beer,' Jeb suggested. 'Watch me eat.'

'That sounds even worse,' said Angel.

'Come on,' he cajoled. 'You've got to keep a lonely stranger in town company.'

'I don't,' she said.

'Come on, Angel. I'm just being friendly.'

'Fuck you, I don't need friends.'

'I can tell you how the search for Fournier's going.'

'How is it going?' asked Angel.

'We finally got a position on the last picture he posted, asking who could guess where he was skiing. It's a copse of firs that's due north from his cabin, halfway to Devil's Peak.'

'You didn't find him?'

'Not yet,' said Jeb.

'Then what's to tell?'

'It's fucking cold out here. You going to ask me in?'

Angel didn't move.

'Then I guess I have to ask my questions out here then.' He gave a little smile. He knew he'd got under her skin. 'What were you doing up at Fournier's this morning?'

'Fetching Trotsky's food from the cabin.'

'That's a long way to drive for dog food.'

'It's specialist food. She's got a liver condition.'

Jeb scrutinised her face.

'I don't believe your story, not for one fucking minute. This is not where you belong, so what are you doing here?'

'I'm interested in predators – those wolves in there.' She pointed to the pens where the animals paced, watching them. 'I love them and they love me.'

'I'm going to find out why you're here sooner rather than later, Angel. So why not just tell me yourself?'

Angel cocked an eyebrow at him. 'It's nothing to do with you.'

'You've been inside.' Jeb stepped closer to her. 'I can smell it on you. I know where to look, and when this snow is over, I'm going to check you out.'

Jeb moved towards Angel, but Trotsky bared her teeth and he retreated. Angel slammed the door shut and leaned against it. The door was steel. The cold would drive him away. She was right. Before too long she heard him curse, then the crunch of footsteps on the snow, a car door slamming, its engine gunning and then silence.

Half an hour passed before Angel lay down on her bed. When she did, Trotsky came and lay beside her as if she sensed her fear. Angel put her arms around the warm animal and waited for morning to come.

TWENTY-FOUR

Cora had carried Yves' tale home with her as if it were a bomb he had strapped to her body. She was afraid that if she moved, if she spoke, if she told anyone, it would blow up and everyone she loved would be destroyed. But she passed unnoticed through customs with it and brought it all the way home. It was only when she was sitting in the silence of her own kitchen that she checked what he had told her.

It took her a while to find the reports but there they were, in a French tabloid, *Le Journal de Montréal*. The police raid on his house, his arrest, the months of investigation, the search of everything he had ever trawled on the subterranean ocean that is the internet, the charges made and then dropped. His name had been kept out of the press – he was simply referred to as a 'leading cultural figure'. That she would not have found him unless she had known what she was looking for gave her no comfort.

There was a brief report in a newspaper, which carried his lawyer's terse statement saying that an admission of guilt fine had been paid for two pictures, one of which, according to the dry statement, was of a clothed person and the other a drawing. Dead, neutral language, the kind that could stifle a scandal by bringing press speculation to a halt. There was naturally no mention of the charges against him that had been dropped. There was no mention that somewhere in a police file there was a transcript of an online conversation between a group of men about a twelve-year-old girl in a hotel and what might or might not have been done to her. Nothing of that, because there had been no case to answer, because there was no evidence. Instead, the lawyer, plain and prim in her dark trouser suit, had stated that Yves was a man who had made a mistake. He had paid his dues. He was sorry for harm done. It was time to move on, as he had moved on.

As soon as Cora had landed back in Scotland and switched her phone on she had received a flurry of messages from Yves. He missed her, he wrote. He sent her more song lyrics. Leonard Cohen's lyrics spoke his heart for him, he said. He sent her photographs of the two of them in the snow. When she asked him more questions – *Your telling me that,* she wrote, *brought me to a halt* – about the images, he deflected her, amused at first and then firm.

It's done. Debt paid, he wrote. *Put it behind you as I have had to. It was a difficult time of my life. It's over. I have you now. We have each other . . . ♥ Who would have believed I would find this happiness that is you? You will be back – in the spring?*

Cora could not bear not to believe him. She suppressed as well as she could her wilder imaginings, swept along again by his virtual attention that got her through the winter and into the spring, when she visited him again.

Yves picked her up at the airport and they drove up to the cabin. It was unseasonably warm and she sat on the rocks by the lake and watched him swim. The sun shining through the clear peat-brown water caught his body thin and pale as an eel under the surface. He surfaced, the water cascading off him. She saw the grey tinge of the skin on the high cheekbones, the beaked nose and the skull beneath his wet hair. She stared at this man on whom death was beginning to settle. She saw his decay, but it made no difference. He had burrowed deep into her heart and this was the only place Cora wanted to be. She could not shake off the feeling that to be with him was to be at home and that – at last – she had been taken in. He climbed out of the water and sat beside her.

'It's good to have you back,' said Yves, pulling her against his cold body. She leaned into him, as if no crimes had been committed. They went back up to the house, and a flock of birds, white and buff with russet breasts, appeared on the windowsill. They pecked at the sunflower seeds Cora put out for them.

'The girl,' said Cora.

'No girl.' Yves was towelling himself so she could not see his face.

'But the transcript, what of that? Even if it was only in those men's minds, that's bad enough.'

'Men,' he said, 'making things up in a chat room.'

'How do you know?' she asked.

'I don't,' he replied. 'I wasn't there.'

'And the other images?'

'The prosecutor in charge. She went after me. A vendetta. They don't like to be made fools of. You know what they can be like.'

Cora didn't know and she did not know what to say, so she said nothing. Later, when they were in bed, he held her as if she was rare. As if she was precious. 'Those pictures,' she asked again, despite herself. 'What were you looking for?'

'All men watch pornography,' Yves said patiently. 'They're lying if they say they don't.'

Cora had to believe him. How did she know what men wanted to look at in the secret parts of their minds? She wasn't one of them, but she did try to imagine it. That made it easier to take the cruelty that came later, his hand over her face, his other hand pinning both her wrists to the mattress. She moved as if there might be a release but there was none, even though she faked pleasure. She could find no way to refuse him the small, strange humiliations that fuelled his desire.

Cora could not fathom her own compulsion to submit, but she did know that a stubborn secret part of herself wanted him with a desire that split her apart, because her body did not trust him. Her body did not trust her either and, although she acquiesced to Yves, she remained numb, those unseen images haunting her.

She wanted to see what he had looked at because she wanted to believe his claims of innocence and persecution. Everybody said that seeing was believing so if she could only see them she would then know that what he had told her was true. She would then see for herself that they were what Yves said – *so unimportant, such an error, just the normal way one goes click, click, click and there you are, an innocent lost in the Web.*

'I want to know what you looked at,' she said one morning.

'What will that do?' He was weary of this.

'You say they were nothing. If I see them then I don't have to imagine them.'

'Well, don't imagine them.'

She was exposed before him. He gave her the briefest of smiles: her silence meant that he had won and they both knew it.

The crows settling in the spruce outside Cora's studio drew her attention back to where she was now. She watched one of them sharpen its beak against the branch, thinking that it was true that she went to Yves' cabin the first time of her own accord. The second time, too. When she had tried to escape him – her mind getting temporary control of her heart – he had known her vulnerabilities too well and he'd reeled her back in every time she'd tried to break off their affair. It was a cruel and humiliating kind of sport that seemed to amuse him.

Cora turned back to her painting. This last weekend she had not gone freely. Instead, she had been driven by the compulsion to be free of Yves. To do that, she'd had to amputate the part of herself that he held in thrall. She brushed her hand over her double-skinned canvas, feeling the portraits of the girl that she had hidden by turning them into snow-fringed trees. She shivered, as if she had touched a ghost.

TWENTY-FIVE

reya collected the projector and lugged it home. She set it up on the table in the living room and threaded the first reel of film onto its little metal teeth. She suspended a white sheet on one wall and switched the old machine on, bringing another world – another time – jerkily to life. On the makeshift screen was Eden. The camera lingered on a bullet-riddled sign, then the gravel road, then it panned onto the pale khaki scrub. There was out-of-focus footage of cattle. Then a whitewashed farmhouse with a deep verandah, and on it, a dark-haired woman in a short dress, her belly tight as a drum against the yellow fabric, a cigarette in one hand, a martini glass in the other. *That must be Mum in there*, Freya thought, stopping herself from putting her hand on her own belly.

The second reels were of more cattle, cycles of drought and rain, footage of men and women queuing up with their hands outstretched, Cora's mother handing out parcels. Second-hand Christmas presents. The men getting carefully measured shots of brandy. Cora standing off to one side with a little boy her own age. Freya looked at him closely. That was Dawid. She had seen him in the photos and in some of Cora's early paintings. The way they stood showed an affinity between the two children that exists between best friends or siblings.

The third reel would not work – the film had been corroded and it broke apart in her hands – but she managed to get the fourth one going. She watched the house with its cool white verandah, dogs scattered in the shade. More cattle. The grass gone and the sky a pitiless blue, vultures circling where the drought-starved cattle had fallen. And then it must have rained again because the grass was waist high and there was a snatch of footage of Cora and Dawid cartwheeling across a lush green lawn. The film jerked upwards, as if whoever was filming had stumbled. There was a shot of the sky – blue above the farm, but with storm clouds gathering on the horizon – and then it was another day and there was an unsteady pan of the stables, the grain silo.

Freya was transfixed by the stand of gnarled old trees that came into view next. Six ghost gums, a table set with a picnic beneath them. It was the original view of the painting that hung in her room at Lawhead. She and her mother would lie in bed and look at it and talk about Eden and stars – the Southern Cross, the Milky Way that Cora said was the backbone of the sky – and Dawid, the boy who had been her mother's only friend before he was sent away. It disturbed Freya now to see the bench in this bland, silent footage that panned across the acacia scrub, the gum trees, the stables, and Cora, looking towards the dilapidated huts where half naked children were playing in the dust.

Whoever was filming must have called Cora's name because she turned and stared mutinously out of the frame. She looked about twelve – she no longer had the body of a child. It was not so much that she had the start of breasts under the yellow bikini she was wearing. It was more that her body was tense, as if she had learned what it meant to be looked at. Freya remembered that feeling herself – the first transfixing stare from a stranger – admiring and predatory in equal measures. It was that gaze, her mother called it the male gaze, that sets a girl outside herself forever. She stopped the film and looked back in time at her mother.

What happened there? she wondered. Who was she looking for? What had her mother seen that made the expression in her eyes so guarded?

In the painting – Freya took down the print she had stuck on the wall of the flat – Cora stood in a gap in the scrub, and stared at the bench under the trees that seemed to Freya like a haven from the sun. Her mother's rendering of it, however, infused that shady place with an unbearable sense of jeopardy. Cora had painted this place – the trees with their amphitheatre of shade, the bench beneath them an altar – over and over.

In all the versions she had seen, Cora had painted herself standing half hidden in the scrub. It was one of those bright revelations of her mother's childhood, so precise in their remembered detail, so unilluminating about what happened before and after the slice of time Cora captured. Freya shivered as if uninvited fingers had brushed her skin. She turned her attention back to the film: Cora had the same expression of inarticulate fury in her eyes that the girl in the *Forbidden Fruit* paintings had. Violence and an eroticism that had been captured on this fragile old film.

The reel was blank for a few minutes after that, and she was about to switch it off when Cora reappeared. This time she was standing on a stage wearing a maroon school skirt and white blouse, and her wild black hair was tied into bunches. Freya watched, fascinated, as Cora, who looked about twelve or thirteen, walked across the stage towards a bearded man who held a silver cup out to her. She took it and moved away quickly, but he pulled her back. She flinched, jaw tight, when he draped a sash over her. He took hold of her shoulder and turned a sullen Cora to face her audience. 'Victrix ludorum' was emblazoned on the white satin across her chest.

The bearded teacher kept his hand on Cora's narrow shoulder, but she did not smile. Her blank eyes deflected the obvious pride of both the photographer and the teacher. Then the film cut to the paintings on display behind them. Freya knew they were Cora's because of their distinct style: the strong sensuous lines and the rich colours had endured in her mother's work. And then the tantalising film ended. Freya looked once more in the trunk, but there was nothing more.

She rewound the last reel and watched the scene again, filming it on her mobile. This time she noticed a green banner at the back of the stage. 'Sacred Heart, Vrededorp' hand-stitched in gold on it. She was now certain that Cora had never mentioned going to this school, but her twelfth year had been a pivotal one if that was the first time she had left Eden. She checked the introduction Cora had written for *Eden*, but there was nothing about it at all.

It seemed so strange to Freya that her mother, who used everything that came her way as material, would have left this out. She was puzzled that her mother had never mentioned this school before, or why she had not mentioned the paintings that were on display behind her in the film. In a way, it had been her first exhibition. Cora had obsessively documented everything about her life, so why not this? Freya knew her mother. If Cora was silent, it was not because there was nothing to say, but because she did not have the words to say it. This gap, however, Freya was determined to understand. Her mother's first show – that would be the place to start the essay she was going to write for the art curating application. This would give her a new angle. Cora would have to tell her why she had never mentioned this school, or the fact that it was where she had started painting, and that it must have been the place where Cora had first displayed work in public.

Freya opened the laptop and typed 'Sacred Heart, Vrededorp' – the dusty mining town twenty miles from Eden – into her browser. The town still had a school of that name and she scrolled eagerly down the page. It had been a mission station originally and had a pretty stone chapel. It was surrounded by lawns and its classrooms had big windows. The school provided an education for rural children, according to the website. There were pictures of grinning children – the boys in khaki shorts and white shirts, the girls in the maroon uniform that Cora had worn decades earlier. There was a fundraising drive for a new building project to make the school water and energy self-sufficient.

Freya was about to leave the page when she noticed a link

with the school's emblem right at the bottom. She clicked on it. There was a statement from the school board, dated two years earlier, in response to the discovery of human remains during construction work. An old well, which had been covered over almost forty years earlier, had been opened up again because of water shortages in the town. Due to climate change it was better for schools and hospitals to have their own generators and water sources. The wider community could be reassured that the bones had been there for decades and that the children were not, nor ever had been, in any danger. Reports that it might be the remains of a teacher who had left the school several decades earlier were speculation. The remains were subject to forensic tests in an attempt to identify them. There was the possibility that the bones could be archaeological. That needed to be ascertained. All queries should be directed to the headmaster's office, but there was no risk to either staff or students, etc.

Freya searched for more on the story. She couldn't find anything in English, but there were a few articles in Afrikaans. She tried Google Translate, but it was garbled and did not reveal much. One article had a photograph of a colonnaded walkway and some girls in uniform – maroon skirts and white shirts – walking through the shadows cast by the sturdy columns with their arms linked. That was the place that Cora would have walked through. The other photograph was of a deep hole in the ground, with a blue arrow pointing to where the skeleton had been found.

Freya picked up her phone and called Johann. 'Hey,' she said, when he answered. 'I need you to translate something from Afrikaans for me. Can I send you a link?'

'And there I was thinking you were missing me, babe,'

'There is that, too.'

'Is it to do with your mom?'

'I don't know,' Freya replied. 'Maybe.'

'Did you ask her?'

'Not about this, no.'

'I'll look at it when I get back home,' said Johann. 'I'm on my way. Can I tempt you with takeout?'

'Yes, please,' said Freya. 'I've had a craving for Thai. I'll have some chicken satay skewers and a massaman curry with jasmine rice.'

TWENTY-SIX

Cora, balancing on the top rung of the ladder, lost herself in the pristine wilderness she was conjuring from fragments of remembered light. She had been running, the cold tearing at her lungs, the dog behind her, her torn paw planting petals of blood on the snow. Snatches of the dog's remembered howl, carried on the wind that blew across the frozen lake, reached her again. Cora flicked through her playlist, selected Sibelius' *Finlandia*. She turned up the volume, and the music, heroic and grand, drowned out all other sounds.

Cora fished a tube of red paint out of her pocket, squeezed it at the waist. As the pigment marked the injured dog's poppy tracks on the ice, she felt easier. Painting had always been her shelter from the things that could not be said, but it worked only if she did not stop, did not eat, did not sleep. If she painted, then she did not need to think. If she did not think, then there was no need for language. If there was no language, then she did not have to remember. So, brushstroke after careful brushstroke, she created this skin to separate the present from the past. To reconstitute herself.

She had done that after Yves' confession, when all he had offered her were the colourless words chosen for him by a lawyer, that conveyed neither image nor feeling. The very things that were her currency. She could not bear to think of him descending into the internet's cinema of hell and returning to the surface, his eyes poisoned. What Yves had looked at haunted her. Once, those girls had been real. Once, they had been in rooms with men with cameras – they must have been, in order for Yves to find them on the internet. Cora tried to picture those nameless girls, but their contours refused to come into focus. To release herself from her obsessive imagining, Cora needed an outline of the girls' faces, of the narrowing of their waists, the tender backs of their knees.

When she had asked Yves to show her what he had looked at, she had felt the hum in his body and she was afraid. His anger silenced her. His love was conditional on her not questioning him, and she wanted his love more than anything. She wanted to be convinced. She wanted to believe, but her eye was trained to look at things until she understood the truth, and Yves could not – or he would not – put her mind to rest. There was no way she could take herself into the dark places of the internet where he had gone, but she could not stop her mind's eye from imagining. Yves' secret opened up an abyss in herself and everything else in her life circled around it.

When Cora got home, she went through her photographs from Eden, searching for the pictures of herself in the yellow bikini. The first painting she had done for Yves and given him had been an innocent gift. She had painted herself in her yellow bikini on Eden because she had wanted to show him the feeling he had restored in her – a joy in her body's potential, its strength and beauty.

When she had found the pictures and looked at them again, she recognised the darkness that underpinned that memory of her pubescent self – her child's body budding with womanhood and the way men had started to look at her. Those photographs – taken by her father, who had followed her about with his Kodak or the old 8mm film camera until she had wept with shame at his intrusion.

That old shame merged with the shame of what Yves had done, something that he refused to own, and it was overwhelming. It drove her mad, not knowing what he had looked for – the man she had loved. To try and understand her distress and shame, she had painted a series of imaginary self-portraits. The images she made of herself were overlaid with her imaginings of the spectral children on the dark web, stripped and captured on camera with their limbs in lewd tangles, their eyes dead: condemned to an eternity in that electronic abyss. Permanently available, unable to escape, unable to shield themselves from view. The combination became the works she had called *Forbidden Fruit.*

But Cora could not free herself of Yves. He had seduced her privately and he had, so quickly, enmeshed himself in her professional life. She had asked him to leave her alone if he would not answer her questions, if he could not put her mind at rest, but he had flown to London for her last Art for Justice event, walking in as she stood on the stage to introduce the work that refugee women had made about their perilous journeys to a precarious safety in England. Then she had Yves' undivided attention. He loved her in public. He could love her when he saw her through the eyes of others. He claimed her unequivocally for himself when she was all frocked up and glamorous, telling stories of loss and beauty to a rapt audience. It was when no one was watching that he cut her down to the size he needed her to be.

When Cora had finished speaking that night, she stepped down and took a glass of champagne from the event's host. As she spoke to him about the evening's success she saw Yves join a group of people smoking outside. She watched his rapid assessment of a young woman – an artist who had fled a war-torn country. She watched the angling of his body, the effortless way in which he distracted the girl from the rest of the circle and held her attention. He was so practised, listening to the girl intently, making her laugh, his attention bringing a flush to her throat. Watching Yves was like watching a wolf separating off his prey. Cora was unable to look away; it was a way of watching herself and seeing how easily she had been caught.

Run. That was her thought, but then he came towards her and kissed her cheek and said how marvellous she had been, how beautiful she looked – it was as if she had hallucinated. His was a hall of mirrors in which any cruelty was possible. She had sensed it in the beginning, but she had put her instinct aside. She accepted his invitation to dinner that evening without saying a word about what she had seen or what she felt.

* * *

The city streets were busy. They found a bistro and ordered wine and watched people go past. The conversation, so easy and fluid at the start, was stilted. She had no idea how to fight him, or how to fight herself, this ice around her heart that trapped the unspoken anger she harboured in it – but she couldn't stand another second of small talk.

'I need to understand.' She had hated the break in her voice. 'It's always only on your terms, but I need to know. I need to see.'

'Darling.' He put his hand on the nape of her neck. 'Why do you make a problem where there isn't one? I love you. You know that.' The same hand slid down her throat and she gave way, despite herself, and put her hand over his. 'Don't spoil such a beautiful evening. Let's go for a walk.' He guided her away from the crowds and into a park.

He picked a late-flowering daisy. 'This is a test,' he said, 'to see if you love me.' He plucked one petal. 'You love me.' He plucked another and pulled a face. 'You love me not. You love me . . .'

And so he went around the flower, tearing off one petal after the other, Cora's heart beating faster and faster as if she was watching her fate unfold in this tiny form of Russian roulette.

He reached the last one. 'You love me!' Yves crowed. 'I knew it.' He pulled her against him, tilting her face up towards his so that he could kiss her.

The foolish tenderness of the moment brought tears to her eyes. She did not resist, even though she was aware of the dexterity of his seduction of her. He made her into a child, unable to control anything. That, thought Cora, as they walked deeper into the park, was the true horror of love. She reached for him and he held her against the old leather jacket he always wore. The necklace she was wearing snagged on the zip and came off. Cora caught it in her hand.

'Won't you fasten this for me?' she asked.

'Turn around.' His fingers were gentle on the back of her neck. 'Women always ask you to do this,' he said, 'to draw attention to their bodies.'

Intimacy turned to artifice. Cora thought of the young woman she had seen him flirting with earlier in the evening. Of how she had turned like a sunflower to the sun of his attention. How Cora had done the same. 'How many women have you slept with?' asked Cora, turning to face him.

'I haven't counted,' he said. 'Many.'

That couldn't be true. He knew so little about what gave a woman pleasure. It infuriated her that she did not have the courage to say so.

'There have only been a couple that mattered,' he said.

'Who?' she asked, despite herself.

'You, of course,' he answered. They walked on. Several lights on the path had been knocked out and it was dark – the night was cooling rapidly and mist rose up from the streams. The darkness seemed to open something in him. 'And a girl who worked at a radio station where I did a weekly arts programme,' said Yves. 'It was her first job and she was alone in the city. There was something so new and fresh about her. I made her laugh. She adored me. I insisted she come and work for me. She resisted. She loved her job but I had to have her.

'I saw her all the time in the beginning, of course,' he said, 'but I am a busy man and so after a while I saw her less.' He stopped speaking, but Cora said nothing. He so rarely told her anything private. She was close, she felt, to understanding something about him.

'It's having something, I suppose. One gets bored when the chase is over. I was a busy man. She learned to wait.'

Cora could not tell if the twist in her heart was for that leashed girl or for herself.

'What about your wife?' Cora asked.

'I would never have done anything to harm my family,' said Yves.

Cora stopped and stared at him. 'Are you serious?' she said. 'You, who put everything at risk?'

'I had a mistress,' he said. 'So sue me.' His flare of anger made Cora step back, but then they were walking on again, away from the lights, and he seemed to soften.

'I had everything when I met her – money, success, power – but I was bored,' said Yves. 'Not everyone has what you have, Cora – that gift you have for art. You wouldn't understand it, but with her I escaped the boredom. We explored a foreign land, one without restraint. One without maps.'

It felt like jealousy, but jealousy was easier. Jealousy made sense – there was a language for it. She had no language for what she felt then – as if a distressed animal was pacing the confines of her chest.

'Each time we found a boundary, we crossed it,' he went on. 'All of them. One after the other. Her trust. Her acceptance. I went further and further. My own power, the feeling of being able to do anything, but once you start it's impossible to stop, and we went too far down that road into the darkness. I had to put a stop to it.' He broke off.

'What happened to her?'

'I don't know,' he shrugged. 'Perhaps it was her that led to the other thing.'

It was so dark where they were standing, the moon behind a cloud. 'Those images?' she asked.

'You should know this, Cora,' said Yves. 'Once you have broken one taboo it's not so hard to break another.'

'You said it was an accident, how you got there. Click, click, click and you were there – that's what you said.'

'She is part of why it happened.' A shadow passed over his face. It could have been shame. 'We went too far down that path.'

'What do you mean,' she probed. 'You went too far?'

'We had – she and I – what you want,' he said. 'I feel it in you. The desire you have for me to hurt you.' He twisted her hair around his hand. 'It's what you want.'

'No,' she whispered. 'I wanted you to love me.'

'I know you want it.' His grip on her hair tightened. 'It's written all over you,' he said. 'It's what you all ask for, in the end.'

'Because it's all you give,' Cora stated. 'It's that or nothing. I cannot bear nothing.'

She tried to pull away from him, but he put his arm around her shoulders and held her, as if she were a skittish horse. 'Come on. Don't be angry.'

'Show her to me – this girl you blame for opening that forbidden gate,' said Cora. 'I know you. You'll have a picture of her.'

Yves took out his phone and scrolled through the pictures. He held it out to her. A girl, fragile, blonde, anorexic-looking, sat on the edge of a bed. Naked, except for a velvet ribbon around her neck. A man's shadow loomed behind her on the wall. It was Yves. Cora would know it anywhere. 'It's a painting.' She was taken aback. She had seen his lifeless landscapes.

'She was my muse,' said Yves. 'I made her sit for hours. It teaches the art of perfect patience. Perfect endurance. The eyes on the skin can be like fire.'

'You have a studio?'

'We all have our hidden places,' he said. 'Now, stop this and look at this beautiful night. This city. This park. These stars. If this isn't perfect, what is?

Except nothing was perfect. 'Those pictures—'

'Why do you ask over and over and over, Cora?'

'Because it's looped in my head. That girl, she goes round and round in my head. Who she was, why she was there, what happened to her—'

'It was one picture,' he said. 'A clothed person. And a drawing.'

'You repeat that every time as if it makes it go away. But she's there. Looped forever, that little "clothed person", as you describe her, caught in the sequence of whatever it was that was done to her.'

'And you want to see the images.'

'Yes,' she whispered.

'You want to take part in a criminal act?'

'No, Yves. I want it to stop.'

'To view them is to commit a crime,' he said. 'It happened. Now leave it in the past: that's where it belongs. It happened to me. Not to you.'

'*You* happened to me,' she cried. 'It *is* happening to me. What did you want? What did you look for? What do you want? Tell me that. It's as if there is a wall up. You took it down and invited me in and then when I had nowhere else to go, you closed it off again. Me on one side, you on the other.'

'It's nothing to do with you.' There was menace in his tone and she was afraid of him, but the path they were on led towards a denser darkness and thick scrub where there was movement, sound. Not the comforting shrillness of a fox, but the grunts of men sleeping rough. She had no choice except to walk on beside him at a pace that was not hers. She could not pretend that this was a place where women were safe in the dark. Thankfully, soon they were in the light again, and in the hotel lobby, and going up to their room where their belongings were scattered.

When they were in bed there was no kiss, no touch, just his hand between her legs, bony fingers pushing her open.

'No.' She pressed her knees together. 'I don't want to.'

But this struggle, the eventual acquiescence, it was the only thing that aroused him and because of that – in the beginning – it had aroused her too. The play fight, the giving over, him holding her so close that she could not breathe. There had been no other way. He knew no other way, no other touch. He pinned her down.

'No,' she begged, 'not this time.'

But he was on her. He had her wrists in his hands and his knee between her thighs and he drove her legs apart. She stopped fighting and Yves slammed into her. She caught a glimpse of herself reflected in the hotel window. Naked and on her back. Arms and legs splayed. He grunted and finished and collapsed on top of her, his face against her neck. 'Darling,' he said, 'I love you. You know that.' He rolled off her and fell asleep.

Cora lay there, her body numb, her mind blank. She could not move. She could not leave, despite the hurt he inflicted on her. She searched in herself for the warrior that could fight on behalf of others, but she was nowhere to be found. She could not bear giving up on the hope of being loved. She listened to her heart, trying to quiet it, as she had done many times since she had discovered the truth about Yves. There was a part of her that wanted to be hurt, that wanted to be erased, that wanted to die.

If she closed her eyes, she saw again the glimmering fire, above it the painting she had given him. She thought of the inscription written at his request - THE GIRL, for Yves, a private view. She had distilled the moment of protest against the lost innocence that drives a girl to cover her body. She had offered up that image of herself as a girl trapped like a fly in amber.

She wanted to take it all back but she could retrieve neither herself nor the painting. Yves had taken possession of the girl she had been because he had the woman she was now. She had given him her heart. If she was going to survive, she had to work out a way to take it back.

She had gone with Yves the first time forgetting that with a stranger - no matter how intimate - there is always danger. Despite the light and the beckoning curl of smoke coming from the chimney, his cabin had been no sanctuary. Yves' secret had become hers to keep. Because he felt no remorse, his shame had become hers and it bound her to him.

She had gone there again because she had invested her whole self in him. Even though she knew the truth from the very first telling, she could not take it in. She had needed him to be what she had imagined him to be. In order to go on, she had made the eye of her heart blind. She looked for tears and didn't find any. She found anger instead, but that anger was not directed at Yves. It was directed at herself.

She wondered again how long she would have to endure her heart's stubborn beating. On and on and on. She'd wanted it to stop before. Walking along the banks of rivers, she had looked with longing at the quick dark water that offered her its cold embrace. At stations, she'd felt the lure of trains rushing towards her, the slash of the wheels on the silver tracks. Once they passed, she had always been amazed to find herself still intact and on the platform.

In the morning, Yves woke and pulled Cora into his embrace, running his hand with infinite gentleness down the inside of her thigh. When she turned to him he put his finger on her lips. 'Shh. Don't spoil the moment.'

Then room service arrived with coffee. She lay in bed watching him pack his suitcase, thinking that the first time Yves had taken her in his arms – her body crushed against his bony chest, unable to breathe – she had felt as if she had come home. She had failed to ask herself then what it was she was returning to. She had failed to wonder why in the airless circle of his arms, unable to move or talk or think, she had felt calm. She had not considered any of this the first time he had driven her up to the cabin – everything new, his hand on her thigh, her feeling that she had at last found a person in whose embrace she could be safe.

He sat down next to her on the bed and said, 'See you soon.' He cupped her face in his hands and kissed her.

There had been silence and calm in the room after he left. For the first time, Cora had pictured life without him.

TWENTY-SEVEN

Freya smiled at Johann when he came in and put the fragrant Thai takeaway on the table. 'Jesus, London can take it out of you some days.' He kissed the top of her head. 'How are you, *skattie*?'

'What does that mean?' asked Freya.

'*Skattie* means "little treasure" in Afrikaans.'

'Oh, I like that.'

'You want a beer then?' he asked, walking towards the kitchen.

'No, thanks. I need you to translate some Afrikaans for me.'

'Okay, just give me a minute.' He fetched two beers from the fridge. 'You find some state secrets?'

'I found this.' Freya turned her laptop towards him. Johann opened both beers and gave her one.

'I said no.' Freya pushed it back to him.

'Don't you want to eat while the food's hot?' asked Johann, opening up the containers.

'Okay, but look at these.' She showed him the newspaper articles she had found.

'You really are looking for skeletons now.' Johann ate as he clicked through the stories.

'I'm not,' Freya argued. 'I was just curious about it because I saw my mother's home movie that her father shot at this school. So I looked it up and there was the report of the skeleton of the man found in the well.'

'Did your mom ever say anything about this place?'

'Nothing. I didn't even know she went to that school until this afternoon.'

'Well, then, it's probably some guy who passed through the town and met the wrong people.' Johann searched for some more reports. 'Here's a more recent one,' he said. 'Not much on it – the dead don't make the news in South Africa really . . . Well, he wasn't robbed. He still had his fancy shoes on.'

'Where does it say about his shoes?'

'Look here,' said Johann. 'There's a list of objects the cops found that might or might not have belonged to him. It's in Afrikaans. *Skoene* – that means shoes. The dead man was wearing a leather pair. Size ten. *Horlosie* – a watch. Seiko. *Broek* – trousers. *Jas* – a jacket. Same fabric, so probably a suit. *Koper knope* – brass buttons. A handful of coins. Some jewellery. Rings and a *skoenlapper ketting.*'

'*Skoenlapper.*' She tested out the word and Johann laughed.

'It's cute when you say it.' Johann smiled.

'Does that mean shoe?'

'That's funny,' said Johann. 'No. *Skoenlapper* means butterfly. *Skoenlapper ketting*,' He leaned over to check. 'It means butterfly necklace.' He tapped the silver pendant around her neck. 'Just like yours. A butterfly necklace, like the one in those porn-paintings of your mom.'

'Don't call them that,' she said sharply.

'Sorry, baby,' he said.

'Don't call me baby.'

'Sorry times two for that.' Johann gave her a rueful grin. 'But it's a funny thing to be there.'

Freya put her hand on her necklace. The butterfly's silver wings were cool and hard against her palm.

'This is more helpful,' said Johann, looking at the next article. 'This article says that although no dental records have yet been found, it is possible that the remains were those of a teacher – a Mr Jacques du Preez – who was leaving right at the end of the school year to take up a post in Zimbabwe. Most likely cause of death is a head injury caused by falling. Consistent with falling into the well, hitting his head. They cannot say if he was dead when he fell into the water because there was no soft tissue left. The ruling is accidental. His only family – a sister who had emigrated to Australia – say they were estranged.'

Johann closed the laptop and picked up his fork again. 'Did you ask your mother if she heard anything about this?'

'She didn't answer when I called.'

'Oh, of course. I forgot. Your mother only speaks to you when she feels like it.'

'Just leave it, Johann.'

Johann took her face in her hands. 'You can't fix the past and you can't fix your mother. It's a cool place, South Africa.

It's not all murder and shit like you see in the papers here. Come back with me and I'll take care of you.'

Freya leaned against him for a moment. Part of her wished that she could just escape and make herself up somewhere else, but then her phone rang, her mother's name flashing on the screen. She took the call.

'Mum.' Johann frowned at her delight at hearing her mother's voice. She turned away from him, the phone pressed against her ear.

'Is there something wrong?' asked Cora anxiously.

'No, nothing's wrong,' said Freya. 'I just wanted to tell you about those old home movies of yours. I hired a projector and watched them all. I felt like Alice in Wonderland going down a rabbit hole.'

'Oh, wow,' said Cora. 'That must've been strange.'

'It was a bit. Amazing to watch you as a girl. You were so fierce. Not a smile, unless you were forced to give one.'

'I loved Eden,' said Cora.

'It wasn't the farm, Mum. I was curious about the school.'

'I've told you so many stories about that boarding school in Joburg that you got sick of them. The smell of cabbage and all those posh blonde girls in bottle-green uniforms.'

'Not that Johannesburg school,' said Freya. 'It must have been before that, because you look about twelve, and the girls are in maroon skirts and white shirts.'

Cora did not say anything, but she was still there because Freya heard her sharp intake of breath.

'Sacred Heart in Vrededorp, I don't remember you telling me about it.'

'Oh, I was only there for a few months. That's probably why.'

'You've never painted it, Mum. I looked through everything I could find. What was it like?'

'Awful,' Cora answered. 'So strict. But I wasn't there for long. I just put it out of my mind.'

'Why were you there at all? I thought your mother home-schooled you?'

'She taught me to read and write, yes but then your grand-mother got it into her head that I was too much of a tomboy and that I needed the rough edges knocked off me. What she meant was I was too old to play with the other farm children. What was I then, twelve? That meant puberty. There were strict rules for girls.'

'White girls?' asked Freya.

'Yes. White girls. No binoculars, no guns, no running around with Dawid for me.' Cora's voice had a catch in it. 'How did you find out about it?'

'It's on the last reel of your dad's home movies,' said Freya. 'The final assembly, it must have been – you were the *victrix ludorum*.'

'Oh, yes. I had forgotten that.'

'And your paintings were there, Mum. The earliest ones of yours I've seen. I wanted to know more about them for the *Self / (M)Other* application essay.'

'I don't really remember them.' Cora sounded evasive.

'It's your stuff, Mum. For sure. That same deep blue you you've always used and the red and ochre. Even in the flickery old film you can see it.'

'Let's watch it when you come home,' Cora suggested.

'Okay,' said Freya. 'But there is this one weird thing. I looked the school up online and there was this weird story from a couple of years ago.'

'I wouldn't know . . . I haven't really kept up with South Africa.'

'Johann translated it for me. A man was found when workmen did repairs to an old well that was closed up years ago. The police think it might be a teacher who worked there. They think no one realised because he was leaving the school,' Freya told her.

'I don't know. After I left I went to Johannesburg and I just put that Vrededorp school out of my mind.' Her mother's voice was tight.

'The newspaper said that when they found him, he seriously was a skeleton, but his shoes and the buttons from his clothes were still okay and there were all these coins and rings and things there.'

'It was a kind of wishing well,' Cora said. 'I remember some of the girls would throw things in for luck with exams or boyfriends.'

'Oh, that makes sense, then. The Afrikaans paper said they also found a *skoenlapper ketting*. Did I say it right?'

'Yes,' Cora said faintly. 'You said it perfectly.'

'Don't you think it's weird about the butterfly necklace?' asked Freya.

'They were fashionable then.' There was an odd sound, as if Cora had dropped her phone.

'Are you still there, Mum?'

'I'm here,' said Cora.

'I thought maybe the line cut out. You were so quiet.'

'I'm here,' Cora reassured her. 'Don't forget to bring that film on Friday.'

TWENTY-EIGHT

The scene Freya described tumbled Cora back decades. Back into the heat which had been building in the shabby Sacred Heart school hall. On the stage it had been even hotter, standing there in her maroon skirt and white blouse and blazer. Her name was called and she had no choice but to walk across the stage to her art teacher, who held out the cup. His fingers had brushed her neck when he put the sash across her body and turned her, unsmiling, towards the audience.

Cora tried to stop it, but the tide of the past could not be held back. She had dammed it for too long. She stared at the fire in the grate but she did not see the flames leaping orange and red around the dry wood. She saw, instead, the colonnaded walk that led to the art room at the back of the school.

Prize-giving was over and the Sacred Heart school had emptied, but still Cora waited to be fetched by her mother. It was her last day and the thought of never having his eyes or his hands on her skin again gave her courage. She had felt a glimmer of her old self return – her defiant self, the one who used to run through the grass pretending to be a lioness hunting.

The school was deserted and the sun was sinking in the summer sky when the art teacher summoned her. She was to help him tidy the art room one last time, he said. She was to fetch her prize-winning paintings. He had something special for her.

Cora jumped to her feet, and the cat, which had settled on her lap, glared at her as she pulled on her coat and beanie and banged the door of the studio shut behind her. She strode down the empty road that cut between the fields. By the time she reached the loch, silvered by the moon, she was running. She stopped when she reached the shore of the loch and watched the little waves chase each other up the shingle, focusing on them in an attempt not to be flooded by her memory of the colonnaded walk that wrapped around the Sacred Heart building. But it was no use. Freya's questions had pierced the membrane of time.

The walkway had been barred with the shadows the columns made. Cora's legs had been heavy as she was walked by the art teacher, his hand on the small of her back. That, she could recall, because the heat of his palm had seared the memory into her skin. He took her into the art room and it was true, he did have a present for her. A box of chocolates, which he handed to her with a flourish, saying, *because the lady loves Milk Tray.*

She had refused to accept it. Cora's lioness-self told the art teacher that she was free of him now, because she was leaving the school and going to Johannesburg. He had laughed and said so she was, but not to worry, he would find her wherever she went, because she was his. He had made her into clay and moulded her to be his own creature.

It was the lioness who had refused when he spread his legs and pointed to where she should kneel again on the ground in front of him. It was the lioness who had put her shaking hands on her hips and shouted that she would tell everyone what he did.

He had said that no one would believe her because she had kept on coming back. They would say she was a whore, which she was, and that was why her parents had sent her here to this school, because of what she had done with that farm boy. He said he would teach her what happened to little girls who told tales. And he had grabbed at her and Cora-the-lioness had evaded him and bolted out the art room.

He had chased her, catching her and dragging her towards the wishing well. There he had bent her over the rough stone lip so that she was staring down into the darkness. She breathed in the rotten smell of stagnant water deep in the earth. *That's where you belong.* His breath was hot against her cheek.

But she was a lioness and so she bit and twisted and kicked him and his grip on her loosened for a second and she broke free, and when he lunged at her again, she shoved him and ran for her life, her footsteps ricocheting off the colonnaded walls of the deserted school. As she reached the front gate, her mother pulled up and Cora opened the door and climbed in.

'Hello,' her mother said. 'Sorry I'm late. It was your father.'

'It's okay, Ma.'

'What were you doing?' asked her mother.

'Nothing, Ma. Just waiting for you.' The afternoon was blank; she must have stepped out of herself, stepped out of time. All she could remember was the waiting.

'The car wouldn't start,' said her mother, the irritation still in her voice. 'I had to wait for your pa to help me.'

'That's okay, Ma.'

'Did you get your paintings?' her mother asked.

'No, Ma. Mr du Preez was gone.'

'Don't you want them?'

'I will paint more,' Cora said, keeping her eyes straight ahead on the deserted road, and the two of them drove back to Eden in silence.

Cora moved away from the shore and back to her studio, her arms wrapped around her body to fend off the cold. There were fissures in time within her memory of that last day at Sacred Heart that Cora had never been able to account for, because she had vanished into them. But this time she could not banish the smell of the fetid air drifting up from stagnant water and the shout of *CoraCoraCora*.

TWENTY-NINE

Angel packed her passport, her papers, the stuffed bear, and the painting of the girl in the yellow bikini into a bag. She drank a glass of milk while Trotsky finished her food, grabbed her bag and went over to the office to leave a note for Tina asking her to feed the animals for a few days while she went to check in, as scheduled, with her benefactor. Trotsky circled around her in excitement and ran for the truck. She looked puzzled when Angel walked to the cages, opened an empty one and called her. The dog slunk into the kennel.

'I'll come back for you, girl,' promised Angel, her voice tight, but Trotsky turned her back on her and started a mournful keening.

Angel walked over to her truck with the burn of tears in her throat. She got in and drove with the heat up as high as it would go. She put on the radio for company.

The bad news is that another blizzard is on its way, announced the station host, *but the good news is the family who went missing while skiing were found sheltering in an abandoned forest hut. The rescue chopper spotted the smoke from a fire they managed to make. Found them alive, though only just, which means there's hope for the others –* the announcer listed the names of those still missing, Fournier's just one of them – *caught in the storm. So, time for some music that will warm your souls: here is Johnny Cash singing 'Ring of Fire'.*

There were a few stars suspended on the horizon. She passed one other vehicle on the road that took her to the highway. The driver flashed his lights at her, blinding her momentarily as she headed south, away from the forest, listening to the all-night lonely hearts requests. She didn't like the sad twang of the country music that these broken-hearted people asked for, so she switched the radio off.

There was a sullen grey light spreading in the east when she joined the streams of cars that filled the arterial roads into the city. She took the turning to the airport, parked her truck in the long-stay garage, slung her bag over her shoulder and went into the international terminal. She followed the signs towards security and shuffled along with the other passengers in the security queues. She'd been taught how not to draw any attention to herself in public places, how to avoid making eye contact without seeming to be furtive.

Nothing beeped on the security scanner and she was waved through to border control, her passport stamped, and then she was on the plane, curled up under a blanket. The plane took off and climbed steeply. She pressed her face against the oval window. All that was below her was an ocean of clouds. It felt strange to be flying so close to them; it made her think of her mother, the two of them lying on the porch, looking for the shapes of their dreams – castles, knights, horses – in the clouds that sailed above them.

They had been such innocents, her and Charly, with the dream-catchers Charly made and tried to sell at the Saturday markets. Charly telling her, as she wove the silvery threads into a web, that people were good, that men were good. A bit like over-grown kids, so if they got a little rough as they sometimes did, you knew it meant they must be secretly hurting. That's what she said when bad things came up while they were watching the news. School shootings. Men killing their wives.

They had lived alone for so long, just the two of them, her mother conjuring the world for Angel, making it safe for as long as she could. Until she was killed on that sunny afternoon when Angel had been at summer camp, instead of at home, protecting her mother. Which meant that her mother had not been there to protect Angel when the lodger had come to collect her.

It hurt Angel to think about, so she took her bear out of her backpack and, like some dumb fucking kid who didn't know any better, held it on her lap. This same little bear had been the only comfort her stepfather had allowed her when he'd taken her to the drab house on an anonymous street he had rented. 'Just for you and me, Angel-babe.' And where he had made her do all the webcam work. Her afternoons and nights were spent performing for the camera with a black cat's-eye mask on her face, so no one would know who she was, doing what she was told to do.

* * *

Looking out of the plane, Angel felt the absence of her mother as sharp as a knife between her ribs. She closed her eyes, yet try as she might, her mother's face would not come into focus. They had been so close that perhaps her mother's face had never been in focus for Angel, but she could remember the feel of her, lying curled up against her mother's full breasts, her belly. Charly's soft arms tight around Angel, murmuring stories in her smoky voice until Angel fell asleep.

Her stepfather had told Angel that Charly had been jealous of her. That she had wanted to get rid of her because she knew how much he, her stepfather, loved her. He always lied. He always messed with her head. He made her cry so that he could comfort her. That's what he called what he did to her – comfort. Angel would not believe that her mother had known anything about the evil in her stepfather's heart.

That evil was infinite – Angel understood that on the first Christmas after her mother was killed. Her stepfather came downstairs to her basement room to announce that she would be doing her first 'hotel special'. And that she must make herself look as pretty as she could and come with him. She had done as she was told and her stepfather had driven to a hotel.

He had parked in the basement. 'You just say I'm your daddy, if anyone asks,' he'd said to her before they got out of the car, his hand a vice on her arm. 'This is a special job. We do this one and you won't need to work for a week. Isn't that what you want, babe?'

She'd said yes.

The hotel was an anonymous place with ugly carpets and a bar in the lobby and staff who never asked questions about who went in and out of the rooms, as long as they paid. They took the elevator up to the top floor. People got in. People got out, but nobody paid her any attention. Nobody asked her a thing. When they stepped out on the top floor there was floor-to-ceiling glass, the city rolled out below. Her stomach clenched when her stepfather opened the door to a room. There, a camera pointed at the double bed.

She did not fight; she did not cry. She did not know where she was and she had nowhere else to go, so she followed him into that room that smelt of smoke and aftershave and old carpets and she did not try to escape when he did to her what the men watching asked for. Afterwards, she walked as best she could back to the elevator.

While they waited for it, she looked down at the dark streets far below, where the lights of cars winked red, white, orange. Because these grime-streaked windows did not open she could not jump, no matter how much she wanted to fly to wherever her mother was. But that was impossible, so she went down the elevator and got into the car with her stepfather. When they got back to the rented house, he took her back to her room.

It had been a lie that she would have a week off. The following day, the camera was on again and the internet men were back, telling her what to do to keep them happy.

The bear with its satin heart, which Angel held on her lap as the plane flew to Scotland, had been her only companion during the subterranean hours she spent wearing her masks so no one would be able to identify her. The teddy next to her on the bed never judged her for what she did. For three years, the teddy bear was her witness. He had been her companion when Angel fashioned a weapon from a strip of metal that she worked loose from the bedsprings when it was dark. The metal spoke was as sharp as a fish-filleting knife when she was done with it. When it was ready, she inserted it into her teddy bear; after that he sat there, ramrod straight. All that was left was to wait for the right moment.

Angel was good at waiting. She had nothing else to do in that house where her bedroom door was locked from the outside. She never went out – except for school or when her stepfather took her to McDonald's for a burger and fries, and a chocolate milkshake when she grew too listless. She would eat it all and then say *excuse me* and go to the bathroom and put her finger down her throat to throw it all up again like he told her to, because it was important that she stayed skinny. Because if she didn't stay skinny and pretty there would be no money and then where would they be?

On the last day that Angel spent in that room in the basement, she put on her mask at three in the afternoon. That was her slot – fifteen minutes after school, just enough time for her to get home and start 'work'. Angel switched the webcam on and the waiting men's names swarmed at her like spiders. Angel shut her mind down.

Hello, the first man wrote.

Angel, time to play, the second one.

And then she would do everything the men told her to do on that bed in front of the camera.

At seven, her stepfather called her for supper and she shut down the computer. Usually that was when her mind opened again. When the noise of the street outside came back in. When the world returned. But this time, Angel's mind stayed shut down. And the voice in her head said, *that's enough, Angel*. So she held the teddy and she felt the knife hidden inside him as stiff and hard as her own backbone and she knew that today was the day. She sat the bear on her lap and pulled the stuffing out of the hole between its legs and she went upstairs to the kitchen. The knife hidden up her sleeve, the tip of the blade cradled in her palm, she went up as docile as ever. As she reached the kitchen the weapon slithered into her hand and when she was close enough she slipped the blade between his ribs and pushed it up into his heart. She held it there until he grunted. She pulled the knife out and plunged it into him again to make sure he was dead, then she went to sit down at her place at the table.

Good girl, said the voice in her head. It was her mother's voice. She watched the blood change colour: fresh pumped vermillion to red to scarlet to crimson. It thickened into burgundy. Angel just sat. The police came. Perhaps a neighbour had called them, or the new woman in her stepfather's life – now, when it was all too late. She did not think to avoid saying that it was she who had done it. That she had sat and watched him die, and that it had not taken as long as she had thought it would.

Angel did not say anything about what she had done in the basement until a blonde woman with kind eyes and careful questions sat down next to her. Angel told her about the webcam and the knife she had made and how good it had felt to push it up inside him, and then she got tired and she asked for her bear and the woman went downstairs with her. The woman's eyes had widened when she saw Angel's room, but she said nothing, just called the police in the uniforms to come down. They had crowded into her window-less bedroom and looked at the camera and the computer and the bed. The blonde woman took her away but she had let her keep the bear. She said they had enough evidence against the stepfather without it. After that, they stopped asking her things.

Later, she told the nice blonde woman about the hotels. The police went looking for the places she described but they could not find them. All hotel rooms look the same and in the morning the chambermaids clean away what happens during the night.

Angel felt something tight and hard shift within her chest. First one and then two tears welled and spilled from the corners of her eyes. They were so unfamiliar, so startling that she kept still and because she kept still, more came and they flowed down her cheeks and into her mouth. But then she straightened herself out, stuffed the toy back into her bag and swallowed her tears so as not to lose more of herself. That no evidence was found did not mean that no crimes had been committed, that they did not keep happening. That they did not multiply ten, one hundred, ten thousand times each time a video of her was viewed and shared online. Angel would never be able to find out who all the men were who had watched her. But there was her stepfather in the hotel room with a web camera, and the police had tracked IP addresses of the four men who had watched it live the first time. One of them had belonged to Yves Fournier but he had managed, with his expensive lawyers with all their *benefit of the doubt*, to get away with what he had done because no one could prove he had been there, watching. But Angel knew the truth and surely Cora Berger did too. She must have felt in his touch that it was not *her* that he wanted?

THIRTY

The oak branches, blown by the rising north wind, knocked on the slate roof when Cora returned to her studio. She was chilled to the bone from her walk by the loch and with each knock she felt the familiar throb of pain in the back of her head. A migraine starting. Coffee and a painkiller might head it off. She got up and piled logs into the woodburning stove and set the Italian moka pot on it. Then she splashed her face in the sink, while Kit-Kat curled up by the fire. She knocked back two pills with her espresso and waited the requisite fifteen minutes for the caffeine and codeine to do their magic. To her great relief, the pain receded.

Cora replenished her palette with the myriad shades that

make white and climbed her rickety ladder. She went higher this time, balancing herself on the top rung, losing herself in the world that she had created for herself. A line from a T.S. Eliot poem – she couldn't remember which one – came to her: 'Winter kept us warm, covering Earth in forgetful snow.' That would do well as a title, she thought, turning her attention to the pale sky above the cabin on the canvas before her, building a pristine whiteness, brushstroke by brushstroke, erasing from her mind's eye the last time she had seen Yves. The distortion of his face, his mouth open, accusing her.

Cora had woken in her Montreal hotel room long before dawn. She had known then that she should be flying home but, against her better judgement, she was going to give Yves one last chance to fully explain himself. To prove the innocence he so vehemently claimed. She was aware that it would bring her more pain and yet, after she had been to the opening of her École Polytechnique massacre exhibition, she found it impossible to stop herself from hiring a car and driving north. The temperature outside was dropping fast, the radio warning of severe winter storms, when she turned off the freeway and took the road that went towards the mountains.

The sky was leaden, streaked with wild white clouds that hung low on the horizon. She passed a straggle of houses, then the animal sanctuary on the right – a girl carried metal trays towards the enclosures. Shortly after, she turned onto the track that led to Yves' lakeside cabin. He was out skiing but he had left the door unlocked for her, so she opened it and went in. It was silent inside. As she stood on the threshold, she felt again that she was unable to rid herself of that last shred of hope that things could be different, that she had not seen things how they were. She had loved him and she was unable to rid herself of love. Love, she had learned, was the worst thing to bear. Worse than grief. Worse than hatred. It was a parasite and she was its host. It would kill her unless she found a way to free herself of its ties.

Cora put her bag down and went into the living room. The painting she had given Yves was on the bookshelf and her own eyes followed her accusingly. She shifted some books so that she did not have to meet her own gaze, knocking off the handaxe she had given Yves at the restaurant after their first evening together. That warm May evening, and who she had been – so full of hope – seemed unimaginably distant. She picked up the knapped stone that fitted perfectly into the palm of her hand. She closed her fingers around it. It was a comfort to have it back – as if she had retrieved at least something of what she had given him. She put it in her pocket and then knelt in front of the fireplace. She layered twigs and twists of paper and struck a match. The kindling took and, as she added logs, the fire sprang to life. She put the food she had brought for supper on the table. Wine. Two glasses. Bread. Olive oil. Cheese. Tomatoes. A Mediterranean meal arranged like a still life.

She poured herself a glass of wine and sat down in her favourite seat, a bench built into the corner window, lined with sheepskin. There were cushions on one end, and a pile of rugs. Curled up and warm, a lassitude that she could not fight overtook her, so she pulled a rug over herself and fell asleep. When she woke, Yves was standing over her. She had the unnerving impression that he had been watching her for some time. She reached for his hand.

'You look like a child when you are asleep.' He pulled her up. 'So sweet. Shall we eat?'

They ate the food she'd brought and the steaks he cooked. They made small talk. They drank the wine, enough for her to find the courage to find the words she had to say.

'I've loved you,' she said, simply. 'But there is so much I need to know – I need to know what you looked at. What you saw when you went into the dark web. What you wanted.'

'For such an intelligent woman, you can be remarkably stupid,' Yves said, pushing his plate aside. 'We go round this all the time. And each time we come back to the same point. Do you want me to go back there and find those images that ruined my life? Do you want to be party to a crime? Is that what you want?'

'No, no,' she said. 'I want . . .' She stopped. What did she want? She did not have the words for it. She wanted things not to be what they were. 'I want you to be able to love me.'

'I do love you,' he said, his voice hardening. 'In my way.'

'No,' said Cora. 'The last time we slept together, I said no and you forced me.'

'Don't even go there.' Yves' eyes were cold. 'You're the one who always wants to play that game.'

'No. I'm not.' She wanted to say that it was the only thing that brought him to life, but she could not find the courage and so she was silent. When they went to bed she lay naked beside him. Skin to skin. He cupped a breast – her breath quickened despite herself – but he quickly lost interest and his hands slipped away from her body and he slept.

Cora got out of bed, put on what warm clothes she could find in the dark, went into the living room and got the fire going. She sat in the window seat. The words she wanted to say to Yves, words she had tried to say and failed, words that had crowded in her throat for so long, hummed like angry wasps . . . She opened her sketchbook, uncapped a pen and composed her letter in one furious rush. She felt unburdened but she did not want him to read it when he was with her, so she folded the letter and tucked it into the inside pocket of his skiing jacket. As she did so, her fingers brushed against a cold metal object. She took it out.

Her heart skipped a beat when she saw the intricate brass key. *The key to the innermost gate of his mind*, was what he had said when she had found it in his jacket the first time they had gone for dinner. She had felt like she was standing at the edge of a brave new world then, intoxicated by her own desire for Yves as much as by his attention. *The innermost gate of his mind*: that had been the border she'd wanted to cross. The key was too big to fit any of the flimsy doors in the cabin, but she was angry and she was unhappy so, instead of putting it back, she hung it around her neck, where it lay heavy and cold against her skin.

Cora returned to the window seat. Trotsky jumped up beside her. She stroked the dog's ears and watched the sky turn from black to charcoal to pale grey. She heard Yves get up and go to the bathroom. 'The drains are backing up,' he said when he came into the kitchen. 'But look at this day – not to be wasted on plumbing.' He ruffled her hair. 'You here, all this snow. If this is not the perfect morning then what is? You coming skiing?'

'No.' Tears caught in her throat and she turned her head away. 'I'm leaving.'

'Cora, don't be such a child.' He took her chin in his hand and turned her face towards him. 'I brought you back to life, don't you remember? Those were your words, sweetheart.'

'I can't do this any more, Yves,' said Cora. 'I can't pretend you didn't—'

'It's in the past.' He cut her off. 'Why can't you just forget it?'

'The past is never over.' Cora gazed at him. 'We carry it with us.'

'Not me,' he said. 'When we meet it is always perfect, but you won't accept that.'

'You torture me.'

He touched her cheek and despite herself she leaned her face into his palm – his touch erasing all time except for the present. In that moment all she wanted was for him to say that she could stay here in this cabin, set in a magical winter that had no past and no future. That desire had kept her tethered to him for so long.

'I know you,' he said tenderly. 'You'll be here when I get back.'

She watched him ski across the lake, sick to the stomach, until he disappeared from view. It humiliated her to be doing that – watching him and hoping for his safe return. Yves made her feel that beyond her capacity to submit, she was worthless. And she had submitted. Sullied: her skin was marked by his disdain. It had seeped through every pore, carrying shame with it. Her shame, now, of being a woman was the shame that had first been put into her by her teacher's hard, thrusting hand between her legs. The shame that to Yves she was nothing more than legal flesh, an undesired substitute for the images he had sought out, a disguise.

Cora's skin crawled at the unspeakable shame of having loved a man like him. His touch had erased everything she was, everything she had made of herself. It had collapsed the distance between the girl she had been and the woman she had become. Being able to say those things so clearly, if only to herself, gave her the strength she needed to leave.

* * *

And she had left. She had escaped him. Cora said that out loud and her own voice startled her, but it was a relief to realise where she was. In her studio, alive and surrounded by the work she had made. Cora stretched and then decided it was time for a change of music. Maria Callas now. Bizet's opera, *Carmen*. She turned the volume right up. Transported by the soprano's soaring voice, she lost herself once more in recreating the ellipse of the lake shore and the storm clouds that had scudded across that immense sky.

THIRTY-ONE

Cora was so absorbed that she did not hear Leo's car, but Kit-Kat did and pricked up her ears. She knew the sound of the vehicle that brought her nemesis, Toby, here, so she left the fire and sauntered over to the ladder to seek protection while the music rose and fell, the majestic sound filling the studio. Cora was nearly done, so nearly done. When she was finished, everything she could not say, all the secrets she had to keep, would be laid out on this, her last painting, and she would be free.

Cora did not hear Leo's footsteps on the path, nor his knock, as Callas' voice crescendoed and filled the studio. She did hear the door open and when she turned to see who was there, for one hallucinatory moment she saw Yves standing in the doorway before she realised it was Leo standing there, with Toby's lead slack in his hand.

Then the dog broke loose and charged for Kit-Kat. To escape him, the cat leapt up a rung towards Cora. Toby crashed into the ladder and sent Cora flying, her arms winged against her own weight. The soles of her feet pushed at air. The glint of the spikes in the flagstone floor rushed towards her. The seconds split. Skin, muscle, bone pierced. Pain exploded in her ripped shoulder, her spine . . . Her head hit concrete, then darkness.

Leo was saying, *Cora, Cora*. She tried to move but she could not make her body work. The dog's nose was wet on her neck, then there was a thud as Leo kicked Toby out of the way and the dog howled her pain as he fled. Then it was just the two of them, Leo on his mobile phone, but the words did not reach her. He put the phone back in his pocket. Time passed, she did not know how much. Sound returned, but not sight. Leo walked to the door and back to her – she heard him. He asked her if she was all right but she did not know if she spoke or not.

An ambulance siren wailed. The crunch of gravel on the drive. The studio door opened.

'Jesus.' A man's unfamiliar voice. The tramp of feet as the paramedics came through the door. 'What happened?' the same voice asked.

'It was an accident,' said Leo. The medics made no comment as they knelt beside her, two of them, and did things that loosened the scream trapped in her throat.

Cora was on the stretcher. The medics did more things to her. They staunched the blood. Talked to her. It was a young woman talking. Her voice was Freya's voice. Cora was shaking and her fingers were crushed in the girl's hand, but her own hand was numb, no feeling, just the pressure of their fingers entwined.

'Don't go, don't go, don't leave me. Stay with me. Stay with me. Stay with me,' said the girl talking in Freya's voice. Except she wasn't Freya. Freya wasn't here. Freya was gone. Where had she gone, her baby? *She was my baby*, Cora was saying this, but no one heard her.

'Keep calm,' the young woman said. 'Keep still, Cora. Stay with us.'

The light was fading. Cora heard the sound of her own breath. In and out. In and out. She counted them. Each one hurt. None of them sounded good. She thought about Freya and she thought about Toby. She thought about Yves' dog, Trotsky. That stupid name he'd given her. She wondered where she was. If she'd made it. She must have. She was tough. Half wolf, half husky.

'Keep still,' the girl with Freya's voice repeated. 'Don't move, Cora.'

'Freya,' Cora whispered. 'She's gone. She left. Tell her I'm sorry. Tell her I love her.'

'She'll come back for you, Cora,' she heard Leo's voice say.

'You wait for her, Cora,' said the girl. 'She's coming. You tell her yourself.'

But her voice faded till Cora could not hear her any more. Freya's face, her beautiful face, was fading. Cora was also fading and the medics were doing things to her again, but she kept falling out of time.

'Keep her talking. Keep her here. We need her conscious, with that head injury.' A man was saying this, but she was almost sure it wasn't Yves Fournier, even though his hands were on her. Holding her down. Bringing the darkness that was closing in on her. Fading out the sound and the light.

'I want Freya,' Cora begged. 'She was here. She was holding my hand.'

'I'm here,' the girl who had Freya's voice was saying, her mouth close to Cora's ear. 'Stay with me. Stay.'

'Why can't I see?' asked Cora.

'Can't you?' said the paramedic. 'Look here towards my voice. What do you see?'

'I just hear you . . . It's dark now . . . My daughter,' murmured Cora to the girl who was and was not Freya. 'I must tell her it was an accident.'

'Your husband will tell her. You just think about breathing. We're going to move you now.'

Cora breathed. And then there was movement – sudden and violent – and she was outside, and the stars were streaks of light above her and she drifted towards them as they carried her to the ambulance. The doors slammed. The ambulance siren screamed again. Cora was cold, so cold, so cold on that journey. It was Yves that the ice should be holding fast. He was here. He had come for her after all. He had her. The ice had her now and she couldn't endure it, this zero at the bone.

THIRTY-TWO

Freya was on her way out when her father rang. The line kept cutting out so she leaned against the front door, pressing her phone to her ear and trying to make sense of what he was saying. Something about an ambulance and Cora and a terrible accident.

Freya's grip on the door handle loosened.

'She's alive,' Leo was saying. 'But she's badly injured. Bones broken and a head injury. That ladder, it wasn't stable.'

'What happened?' Freya's knees gave way and she slid down to the floor.

'She fell,' he said. 'She just fell.'

'Mum's never fallen in her life.'

'Darling, I'm so sorry,' said Leo.

'Just tell me, Dad,' begged Freya.

'I went there to return Toby. I said hello. Toby chased that half-wild cat you and Cora rescued and he knocked the ladder and then she fell. She was up there working on this snowscape—'

'Snowscape?' she interrupted. 'What do you mean, snowscape?'

'Her painting, this huge mad painting she's working on. It's why she was on the ladder. No people in it. Just trees and ice and snow. None of her colours, nothing familiar. It's some kind of hellish Narnia that she's working on.'

'She's never painted snow,' Freya said, fear making her voice sharp. 'What are you talking about?'

'I'm sorry, darling,' he said. 'I never had a chance to ask her. I brought Toby home and she was in her studio. Toby saw that cat and he went after her.'

'Kit-Kat.'

'What?'

'Kit-Kat,' she said. 'That's her name. My cat's name.'

'Yes,' said Leo. 'Toby knocked over Cora's ladder and that's why she fell.'

'That's why she fell,' Freya said, taking a deep breath. 'Okay, so what did the doctors say?'

'They didn't say anything,' Leo responded quietly. 'Because we're divorced, I'm not next of kin any more. You are. You're the one who'll have to help her decide.'

'Decide what?' she whispered.

'I don't know, Freya,' said Leo. 'Whatever needs to be decided.'

'What's wrong with her, Dad?' The pressure growing in Freya's head was unbearable.

'She smashed her elbow—'

'That's fixable.'

'She hit her head too,' said Leo. 'Badly.'

'She's concussed?'

'She can't see.'

'What do you mean?'

'Her sight,' said Leo. 'She might not get it back.'

'I'm getting the next train,' Freya said.

'I'll be waiting.' Leo sounded relieved.

Freya was unable to move after her father ended the call. The living room was silent. The space was filled with her mother's work. It covered every piece of wall space. There was no snow anywhere. There was blood and heat and the texture of the soil that she mixed into her paints, but there was no snow. Everything was on display. Or was it? Freya was filled with doubt. Everything she had been sure of was unstable. The ground beneath her feet, made unstable by her own mother.

'Who was that?' Johann was standing in the doorway, his hair wet and a towel around his waist.

'My father,' she replied. 'My mother's in hospital.'

'What happened?' He tried to put his arms around her, but she pushed him away.

'The dog knocked the ladder over and she fell. She smashed her right arm. She hit her head too. She can't see.'

'She's blind?'

'They don't know for how long,' said Freya. 'I'm going home now.'

'Fuck, Freya.' Johann frowned in sincere concern. 'I'm sorry. Let me come with you.'

'No. This is for me to deal with on my own.' She went into the bedroom. She opened her cupboard, but her vision blurred and she could not see what she needed to take. She put her hands into the shelves and felt amongst her sweaters. Soft and thick. She pulled two out and stuffed them into a bag, opened her underwear drawer and did the same, grabbing whatever was on top. Then she gave up and put on her coat and boots and grabbed her handbag.

'I'll get you a taxi, then.' He picked up his phone and tapped in the instructions. 'Two minutes.'

She opened the door.

'Freya, wait,' said Johann.

'What?' asked Freya.

'Say goodbye.'

'Goodbye, Johann.'

'When will I see you?' he urged, catching hold of her.

'I don't know,' she said, looking at him as if his face was coming into focus for the first time – high cheekbones, sun-bleached hair. A stranger. She could remember no connection to him. There could be no connection between them, when her mother's broken body was hooked up to hospital machines. 'I'll call you. I have to go. There's my taxi.'

She ran down the steps and got into the car. The driver smiled at her in his rear-view mirror.

'Euston Station?' he asked.

As she said, 'Yes,' a pain deep in her pelvis doubled her over.

'You all right, love?' asked the driver.

'I'm okay,' said Freya. 'I just need to get home.'

THIRTY-THREE

The tumult of the hospital. The sound of doors opening and closing. The hands. The urgent voices of the doctors in the white chamber where they took Cora and dismantled her and put her together again so that pain surged through her. Stole her tongue. Rattled her breath in her chest. A heavy hand, pressing her down, and then the room around her disintegrated.

The pain moved like a serpent from her arm and her head and her ribs to her heart. She remembered falling – the ground rushing up at her, the stake glinting in the light, her chest hurtling towards it. She had registered that in her mind's eye in the moment of her flight, and had twisted away from the impalement that would have ended things. But was that possible? The blur that came with the pain in her ripped arm and her head was returning and it was a relief when she heard the nurse come in and give her something to keep the pain at bay. Everything faded again except for one piercing moment of clarity.

She opened her eyes: she could see nothing except a narrow band of light down the centre of her field of vision. That blindness filled her with fear, so she closed her eyes again and focused on the pain. The ice had her heart in its grip and it was slowing its rhythm. Stopping it. The darkness had its appeal. It was familiar. Unlike these hands on her. These machines. This hum of the hospital. The nurses. The X-rays. The young doctors. The phone calls. The brusque consultant. The concern.

An alarm went off, a low whooping noise that sounded like Yves calling her – *CoraCoraCora* – his voice gentle but his hands hurting even as he coaxed her towards him. She tried to retrieve what had happened to her, as if knowing it would raise her up like Lazarus and return her to the top of the stepladder where she had been balanced with paints in one hand, brush in the other.

A bell rang three o'clock two o'clock ten o'clock; she couldn't be sure which o'clock it was because day and night merged in the perpetual twilight of her vision. The pain in her arm again, sharp as a blade. The finality of that bore down on her and her heart pounded at everything she knew and did not know. The pain in her head drummed on. She could see nothing.

Feet coming down the corridor. Doctors, brisk nurses. Doing things to Cora's arm, her chest, her back. The hands were not unkind, but the movement – touch – was agony. There was the young doctor, the outline of him, his solid body. There were beeps and bleeps and hushed voices and the squeak of shoes and there was the smell of a hospital. Cabbage and ammonia and fear. There were voices, but none that Cora knew. None that she wanted to hear. They said words her mind refused. Fracture. Nerve. Disc. Split. Heart. Almost. Lung. Detached. Prognosis. Spine. Arm. Nerve. Uncertain. Curl your fingers. Your left hand. Fine. Good. Your right hand. Nothing. Use. Arm. Work. Uncertain.

A very bright light. A question.

'What can you see, Cora?'

'I know what I saw,' murmured Cora. 'I went underground. I saw what he does. I'm not delusional.'

'You're not delusional, my dear,' said the doctor. 'You're concussed. You had a terrible fall.' He put his hand on her forehead for a moment, his touch as gentle as a mother's, as fleeting. 'Can you see anything?'

Cora opened her eyes. It was dark except for that narrow band of light right in the centre. No colour. No texture. Just the outline of the doctor's hand, his arm, the shape of his head when he moved through the narrow rectangle of illumination, shining things at her, asking her questions.

'I can't see,' said Cora. 'I can't see what's in this room.'

'Can you see light and dark?'

'That's not enough,' she said.

'Don't worry, love,' a woman's voice soothed. A nurse. 'It usually passes.' The scratch of a pen as she wrote things onto Cora's chart, her pain recorded in neat scrawls on graph paper.

'Your left arm, please,' said the nurse. The one that was not smashed at the elbow. It was of no use to her because she did not paint with that hand, so if the nurse needed it, she could have it.

The nurse inserted a needle into the vein in the crook of Cora's elbow, eased it out again and pressed on the tiny painless wound. The liquid measured into her vein floated Cora out of her body and out of the pain.

THIRTY-FOUR

ngel's plane circled above Glasgow. From the air it did not look that different to where she had come from. There was snow, there were lakes – lochs, here – there were trees and there was the runway with its flashing lights. The weather was bad and the landing was rough. She was relieved when she could finally sling her bag over her shoulder and leave the plane. She smiled as she handed her passport over to the border guard and said yes, she was here on holiday. He looked at her photograph, looked at her and wished her a good one.

She tucked the passport in her back pocket, dodged the taxi drivers with signs in their hands and took a bus into the city.

It was cold and bleak with driving sleet and no one, hurrying along with their heads down, spared her a second glance. She found the train station easily enough, bought her ticket and watched the unfamiliar and unpronounceable names of the stops glide past. When the train reached the end of the line she got out and waited for the ferry with a handful of construction workers, who turned their backs on the rain and cupped their hands around their cigarettes.

She boarded the ferry with them and stood in the prow. She watched the water plume behind them as the captain guided the small boat across the loch. The shore come into focus, leafless trees against a sullen sky. The day was dark and lights were on in the houses. Their windows offered snatches of domesticity – a cat on a windowsill, a woman and a child sitting in a kitchen, a man reading a paper. She jumped ashore as soon as they docked and walked past a pub, a shop, a school, a chapel.

The houses fell away, and she was on the narrow road hugging the edge of the water. She kept walking until she reached a sharp bend in the road. There was a gate just beyond it. Angel opened it and walked up the hill towards Cora Berger's house. The front door did not look like it had been used for years, so Angel took the path that led across the frozen lawn to the back of the house. She knocked on the kitchen door. When there was no answer, she turned the handle and, to her surprise, it opened. She stepped inside and listened. A branch tapped against a window somewhere, but that was the only sound.

'Ms Berger?' she called.

Silence.

Angel inspected the kitchen. There was a scrubbed wooden table with an empty vase and some birthday cards on it. She picked up a couple and read the notes. Cora had friends. She was loved. Angel hadn't considered that possibility. It was possible that Yves Fournier had friends too, but she hadn't come across any of them and she had not heard anyone say he was loved.

A wine glass in the sink, coffee cups, and a dirty plate. Glasses, odd plates, an open tin of shortbread on the dresser. A newspaper cutting caught Angel's attention. A photograph of women in headscarves, wiring shoes together. A picture of Cora standing alongside them. The same photograph she had seen tacked onto the kitchen cupboards in Fournier's cottage.

She inspected the photographs impaled on the cup hooks. Cora Berger with a little girl on her lap at a picnic. The daughter. It struck Angel for the first time that she and Freya were more or less the same age. Another one, of Freya in a school uniform. Her oval face with the high cheekbones the mirror of her mother's.

One of Cora and Freya, both of them wrapped in striped beach towels. A man – the father, perhaps. Angel wondered where he'd gone. She studied Freya. She'd seen that butterfly on the silver chain around her neck. It was the same one twisted around the neck of the painted girl in Fournier's house. Anger, hot and liquid, surged through Angel, but she knew enough about hiding secrets and she was patient and she knew how to search.

She opened the drawers. Knives in the top one, silver cutlery in the next. Receipts and unopened mail in the third. She shut them and walked through the house. A sitting room with no fire in the grate, a dining room with an empty fruit bowl, a closet full of boots and jackets. She stood at the bottom of the stairs and looked up at the stained-glass window that stretched up towards the first floor and then the dimly lit second floor. The glass scattered jewels of light on the pale carpet: yellows, oranges, and poppy reds. The wall was lined with paintings.

She was drawn to the faces that looked out at her. Each of Cora's self-portraits held Angel's searching gaze; they seemed to speak mutely of things that were best kept hidden. These were not like the splayed, near-naked child she had found hidden in Fournier's cabin. Angel knew there would be more of those, and those were the ones she was after.

The last painting was of Freya on a swing, flying as high as a bird, her mother pushing her. It was in the same vivid colours that Angel had seen in the painting in Fournier's cabin and it gave her the same sense of unease.

'Cora?' she called. There was no answer.

She climbed the stairs. On the first floor there was a door opened onto a bathroom, then two closed doors beyond that. She opened the first one. The daughter's bedroom. Gymkhana rosettes and photographs of ponies were still tacked up on the walls alongside a poster of the southern skies – the Southern Cross and the Milky Way, stars Angel did not know. She ran a finger over the porcelain figurines on the dressing table. The little Goose Girl, a mare and her foal, a milkmaid. They were filmed with dust. There was a black hoodie on the chest of drawers. Angel tried it on. It fitted perfectly. They were the same size, she and Cora's daughter.

The bedroom across the landing was empty. There were no sheets on the mattress, no bedside light, no books. There were dark squares on the wallpaper where pictures had once hung. She opened the cupboard. A tweed jacket hung there, the sleeves bent in the shape of the arms of the man who had worn it. Freya's father. The husband. She could smell him.

Angel had only one memory of her own father. This: muscular arms, big hands, a dragon tattoo snaking around both wrists, her sitting high up on his shoulder, the world below her distant and diminished. He smelled of smoke. Then he left and that was it. There were no photographs of him, and he never tried to find her after her mother was killed. Not that she knew of, anyway. She had certainly never tried to find him.

Up the last flight of stairs. There was one door and she opened it. After the jewel-bright colours of the house, Cora's bedroom was startlingly white – the walls, the wooden floor, the furnishings, the unmade bed. There was nothing on the walls. She turned her attention to the wardrobe. Not that many clothes. All of them blue or green or black, except for one red silk dress.

On the dressing table: a mirror, cut-glass containers with jewellery in them. A bottle of perfume, Chanel No 5. She sprayed some on her neck. The scent she had detected on the pillows on Fournier's bed. T-shirts and sweaters in the drawers. Underwear in the top one. She rifled through the scraps of black and white silk.

The armchair at the window faced the loch and the mountains beyond. A sketchbook lay on the floor. Angel's hands tingled as she opened it up. A photograph fell out. It was of a white farmhouse with a red roof, dogs flopped on the shadowy verandah, a little girl in khaki shorts and nothing else, sitting on the steps. Cora. The innocence of her, the strength in her wiry limbs, her boyish brown chest, and the grin girls have before men start looking at them. She put the photograph back and flicked through the sketchbook pages and saw a sketch of the lake by Fournier's, the trees coming down to the water, flocks of geese flying overhead.

Angel lay down on the bed. Cora's pillows were as soft as a caress. She pulled Cora's duvet up over her body. The forgotten embrace of a mother's bed softened the piano-wire tautness in Angel for a moment. She lay still for a moment, wondering if Yves had lain here too, then she got up, straightened the bed and went downstairs. She took a piece of shortbread from the open tin, closed the kitchen door and ate the shortbread as she walked up to the stone outbuilding. The pitched roof of Cora's studio was etched against the sky, lichen on the tiles, abandoned swallows' nests under the eaves. There was no sound coming from it, but the lights were on inside. Angel had a lot of questions for Cora Berger. She flexed her fingers. She would subject her to a private inquisition. Only then would she decide if there would be one more dead, or two.

She looked through the window. There were canvases stacked against one wall and a woodburning stove against the other, a cat curled up in front of it. There was a trestle table below the windowsill: on it a jumble of paint tubes, many of them twisted and broken-backed; a bunch of holly in a vase; brushes in a jar. Palette knives marked with shades of white and icy blues and greens. No sign of Cora Berger.

The clouds parted and for a moment the pale sun shone through the round windows in the roof, illuminating one wall. A low sweep of hills, trees marching alongside a lake, a leaden sky, shadows beneath the snow. Angel drew back, disorientated. It was the view from Yves Fournier's cabin. The landscape into which he had disappeared. The scale of the painting took her aback. It was as if Cora had been replicating the exact size of the wilderness where she had been with Fournier. Beneath it, she saw now, the floor was a mess. A splintered ladder lay on the floor, a bucket on its side beside it, from which a white wing of paint arced across the flag-stones, streaked with oxide red.

The door was locked, so Angel worked her way around the windows, looking for a way in. The third window was not quite shut. She worked it open, climbed through and jumped down from the windowsill. The cat arched its back at her and vanished up the stairs leading to the loft. A faint metallic click snapped her attention back to where she was. She turned, her heart racing. A harness, hanging from the ceiling, swayed in a gust of cold air from the open window. Her eyes lighted on a stake protruding from the flagstones. She walked over, crouched down and touched it. Slightly sticky. She sniffed her fingers. Blood.

She looked across at the silent, enigmatic painting. Stepping close to Cora's canvas, she ran her hands across the surface. It was ridged and textured, as if the paint was layered over rock and earth, everything buried beneath the snow. Angel could feel Yves Fournier's malignant presence. She felt along the frame. There were nails along the side, and a small section of fabric protruded. The fabric had been tacked onto the frame, silver tack after silver tack hammered into the wood. She tried to prise one off, but it tore her nails. She fetched the palette knife from Cora's table and used it to loosen the tacks that fixed the top layer of paint-covered silk to the canvas beneath.

A hidden world tumbled out. Sketches, photographs, draw-ings, a stone, six numbered Polaroids of Cora standing naked in a hotel room, an archipelago of bruises on her arms. Long deep scratch marks down the inside of her thighs. Angel assessed the evidence before her. Cora's sketches, her mementos, and the photographs she had taken of her own naked, and sometimes bruised, body. Nothing that Angel had not seen on women, had not seen on herself, before. There was more, there had to be, but if it was here in the studio she couldn't see it.

The cat came down from the loft, curiosity getting the better of it, and Angel picked it up and stroked it. The animal purred, quite at ease in her arms, kneading her claws in pleasure at her touch while Angel stared at Cora's canvas. She walked over to the painting again and, holding the cat in one arm, ran her free hand across its surface. It had two layers – the smooth one on the top. Underneath it, the ridged texture remained, even though Angel had removed everything that she could dislodge. She pulled the top layer back so that she could examine the coarse canvas beneath.

It was covered with a layer of white acrylic paint, but shadows showed through. The outlines of other images – she counted twelve – that were affixed to the frame. She picked up the palette knife and scraped off what she could. Then she unfolded each piece of paper and spread them out on the floor. A girl of eleven, maybe twelve, heart-shaped red sunglasses on, draped across beds in hotel rooms, bent over in recording studios and schools and confessionals, curled up on beds. A necklace with a butterfly around the neck of the girl in each painting. A flash of light, a mark of identity or possession. The necklace Angel had seen in the video clip, flashing around Freya's neck. She took the painting that she had carried from Fournier's cabin out of her bag and laid it out next to the others. The thirteenth one – the girl in her yellow bikini. All of them in place. Cora's secrets undefended before her.

Angel considered them all as if they were exhibits. In a court of law, it would be evidence that lawyers could argue both ways, but Angel was self-appointed judge, jury and executioner, and here she had the proof she needed to conclude that Cora had offered up her own daughter to Fournier. As she, Angel, had once been offered to him, by someone who was meant to have protected her. She refolded the miniature paintings and, using the glue she found on Cora's table, stuck them and the photographs back onto the canvas. She pulled the painted white silk straight and tacked it back onto the canvas, shrouding again what lay beneath it. Angel swept up the fragments of white paint that she had dislodged and tipped them into the cold ash in the stove. She had what she had come for – no one else needed to know. The painting was restored, everything hidden once more in plain sight.

THIRTY-FIVE

Freya had no recollection of getting to the station, of buying her ticket or of getting onto the train, but she must have done all of that, because the next thing she knew she was looking out of the window at the sun, breaking through the clouds for a moment, turning the rain on the dirty train window into liquid gold. Cora used to tell her how welcome the rain had been on Eden, the clouds filling the sky, blotting out the sun, bloody and enraged. Her mother had made Freya feel the hot air, hear the murmur of the wind in dry grass until the first drops suddenly began to fall. How they would soak into the parched ochre soil and how Cora had tilted her face to the sky and opened her mouth wide so that she, like the drought-stricken soil, could drink in the life-giving rain that would bring the veld back to life within days.

Red soil, blue sky, etched with new shoots that were a luminous green. Cora had created worlds for Freya, conjured visions of places she had never seen. Freya could not bear to think of her mother blind.

She caught sight of Leo as she got off the train in Glasgow. He was standing on the platform, his hands shoved deep in his jacket pockets. He had that look of displacement he always had in public places. She saw for the first time that her father's face, crumpled by the neon light, was old. When he saw her, he straightened his shoulders and pulled her towards him, holding her against the warm cave of his chest.

'Freya,' he murmured into her hair. 'You must be exhausted.'

The sob, lodged in her throat since he'd phoned her to tell her about Cora, loosened, but tears brought no relief. She did not know how to share her terror with Leo now that he was no longer her mother's husband.

'I'm okay,' she said, wiping her eyes.

'Do you want to go home first?' asked Leo. 'Have a rest?'

'No,' she shook her head. 'I want to see Mum now.'

She followed him to the car, where Toby's nose was pressed against the gap in the window. She climbed into the back and threw her arms around the dog's neck.

'Your name was the first thing she said after she fell,' said Leo. 'I think she thought the paramedic was you until she put her hand up and touched her face.' Freya didn't know what to say so she leaned against Toby's warm body until Leo turned into the hospital.

'Phone me when you want to be picked up again,' he said. 'Toby and I will be here for you.'

The hospital was a forbidding concrete block, its brutalist façade broken only by strips of narrow windows and the glass elevator shafts. The skin between her shoulder blades tightened as she walked across the wet car park towards the entrance. She pushed the glass door at the hospital entrance. The lobby was warm and busy – patients, visitors, cleaners in high-vis jackets mopping the floor all competed for space. She navigated around them to reach the clerk at the reception desk.

'How can I help you?' he asked.

'I've come to see my mother,' she said. 'Cora Berger.'

He tapped at the computer in front of him. 'Good news is that she's out of intensive care. She's in high dependency now. Ward 7B, private room 4006. Are you Freya Finch?'

'Yes,' she said. 'I'm Cora's daughter.'

'You're listed as her next-of-kin,' he said. 'I'll write that down for you, then. You keep this.' He handed her an official-looking hospital pass. 'Because she's private, you can come and go as long as the doctors approve.'

'Oh, thank you.'

'Fourth floor,' he called after her.

The tears she had kept at bay ran down her cheeks as she pressed the button. The lift opened on the fourth floor and she stepped into the glass lobby. She paused for a moment. Below her was the car park – she could see Leo's car. She squared her shoulders and wiped her eyes and walked past the busy nurses' station. No one stopped her so she continued on until she found Cora's room at the end of a corridor. The door was ajar, and for a moment she stood on the threshold. Fear settled like stone in her chest when she saw her mother surrounded by machines, tubes, things dripping, things flashing.

Freya closed the door behind her and went over to the bed.

She looked at her mother's heart rate beating on the monitor. It was steady – a pulse and a pause, a pulse and a pause. She could match her own heart with its rhythm. Cora's chest was strapped where three ribs had cracked, and her head was bandaged too, the right eye swollen and beginning to blacken. Freya placed her hand on the splint on Cora's smashed arm and said her mother's name.

'My baby. You're here at last.' Cora opened her eyes, but they did not focus. 'I can't see you.'

'Here I am,' said Freya.

Cora lifted her good arm and ran her fingers across Freya's forehead, eyebrows, cheekbones, mouth, chin. 'It's your beautiful face,' she said, her voice so faint that Freya had to lean towards her to hear.

'What happened?' Freya ran her hands over the ridged brace that held Cora's arm together. 'Tell me,' she said. 'I need to know.'

'I was painting, then I went flying. I hit that stake. My arm did. My head hit the floor. People came and then I was here.' Cora stopped so that her breath could catch up with her. 'I don't remember much of what happened in between. I was up the ladder. There was the cat and then there was Toby . . .' Her voice broke. 'I don't know – it hurts. The whole of me hurts and I can't see. What will I be if I can't see?'

'Your vision will come back, Mum,' said Freya, keeping the fear in her voice suppressed. 'It must be just because you hit your head so hard.'

Her mother's heart, beating too fast now, made rapid little spikes on the machine. To calm her, Freya began to hum the lullaby that Cora, with her low, tuneful voice, had soothed her with when she was very young. Soon, Cora breathed more evenly and the monitor slowed. When her mother was calmer so was she, and for half an hour or more the room was very still, then she stirred again. 'You're still here, darling,' she said.

'I am here,' said Freya. 'Till you're better.'

'It feels like there's a bayonet in my head,' murmured Cora. 'The doctors won't tell me if I will see properly again. They say it's too soon to say. I don't want to be a broken thing.'

'You'll see again,' Freya insisted. 'You have to. For me.'

'I was thinking . . .' Her mother lifted her hand to touch Freya's face, but her own face twisted at the movement; pain turned into agony.

'Don't move, Mum. It hurts you too much.'

Cora dropped her arm. 'I was thinking,' she repeated, 'that if I were a horse, or a dog, and still on my father's farm, he would shoot me and the suffering would be over.'

'You're not a horse or a dog,' said Freya, her voice catching. 'You're my mother.'

'Did I tell you about the kudu we found? Me and my father?'

'No,' said Freya. 'Tell me now.'

'I went with my father to check a cattle post. We found a kudu cow. The poor antelope had tried to get to the water and her leg had snapped on the barbed-wire fence. My father got his revolver out and checked the bullets. Two. Enough. He stood by her head, the gun gripped with both hands, and he fired. We loaded her onto the back of the truck. I sat next to her. It seemed right to keep her company.'

'Why did you take her home with you?' asked Freya.

'Because kudu makes the best venison.'

'Oh,' said Freya, 'I see. How practical.'

A nurse appeared with a tray. Chicken soup and a crisp white bread roll and a pat of yellow butter. She set it down and adjusted Cora's bed so that she could eat.

'I'm not hungry,' said Cora.

'Try something.'

'I'll help her,' Freya reassured the nurse.

The nurse left them to it. Freya dipped the spoon into the soup. 'One for you, one for me,' she said, mimicking what Cora had said when she was a child and sick and refusing her food. Cora smiled and took a spoonful and Freya fed her mother. It seemed to be difficult for Cora to swallow, but she managed a few spoonfuls before she said, 'You eat the rest, darling. You must be starving.'

Freya finished the soup and ate the bread and butter.

'It's better with you here, Freya. We were so used to it, weren't we? Just the two of us together. Leo somewhere else in the house or out walking the dog, so just you and me, really. It felt like the whole world. Was that wrong?'

The pain was making her restless again.

'Shall I lower your bed again?' asked Freya. 'It's more comfortable if you're flat.'

Cora nodded almost imperceptibly. Freya worked out the mechanism of the bed. She straightened the pillows and smoothed the sheets. There was a sheen of sweat on Cora's face, so Freya fetched a washcloth and wiped her face and neck and across her shoulders, finding a key on a long silver chain around her mother's neck. There were flecks of blood in the links and she sponged it clean, streaking the rough white towel in her hand.

'What's this?' she asked.

'It's my lucky charm. I was wearing it when I fell. I'm choosing to believe that it stopped me from being impaled by that stake.'

'What's the key for?'

'Bluebeard's chamber.' Cora gave the ghost of a smile.

'Can't be,' Freya frowned, examining it. 'In the Bluebeard story, the woman who disobeyed him and looked in the secret chamber could never get the blood off the key. That's how he caught her. The blood came off your key, no problem.'

'I'll take your word for it.' Cora took the key from Freya and closed her fist around it. 'That man they found at Sacred Heart. You said some things were found with him. You said a necklace?'

'Yes, with a butterfly on it,' said Freya. 'Like the one you gave me as a talisman.' She guided Cora's hand to the delicate chain around her neck, the pendant with its mobile wings settled in the hollow at the base of her throat. 'You had a necklace like this, Mum. I saw it in the footage of whatever ceremony was going on at Sacred Heart. You were wearing it on that stage.'

'Was I?' asked Cora. 'I somehow put that whole year out of my mind.'

'What happened there, Mum?'

'I don't know. I don't remember.' Her mother stared unseeingly at Freya, but she had a stricken look on her face.

'You never heard anything about the art teacher disappearing – a Mr du Preez?' Freya asked.

'No,' said Cora. 'I never heard. I never asked. I never went back. Must have been some accident, if they found him down there. That well was not safe. It was deep because the water table was so far beneath the surface. We used to throw things down – coins for wishing, stones to see how deep it really was. We would count the seconds before they hit the water.'

They were both quiet for some time after that, just the beeps in the room and the muffled hospital sounds beyond the door.

Freya did not know what to make of what her mother had told her about what she remembered of her time at Sacred Heart. All she knew was that her mother carried secrets from her childhood that she could only ever tell obliquely in her enigmatic paintings.

'About *Forbidden Fruit*, those paintings—'

'What about them?' Freya sounded weary.

'I was trying to fix something. Something in myself. They were never you. They were always me. You, I protected always.'

'I know that,' said Freya, a catch in her voice.

'It was me I couldn't defend.'

'I've tried to understand.' Freya chewed at her lip.

'I find it difficult to explain, but I am sorry,' said Cora. 'There sometimes aren't words for things.'

'I have to find the words, Mum. I'm not like you, shutting things away in pictures that you can feel but not understand.'

'I know, darling. I know that. It hasn't been easy. I haven't been easy. I am sorry.' She tried to touch Freya's face, but the movement was too much and she gasped in pain.

'Stop,' said Freya, in distress. 'It's hurting you to talk, Mum. It's over now. It's behind us.'

Freya lay down beside her mother.

'I can't see your face,' Cora said.

'Not at all?' asked Freya.

'Just a shaft of white light and some dark shapes. That's all. What will I be if I can't see?' Cora repeated, her fear palpable.

'You'll still be my mother.' As Freya stroked her mother's hand to soothe her, she remembered the embryo inside her, a tadpole in its amniotic sac. She thought of her mother pregnant with her. 'Do you know what made you keep me?'

'You gave me reason to live, then,' said Cora. 'It was as simple as that. You still do.'

'And if your sight doesn't come back?'

Cora said nothing.

Freya had to gamble this foetus. It was the only card she had. If she played it, maybe she could keep her mother's despair at bay. 'You have to live,' said Freya. 'Not only for me. I could have the baby. Then there would be two reasons.'

'My sweetheart,' Cora whispered. 'You don't have to do that to make me want to stay. You're enough.'

But the pain was returning, the effort of speaking suddenly too much. She moaned and Freya, frightened at how pale she was, pressed the alarm.

A nurse appeared almost at once. Freya stepped out of the way when she saw her taut face. In one fluid movement, the nurse checked the agitated machines. She adjusted the drip that suspended Cora's mind above the ocean of pain in which her wounded body floated.

'It's just the painkiller running low,' the nurse reassured Freya. 'She'll be all right.'

'I'm fine,' said Cora faintly. Her chest was rising and falling evenly again.

'Your mother's a fighter, lass,' said the nurse to Freya. 'She's got us and she's got you here. We'll pull her through.'

'Will she see again?'

'The specialist is the one to discuss that with,' said the nurse.

'What do *you* think?' Cora asked.

'Focus on now,' said the nurse. 'Focus on your daughter. That's all you can do. All I can say is that I've seen head injuries like this before – this loss of sight. And patients can recover. The doctor left a pamphlet about it next to your bed.'

'How is that going to help if I can't see it?'

Freya picked up the sheet of paper. The typeface was small and the words seemed to be crowded together. She could not make sense of it at all.

'It's all better discussed tomorrow morning,' said the nurse, pausing her activity to hold Cora's hand for a moment. 'What you need now is rest, Cora. Give the swelling a bit of time to come down.' The nurse looked at Freya then. 'Looks like you could do with some sleep too, love. It's a shock, seeing your mum like this. You go home. Get yourself strong for tomorrow. We'll take care of her tonight.'

The nurse closed the door as she left the room.

'She's right,' said Cora. 'You need to sleep a bit now. Off you go. Rest.'

'Let me sit with you, Mum.'

'I'll be fine,' said Cora reassuringly. She had sensed that Freya was reluctant to leave. 'Come back in the morning. Go home, darling. Read that eye specialist's pamphlet for me so we know what's going on. I'll sleep now. Those drugs the nurse gave me should knock me out.'

'On one condition,' Freya replied, tucking the pamphlet into her bag. 'You call me if anything happens.' She put Cora's phone into her hand and kissed her mother's forehead.

Cora smiled. 'I'll phone if I need you,' she said, 'I promise.'

When her mother closed her eyes, Freya slipped out and closed the door.

THIRTY-SIX

Freya took the stairs down to the cafeteria in search of her father. Leo stood up when he saw her and put his hands on her shoulders. Warm and big, as she remembered them as a child. The hands that had comforted her when Cora was quick or sharp or absent.

'She would've been fine if that spike hadn't been there,' said Leo. 'She would have been bruised, but fine.'

'But it was there, Dad. Her right arm and her shoulder are badly damaged.'

'She'll make it, darling. I promise.'

'She knows how to fight for everyone but herself,' she replied.

'She's tough, your mother.' Leo put his arm tenderly around his daughter's shoulders, but Freya shrugged him off

'She isn't, and you know it. That was always your excuse because she kept going, even though she was on the edge for so long. Getting closer and closer, and you never even reached out a hand to her. You knew where she came from, how things had been for her. She had no one except you, and you were just quiet, Dad. You let her do everything.'

'You were a child. What could you have known about her, about us?'

'Everything,' she replied. '*Because* I'm your child – yours and hers – and she was an independent woman and that was difficult for you, wasn't it?'

'No, Freya, it's how she is.'

'She's successful with her work, with money.' Her voice was rising and the people at the tables close to them were watching.

'Yes,' said Leo. 'She is.'

'And that can be tough on men.' Freya did not take her eyes off Leo's face. 'Women taking over, running the show. Is that what you couldn't handle? Is that why she left?'

'No. It was her choice. I was always there for her but she – she said she couldn't go on. I thought there was another man.' Leo looked down at his hands. 'Not that she said. Not that anyone would've known if there had been.'

'I'm sorry, Dad.' Freya dropped her face into her hands and began to cry. 'I'm taking it out on you, I know, but I just can't stop myself from wondering why she lost her footing when she was so used to painting up there.'

'She didn't eat. She didn't sleep. She was working day and night.'

Freya looked up at him 'How do you know?'

'I went past the house sometimes,' Leo told her. 'There were lights on in the studio at three in the morning. Her up there on the ladder working, totally absorbed.'

'Were you spying on her?'

'No, of course not.'

'Then what were you doing there in the middle of the night?'

'I couldn't sleep. I went for a walk. I ended up there.'

'Why?' she asked.

'I don't really know. I did it sometimes. I loved her, Freya. I wasn't enough for her and so I lost her,' said Leo.

'I can't lose her, Dad,' said Freya, the tears she had been holding back spilling down her cheeks.

Her father took her in his arms. 'You won't, my darling. Your mother will never give up on you. Now, let me take you home. You need some rest.'

Leo took her hand as if she were still a little girl. He led her out of the hospital, opened the car door for her and helped her in. Climbing in beside her, he started the engine, driving in his meticulous, law-abiding way that had driven Cora mad and now set Freya's teeth on edge. When he stopped at a traffic light, he fiddled with the radio, filling the silence with reassuring BBC voices reporting on far-off conflicts, where the breaking of bodies was an everyday occurrence.

Freya checked her phone. There were five messages from Johann, but she could not face talking to him. Instead, she texted. *Arrived okay. Cora not okay. Too tired to talk.* He called straight back but she let it ring until it stopped.

'Who was that?' Leo asked.

'Just a guy I'm sort of seeing,' Freya replied evasively.

'Who is he?'

'Nobody important.' Freya stared out the window. The light was dying, but she could still make out the landscape she had learned to love. Cora had taught her to see its gentle details around the loch. A down-lined bird's nest, a fox trotting in the undergrowth, the subtle shifts of colour in the heather. Her mother had shown her these things, the two of them walking on the narrow paths that the sheep created, hand in hand. Comrades. Talking about their days. What they'd done. What they'd seen. What they'd been thinking. Stopping to sketch, take photographs, collect stones and bones and flowers. They would take their treasures home to show Leo. Afterwards, Cora would work them into whatever canvas she was busy with, building the texture of the earth into her paintings.

As Leo turned up the steep road that led to Lawhead, Freya looked up at the house – the familiar yellow stone, the pointed windows on the top floor, the smokeless chimneys silhouetted against the clear moonlit sky. He stopped, and she got out of the car and opened the gate for him. He drove on, triggering the motion sensor light. Freya walked up to the house, her gaze fixed on Cora's studio, where the lights had been left on. She thought she saw a flash of movement in the loft window – the cat prowling, or a bird perhaps – but it was hard to tell.

She joined her father, who was standing by the car also staring at Cora's studio, his hands limp at his side as if he no longer knew what to hold, what to relinquish.

'Do you want to come in with me, Dad?'

'I er . . . I am . . .' said Leo, struggling to finish his sentence. Toby whined. 'I'll just take him for a quick walk around the garden now.' He gave Freya the key to the studio and then turned away and walked across the garden with the dog at his side, leaping into the air as if he were a puppy. As if he were forgiven.

THIRTY-SEVEN

Angel heard the sound of the gate at the same time the cat did. They both cocked their heads to listen, then the cat bolted up the staircase and disappeared into the loft. Angel pressed herself against the wall and looked out of the window. She could make out the house and the drive, where a vehicle was coming slowly up the gravel. She looked intently at the driver. A man - the right age, the right height - but it was not Fournier.

Angel turned her attention to the woman who had closed the gate and was walking up the drive. When she stepped into the pool of light cast by the motion sensor, Angel could make out angled cheekbones, dark hair, a slight body in a black coat, boots, hat. If it was Cora – it had to be her – then Angel's waiting was almost over. She picked up the box-cutter on the table. The makeshift weapon made her blood surge, even though now she had to contend with the man walking the dog too. Before she did that, she needed time to think. To think, she needed to hide. The cat's escape into the loft guided her. She grabbed her rucksack and climbed the stairs to the loft. It was half full with hay bales. The cat retreated into a corner, the fur around its neck on end. Angel hid with it, behind the hay.

There was a gap between the wooden slats in the loft floor and when she looked down, she had a bird's-eye view of the studio. The worn blue sofa, the fireplace, the table, and the door. The light falling between the strips in the roof made stripes of grey and black on the floor. She could keep an eye on the stairs that led up to where she lay. She was ready. All she had to do now was watch and wait.

The woman unlocked the studio door. It caught on the grooves left by a century or more of cattle going in and out for milking but, with a shove, she got it open. Angel heard her moving around the studio.

Freya averted her gaze from the stained wing of white paint on the floor and looked at Cora's canvas. Her mother's enigmatic painting filled the north wall of the barn. A long, low line of hills. The Arctic sun not cresting, but illuminating the sky, the hills, the frozen lake. On the one side there were trees, stiff as soldiers, and ice glittered on the frozen branches. On the other side of the painting there was a single russet streak beneath the trees. It was if the land itself was bleeding. It was a thing of beauty, this stark landscape, revealed snowflake by painted snowflake.

Where is this place? Freya asked herself as she walked over to Cora's snowscape, white but for the line of crimson marks. Up close, they looked like tracks, as if an animal had been injured. Freya ran her hands over the canvas. Her mother had covered it with a second layer. She felt along the frame of the painting. A few of the tacks that Cora had shot into the frame to hold the silk skin of the painting had come loose. There were wrinkles at the bottom of the canvas, as if the top layer of silk had just been added. She stepped back again so that she could look at her mother's huge painting as a whole, when her attention was drawn by a sound in the loft.

Freya looked up. A glint of light in the loft floor, there and then gone – Freya sensing, rather than seeing, movement. 'Kits, Kits, Kits,' she called. There was pin-drop silence, but Kit-Kat did not show herself. Freya gripped the stairs, climbed up towards the loft. There was no sign of the cat, but the hairs on the back of her neck stood on end.

Angel lay face down behind the bales of old hay, her face pressed into her arms. Even the gleam of an eye might catch the woman's attention, and it was too soon. Mistakes might be made, evidence left if Angel was forced to act before she was ready. She gripped the blade in her hand and did not look at the woman climbing into the loft, calling, 'Kits, Kits, Kits.'

Then came the man's anxious voice, saying, 'What are you doing up there? I can't stand another accident. Come down, darling. Please.'

Freya looked down to see Leo gripping the stairs, his face stricken. She climbed down. 'Looking for Kit-Kat. I thought I heard her up here, but no sign. I didn't mean to frighten you.' She hugged him tight. The wind blew the door shut, the sound gunshot loud. They both jumped.

'Let's go inside now. Leave this cold place,' he said. 'You need sleep. If you're going to take care of your mother, you need to look after yourself first.'

He put his arm around Freya and they walked down to the house.

'That huge painting,' said Leo. 'What was she doing?'

'I don't know, Dad. I'm not sure if I've ever really known what Mum was doing.'

'The only time we spoke was when I fetched Toby. Then it was as if she was here, but not.' Leo turned to face her. 'She didn't say anything to you?'

'Nothing,' Freya replied. 'She was like that with me too, in the last while. She'd talk to me, but I could tell her thoughts were elsewhere.' She opened the kitchen door and Toby raced in and curled up in his basket. It was freezing, so Leo filled the stove with wood and struck a match. The flames leapt up, illuminating his face, and Freya opened the fridge. Olives and a rind of cheese and wine.

'Mum hasn't been eating much again,' said Freya, taking out the olives and eating them as she pulled out the medical information the specialist who had seen Cora had left beside her hospital bed.

'Is that about Mum?' asked Leo, leaning over to look.

'About her losing her sight, what they can do about it.'

'Is it permanent?'

'They don't know.' Freya gave up trying to read about head injuries and loss of eyesight because her eyes blurred over the complicated words and the uncertainty of the outcome. 'She kept on saying, "What will I be if I can't see?"'

'Maybe I can help you with it?' asked Leo.

'Let me talk to Cora about that tomorrow.' She felt torn

between her parents. 'When I can think better. When we know more.'

'Don't you need something more to eat?' her father asked. 'I could make you some pasta and pesto with Parmesan.'

Freya attempted a smile. Her favourite childhood meal. 'The olives were fine.' She put the empty jar on the draining board. 'I'm exhausted. All I want is to sleep.'

'You going to be okay here?' he asked.

'Of course I am.'

'You could stay with me.'

'And Kayla?'

'Well, there is a spare room.'

Freya shook her head.

'I'm so sorry, Freya. I love you.'

'I love you, too,' she said. 'It's just awkward and I've got enough going on . . .'

'Do you want to keep Toby tonight?'

'It's fine, Dad. I'm going to go back to the hospital early in the morning, so you'd better take him.'

'Don't you want me to give you a lift?'

'It's okay,' she said. 'I'll get a taxi.'

'Well, you phone me if there's anything.'

Freya nodded, the burn in her throat making it difficult to speak. She closed the door on her father and stood for a moment alone in the kitchen, overwhelmed by exhaustion. She put her bag over her shoulder to go upstairs to bed and switched the kitchen lights off, but the darkness was so desolate, she switched them on again. She went through the house, putting all the lights on, one room after the next, all the way up to Cora's room.

She hadn't intended to sleep there, but once she climbed the last flight of stairs, she could not face going down again, so she dropped her bag on the dressing table and took off her clothes. She felt dirty, but she was too tired to have a bath, so she wrapped herself in her mother's green velvet dressing gown and climbed into the big unmade bed, giving herself up to its soft embrace. She turned off the bedside light.

It was so still outside that she could hear the water from the loch break on the narrow strip of beach. The sound was as rhythmic as a heartbeat, and she imagined herself carried away on those gentle waves, rocked by the water, and it dawned on her, just before she fell asleep, that she did not feel sick. The nausea was gone.

THIRTY-EIGHT

A ngel watched the couple walk back to the house and go inside. Fifteen minutes later, the man came out and drove off with the dog. Shortly after, the woman left the kitchen. Each time she switched on a light, the windows revealed an entrancing domestic scene. A vase, a pile of books, a plant. Each one bathed in warm yellow light. It looked like the illuminated Advent calendar Angel and Charly used to take out each year, one light coming on for each day leading up to Christmas. The woman worked her way right to the top of the house, where she switched on the lights but did not draw the curtains. Angel watched her strip off her clothes and then wrap her pale, slender body in a dark robe. She saw her lie down, and then the light went out.

Angel waited for half an hour, but the light in Cora's bedroom stayed off so she came down from the loft. She slipped out of the studio and walked down to the house. She tried the back door – it was locked, but the sash of the window in the scullery was easy to open. She jumped down into the kitchen.

When she was in, she took off her boots and leather jacket and climbed soundlessly to the bedroom on the top floor. The door was open. Angel stood on the threshold. A shaft of moonlight on the bed: the woman lying on her back. Angel listened beneath the silence to her quiet rhythmic breath. She crossed the room and stood beside the bed, letting her eyes adjust to the dim light. The woman slept with the trusting abandon of an exhausted child – her arms flung out on either side of her body, her lips parted. Slowly, the features of the sleeping young woman came into focus.

Angel stared down into the pale upturned face, the flash of silver at the throat. A slender chain, a butterfly dangling from it. The girl in the painting in Fournier's house. Angel recognised the thick brows, the high cheekbones, the wide-set eyes, closed in sleep. It was the daughter who Angel had seen in the news clip, a reporter shoving a microphone at her face.

She made her calculations fast. A handbag lay on the dressing table, its contents spilling out. She rifled through it – purse, phone, keys, notebook – she flicked through the notebook, found nothing. Then a rectangle of card on a lanyard caught her eye. 'New Victoria Hospital Family Pass' it read along the top. With it, a scrap of paper with numbers for a ward and a room – and Cora Berger's name. That's where she was then. That was why she wasn't here, where Angel had come to find her. She was in this New Victoria Hospital but the card in her hand meant that she was alive. Angel pocketed it.

Freya's eyes fluttered beneath their lids – dreams, or the sense a body has of another, even when unconscious. There were such things as innocent victims – that, Angel knew too well. And that was what this girl would be if she woke up and saw Angel by her bed. It was Cora Angel needed to see, not this replicant daughter of hers. But the girl – her vulnerability – was something to use against a mother, that much she knew. The blade that she held in her hand gleamed in the faint light.

The necklace was around Freya's slender neck, the silver butterfly resting on a delicate clavicle, the chain forming a small suspension bridge between the bone and the pale column of her neck. Freya stirred, muttering in her sleep. Angel waited until Freya was still again, then she reached over and – quick and clean – made the cut. The butterfly fell into her hand and she eased the chain away from Freya's neck. She slipped the necklace into her pocket. She had the evidence that she needed to deal with Cora.

She went back down the stairs and into the kitchen, climbed out the window and took the road that hugged the contour of the hills. Mist rested on the fields and dark trees protruded above the stone walls. She walked on until she could cut downhill to the empty road that followed the shore. There was a bus stop not far down the road. Angel got there as a set of lights cut through the darkness. The driver pulled over and she climbed in, handed over the fare and sat down. She looked out of the bus window and saw a fox drinking from a pond. Its russet tail the same colour her mother's hair had once: the thought of her, sharp as hunger.

THIRTY-NINE

reya did not know what had woken her. She tried to move, but her limbs were heavy with sleep. She knew where she was, however – in Cora's bed and in Cora's bedroom. What was disorientating was the presence of the familiar smell of Cora's studio – the ghostly notes of paint and straw were suspended in the chilly bedroom air. She listened intently; there was silence inside and outside, which was no comfort at all. It just reminded her how isolated she was here. She should have kept Toby.

It was dark, except for a narrow band of moonlight cutting through the gap in the curtains. There was no movement in the room, yet she was convinced that someone had been standing beside her in the darkness. She put her hand up to her throat, but her fingers, reaching for the protection of the necklace she always wore, found only bare skin. Cora had given it to her when she'd got her first period, a talisman that would protect her. It was a bad omen that it was gone. How could she have lost it?

Fear of the dark, fear of the night, fear of the angry ghosts that roamed these hills in the winter galvanised her, and she sat up in bed and felt about for the necklace. It was not there. She tossed aside the pillows and the duvet, hunting for it in the bed, but all she felt was the cold white expanse of the sheet. Nothing. She leaned over and looked on the floor. Nothing there either, but as she looked, her stomach cramped so painfully that she had to hug her knees and breathe. As soon as the pain was gone she checked the bed again.

Still nothing, but she was sure she'd had it on when she went to bed, sure she'd touched it for luck before she'd fallen asleep. She was sure, but she had been so exhausted and the chasm of sleep into which she had fallen had been so deep, that it was hard to account for things. The absence of the necklace made her unbearably anxious. Without it, she was unprotected, and so was Cora. Neither of them was safe.

She got out of bed and went to the window. A fox trotted across the field and vanished into the undergrowth. A bus moved along the loch, its red rear lights winking.

The exhaustion and shock made it hard to think straight. Freya had spent her life bargaining with fate for as long as she could remember. Whenever her mother had travelled, her absence had cut Freya off from the comfort of routine and, to soothe herself, she had passed the days until Cora's return with small rituals. If she walked up the left-hand side of the steps only, Cora would come back. If she only wore yellow, Cora would come back. If she didn't wash the cheek where Cora had planted her last kiss, Cora would come back. This hamster wheel of thought whirred on in her head now. The only way she was going to be able to rid herself of the uncanny feeling that the loss of the necklace and Cora's safety were linked, was if she found it.

She tightened the belt of Cora's velvet dressing gown and went down to the kitchen. She searched the table, in the fridge, next to the sink. No sign of it. In the hallway, she pulled on Wellington boots and an overcoat and went up to the studio, lighting the way with her torch.

She opened the door and went in. It had the same smell she had sensed when she woke up – cold and straw and paint. Her mother's smell, when she worked. She switched on the lights. Everything was as she had seen it last. The spectral snowscape, the paint on the floor, the broken ladder propped against the wall, the cluttered trestle table, the blue sofa. She searched, but there was no sign of the silver butterfly.

She was chilled to the bone by the time she returned to the house. She ran upstairs and jumped back into bed, but she was unable to sleep, her thoughts with her mother, lying in the hospital bed like a broken doll. She dialled Cora's number, but her phone was switched off. Filled with dread, Freya searched for the key to Cora's room, finding it in a silver dish on her mother's dressing table. She felt a little better when the door was locked. She took her phone into bed with her and turned off the light.

It was still pitch dark when Freya was driven out of her warm bed by cramps low in her pelvis. She stumbled to the bathroom and sat on the cold white lavatory seat with her head in her arms, clammy with pain. She parted her legs and looked down. There were whorls of blood, dark and clotted, sinking into the water, settling onto the white porcelain. This was not normal. This she did not know how to think about. She flushed the toilet over and over until all the blood was gone, then she crawled back into bed, wishing that her mother was there with her. She wrapped her arms around her aching belly, not sure if she was crying from relief or from grief.

FORTY

Angel walked into the hospital with a group of cleaners all dressed in dark practical clothing similar to hers. No one paid her any attention as she crossed the lobby, which was full of people despite the lateness of the hour. She checked the card she had taken from Freya's bag and took the elevator to the fourth floor. Cora's was a private room at the end of the corridor. The door was ajar. Angel went in and closed it behind her. She stepped closer and assessed the motionless woman lying on her back on the bed. Fluids glided down the drip and into one of her veins. The heart monitor made tiny green blips on the screen. Her oxygen levels were steady.

Angel opened the file hanging at the end of Cora's bed. Cracked ribs, the nerves almost sundered in her elbow, a head injury.

There were X-rays and scans. Angel held them up to the dim light and peered into Cora's body, then replaced the file. She held her hand close to the prone woman's mouth. Cora's breath fluttered faint as a moth's wing against Angel's fingers. Asleep, or unconscious. She put her hand on Cora's chest and pressed.

Cora cried out. It was as if a thousand tiny arrows had passed through her. She opened her eyes to see a raven hovering above her. She closed them again to drive away the hallucination. She had forgotten that she could not see. She tried breathing through the pain as she had when Freya was born, waiting for the arrows to land, for the pain to end, but the pressure on her chest grew, and so did the pain. She opened her eyes again. The raven was still perched on her bed, and its beak was digging into her breastbone.

'You're hurting me.' Cora tried to push the raven's claw away, but the movement was excruciating and her hand was slippery with sweat.

'I need you to pay attention, Cora Berger.' There was no pity in the crow voice. This crow-girl, speaking to her.

'Who are you?' whispered Cora.

'My name is Angel Lamar.'

'I don't know you.' Panic in Cora's voice. 'Where are you from?'

The crow pushed down harder, the pain a beak, tearing Cora open.

'I work at the wolf sanctuary,' said Angel. 'The one near the lake.'

'Stop hurting me,' begged Cora. 'Please.'

'The dog,' said Angel, not moving her hand. 'Trotsky. A woman found her, brought her in.'

'Oh,' said Cora, and just like that she was back in the snow, the fear, the running. 'Why are you here?' This was impossible. She must be hallucinating. 'What do you want from me?'

Angel bent so close to Cora that she could feel her breath on her cheek; smell her – sweat, leather, cold. 'Yves Fournier,' she breathed. His name made Cora's heart skip in terror.

Angel pressed harder. 'Where is he?'

'I don't know,' said Cora.

'I think you do,' said Angel. 'I found no sign of him in the cabin. Traces of you, though.'

'Stop, please.' Cora gasped for air. The crow-girl ignored her.

'What business did you have with him?'

'None,' whispered Cora.

'Where is he?' asked Angel.

'Leave it. Leave it be.'

'It doesn't work like that, Cora,' said Angel. 'Not with me.'

'I can't tell you.'

'But you will.'

'If you hurt me again, I will scream,' said Cora. 'And the nurses will come.'

'That would be a mistake,' said Angel.

She placed the silver butterfly on its delicate chain in Cora's hand. Cora could feel the fragile silver wings. Her heart raced. 'Where did you get this?'

'I took the necklace from your daughter,' she said.

The pain was a hacksaw through Cora. 'How did you get it? She never takes that off. It keeps her safe.'

Her eyes turned towards the sound of Angel's rasping voice.

'I took it while she was sleeping. I stood as close as I am to you now, with a knife in my hand, and I cut it off. She didn't even stir. What you need to know is that I can hurt her, as I am hurting you, and no one will know. I have done it to others, before, and I will do it to her, unless you tell me the truth.'

Cora shuddered with fear. 'What have you done to her?'

'The question, Cora,' said Angel, her hard hand poised over Cora's body, 'is what you did to her.'

'I have protected her,' Cora cried.

'Then why did you offer up your daughter to Fournier?' Angel hissed. 'You know what he is.'

'No,' Cora said. 'No!' She turned her head away. It was her only escape from this nightmare.

'I found the painting you signed for him in his house,' said Angel. '*THE GIRL, for Yves, a private view.* You wrote on it. You signed it with a heart, to him, from you. Your daughter Freya in a yellow bikini, wearing this necklace.'

'I never let him near her,' Cora murmured. 'It was myself, I could not protect myself, not Freya. I kept her from him.'

'I went to your studio,' Angel said. 'I saw the blood. I saw your painting of the snow. The blood you painted on it. I opened it up and I found what lies beneath.'

'No.' Cora tried to shake her head.

'Where is he?'

'Not here,' she said frantically.

'I found the other pictures of Freya you'd sealed inside your painting of the snow.'

'You're looking at it wrong. It's not what it seems.'

'What is it, then?' Angel's voice was as harsh as the rook that sat on the tree outside Cora's studio. 'What did you do for Yves Fournier?'

'Nothing. I did nothing for him!' she cried.

'You can't deny it.' Angel pressed down hard again. The pain stole Cora's tongue as the crow-girl put her mouth right by

Cora's ear and whispered, '*THE GIRL, a private view*. You offered him your daughter.'

'No,' Cora managed to say. 'That was *me*. That painting was a gift that I brought on my first visit to his cabin. Before I knew anything . . . I gave it to him because he had been so interested in me, in who I had been when I was a girl. In the place that made me. I didn't know what he was when I gave it to him. He told me just after.'

'And the rest?' Angel's disbelieving voice was harsh. 'The *Forbidden Fruit*. What was that, if not your daughter?'

'That was my childhood, *my* body that I plundered, and it was not for Yves. I did it *because* of him.'

'Explain.'

'To try and make sense of what he told me,' Cora told her inquisitor. 'When he told me about his criminal record, I couldn't take any of it in. When I got home, I took out photographs that I hadn't looked at since I was a child. I could not help but look at myself through Yves' eyes.'

'Those paintings you did,' Angel's low voice pulsed with anger. 'I saw them. The way you looked at her, it's obscene.'

'They are pictures of *me*,' whispered Cora. 'All of them. That sun-dappled lawn. The sprinkler. That little girl in a yellow bikini bottom with a cherry on the side. That's me.'

Cora paused, waves of pain moving behind her eyes that refused to focus on this dark girl hovering over her. She couldn't see her, but she could sense her rage, a weapon drawn. One that she had to deflect from Freya.

'To understand why he could not love me, I had to understand what he did want. What he loved. What he looked for in a child. So I looked at myself, as if I had frozen a film of my childhood,' Cora continued. 'One frame after another, I found the movements of the girl I had been. A very young girl, coming into the awareness that someone was watching her.'

Angel eased the pressure on Cora's chest a fraction, and she drew breath.

'I dissected the movement of my own body,' she said. 'In the paintings, I stripped myself. I put myself into the images that Yves was found guilty of possessing. The images I could not see – that no one should see.'

'Those images are searched for, looked at, manufactured, each night, each day,' said Angel, her voice just louder than a whisper.

'I know,' said Cora. 'I excavated myself – looking for the freedom that was in the little girl I once was, because it was that freedom that gave me my will.' She paused for breath, letting the wave of pain that surged through her crest and then subside. 'But I could no longer find it. He took that freedom from me. I let him into me, into my heart. I lost my self-containment.'

Angel removed her hand from Cora's sternum.

'You went with Yves Fournier even though you knew what he'd done?'

'I didn't know in the beginning,' said Cora. 'He took me up to that cabin to tell me. I had no idea where I was. It was dark. There was snow everywhere. Wolves, too. I couldn't leave. I stayed the night.'

Angel leaned so close, Cora could feel her breath on her face when she spoke. 'So you're not to blame?'

'Of course I'm to blame,' sighed Cora. 'I was blind enough to fall in love. That was the fall that broke me, not the one that brought me here.'

'You returned.' Angel ran her fingertips over the brace around Cora's body, her touch an ominous caress. 'Why?'

'I've asked myself that question so many times, but all I can tell you is what I told myself – that Yves opened up my heart and I couldn't find a way to close it again. I mistook cruelty for love. He set a trap. He needed me to make himself respectable in the eyes of the world or, perhaps, in his own eyes again. I don't know, by then I was in too deep. I was caught, and the more I struggled to escape, the more entangled I became.'

'What did he tell you?' asked Angel. She cracked her knuckles. The sharp sound jolted through Cora's body.

'Two images that he happened upon were found on his laptop.'

'And you believed that?' asked Angel.

'I tried to.'

'Photographs like the one he was caught with, screen grabs . . . Cora: if there is one, then there will always be a sequence. There's the before and there's the after.'

'Yves said he paid a fine.'

'That is true.' Angel sat down on the bed. 'He had a good lawyer and a judge who was on his side.'

Cora could not see her, but when she heard the girl's shallow breathing, she realised that Angel was afraid too. Cora knew only too well that frightened people do dangerous things. She would have to be very careful.

'He told me it was an innocent mistake,' said Cora. 'The mistake any man on the internet can make.'

'That's a lie. He knew what he was looking for. They all do. He typed in the words that conjured the images he wanted to see. He sought it out. Did you see what he looked at?'

'He said it was nothing. He lied.'

'But you found what Fournier looked at in the end, didn't you?'

Fear made Cora's mouth dry. 'Some water, please.' Angel held a glass to her lips and she drank.

'I did,' Cora murmured. 'But only at the end.'

'This last weekend?' asked Angel.

'Yes.' Cora closed her eyes, seeing again Yves' obscene paintings in the basement. The cruelty in them spiralled Cora back into that subterranean darkness, to that girl down there, that naked child with her masked face, her body braced for what was coming. To Yves coming down the stairs, to the convulsion of violence. 'I found—'

A sound at the door.

'Shh.'

Cora sensed Angel move away from her bedside as a nurse swept in. He asked, 'Who's this with you so late?'

'I . . . I am . . .' Cora heard the shock in her voice. She wasn't prepared for this. She wasn't as hard as she seemed. 'It's my daughter, Freya.'

'Well, hello, Freya,' he said. 'It's a comfort for your mum to have you. But you should know that night stays are not usually allowed.'

'Just a bit longer,' Cora pleaded. 'It's frightening not being able to see.'

'I understand,' said the nurse. 'But you're going to be asleep before you know it, with what you've been prescribed. You go, Freya, when your mum dozes off. I wouldn't like to lie here without being able to see anything, either. How's the pain, Ms Berger?'

'I'll survive,' said Cora.

'Excellent,' he replied. 'I'm just checking the monitors, Ms Berger. The eye specialist will be in tomorrow morning to see if you do need surgery.'

'To save my eyesight?' asked Cora

'You must have faith.' The nurse put his hand on Cora's.

'The doctors do work miracles these days. Now, Ms Berger, do you need anything else? Are you comfortable?'

'I am. Thank you.'

'Just call me if you need anything.' Then he was gone, and the only sounds in the room were the tweets and chirps made by the machines monitoring Cora's body.

'You didn't ask for help,' said Angel.

'No, I didn't,' Cora replied, slowly. 'I have this feeling we must help each other. That we're the only ones who can.'

Angel considered that for so long that Cora began to wonder if she was still there, and asked as much.

'Yes, I'm here,' came the reply. Angel came to sit beside Cora. 'You can't see me at all?'

'I see your silhouette. Dark against the light. Like a crow against an evening sky.'

'Touch my face, then.' Angel picked up Cora's uninjured left hand and placed it on her cheek. 'I won't hurt you again.'

Cora studied the girl's face with her fingertips, trying to know her face, as she would if she were to paint her portrait. She assessed the shape of her face, the sharp angle of her cheekbones, the large eyes. The mole on her cheek – a beauty spot – beneath her left eye. She ran her fingers over the mark again. Trying to understand by touch what she would know at once by sight. The mole she felt was the key to this stranger's face.

She had seen a mole like this on a child's face – just part of it, on her cheek, below the mask. Cora traced the girl's full mouth. The shape of it turned her blood to ice. This was the girl she had seen in the paintings in the hidden room beneath the cabin.

'You,' whispered Cora, moving her fingers across Angel's face. 'You were the girl in his paintings.' Angel was motionless but Cora could feel her tension in her fingertips. She lowered her hand. 'Yves. There was a hotel room. There was a girl. Was it you? Was he there?'

'Yes. Except he watched safe on the other side of a webcam,' said Angel, her voice hard and flat. 'Nothing to smell, not even when I was sick. Nothing to touch, so no reality. Not me. Videos – someone else doing the dirty work at his long-distance direction.'

The raven-rasp was gone; her voice was that of a child again.

'The men say it's nothing. It's only an image. That it's not a real girl. But it's *my* body; it is *my* soul that was taken with those videos, those stills they snatched. That was me, gone. Frozen forever. I never get older. It never stops. I keep getting downloaded. My stepfather's hands with nicotine stains on them, all over me. In the watcher's mind, those hands are his, doing those disgusting things to me, but he is not *responsible* because all he does is watch – a little tiny picture on his phone or his computer screen, which is not big enough for the girl to be human.'

The rush of Angel's words stopped and Cora felt for her hand, found it, the nails bitten to the quick, the cuticles torn back.

'They didn't need to be there in the room with me to direct the hands on my body, the camera angles, the endless shame. They didn't even need to say anything. The men who film girls like me know exactly what the watchers want to see.'

'I am so sorry,' Cora murmured, 'for what those men did to you.'

'That was my childhood.' Angel took her hand back and cracked her knuckles again. 'That's how it lives on. Except now I am hunting them down. One at a time, starting with Yves.'

'I am so sorry, Angel,' said Cora, but the girl continued as if she had not heard Cora speak.

'There's always another one,' she said. 'There is always one more. They multiply, like the pictures of me do. It will never stop. They don't think it's a crime – just pictures, they say. Nothing real, but my skin burns every time I think of them.'

Angel stopped speaking and Cora listened to her breathing. In and out. In and out. Trying to master herself again.

'Those of us who survive live on as dark stars,' murmured Cora. 'We are invisible but we collapse the light.'

Angel watched her, saying nothing, waiting for her to go on.

'That was the man I fell in love with. He made me feel at home so I didn't see it, but it was there from the beginning. I tried to see things the way Yves wanted them seen, but I failed. The signs were there, but I didn't know how to read them. Later' – Cora's voice was fading – 'when he told me his story, he had broken the truth down into such small pieces that it might as well have been lies. It was only when I saw the pictures that I understood.'

Cora's breath came in ragged gasps.

'You saw what you wanted to see in him,' said Angel.

'I know,' said Cora. 'I did.'

'Men like him are vampires. They spread their contagion one bite – one view – at a time. Look how it spread from me to you. They keep doing it unless they are stopped. And that is what I do. I stop them,' said Angel. 'So help me, and redeem yourself.'

'I don't have him.'

'Didn't he come with you?' asked Angel.

'He couldn't come with me.' Cora shivered at the memory of him coming at her, his fist raised.

'Is he alive?' Angel asked.

'He was when I left him.'

'Tell me where he is,' Angel demanded. 'Give him to me.'

'What will you do with him?'

'Finish what you started,' said Angel. 'I've done it before.'

'So have I.' Cora said this so quietly that Angel had to bend close to hear her say, 'I felt so ashamed that I had been taken in again.'

'What do you mean, taken in?'

'I had nowhere to turn when I was twelve and I was taken in,' Cora said. 'I did what it took to get away.'

'Who?'

'My art teacher.' The pain in Cora's chest was easing. 'What he did to me was the secret I had to keep on his behalf.'

'That's how they do it,' Angel said. 'And that's what we do.'

'Until we stop,' Cora replied. 'When Yves told me his carefully crafted version of what he'd done, it was as if he was offering the most precious gift of trust. And that made me that child again, as paralysed as I had been when I was twelve.'

'The man, the one when you were a child,' Angel asked, 'what happened to him?'

Cora could not see his face, but her skin remembered. The hard hurting hands. The pressure on her thighs as he bent her, face down, over the stone lip of the dry well. The rotten smell that had come up from inside the earth.

'I wanted to be free of him and the only way I could imagine being free was if he was dead.' Cora marshalled her strength. 'I wanted him to die.'

'Did you kill him?' asked Angel.

'I don't know.'

Cora had bared her teeth and bitten him so hard that she'd tasted the salt of blood. For one second, he'd loosened his grip. That split moment was all she needed to push him with the strength and wiliness born of desperation. He was already off balance, but he had her by her necklace, and the chain cut deep into her throat when she shoved him – then it snapped, and as she sprinted away there was just his scream, *CoraCoraCora*, spiralling down. She heard it again, but no matter how hard she listened to that lost echo, she never heard his body hit the water. For all she knew, he was still falling.

'Did you want to kill Yves?' Angel's voice brought Cora back to the present.

'I wanted him to die,' she said, 'but I didn't want to kill him. That is always the mistake women make.'

'Not me,' Angel breathed.

'Not me this time, either,' said Cora, as softly. 'I almost did. I phoned his wife, but I couldn't speak to her. I couldn't say, go find him. I did not want him saved.'

'Tell me where you left him, Cora, and I will finish things for both of us.'

'In the cabin, there's a room in the recesses of the cellar. The door to it is hidden behind a bookshelf.'

Angel dropped Freya's necklace into Cora's hand, who closed her fingers over the delicate wings and continued: 'The key is round my neck.'

Angel took the key gently off Cora. She liked the weight of it when she hung the chain around her own neck. 'Sleep now,' she said, then she left the room, closed the door behind her with a soft click and slipped out of the hospital.

ora did not sleep. She thought of Angel making that journey back to the cabin she had once fantasised as a place where she might belong. She pictured Angel inside it, at the window seat where she had been on that last weekend when she had watched Yves ski across the lake. When he had vanished from view, she had taken the key she had given Angel from around her neck and checked each of the rooms of the cabin again. The key did not fit any of the doors and none of the cupboards were locked. She checked under the beds, but there were no locked trunks there either. The absurdity of what she was doing got to her after that. This was not his only house, she'd told herself, and she had given up the search and gone into the bathroom, turning on the hot water.

When the bath was full she got in and scrubbed herself until her skin was raw. She felt more resolute when she pulled out the plug. She hung his key around her neck again. It opened nothing and took her nowhere; it would be the perfect memento. She dressed, did her hair and face and packed, erasing every trace of herself. It was easy – her touch had, in reality, been so light. She carried her bag down to the car and put it in the boot.

The wind was strong and it was driving storm clouds heavy with snow towards the cabin. She had a long drive ahead of her. She put her car keys into her pocket and walked back up to the house. She used the toilet, but when she flushed, it backed up and the water in the bath gurgled. The cold water in which she had lain had not drained. The detritus of her body – the soap ringing the bath, invisible skin cells, three pubic hairs drifting in the cold grey water. She couldn't leave herself here in that way.

She pulled up the trapdoor to the cellar and switched on the light. A dull greenish glow illuminated the stairs, angled steep down towards the damp concrete below. She descended. The air was icy and the light was viscous in the basement rooms. In the first was an old washing machine. A stack of odd skis, a perished trampoline, a deflated soccer ball, a doll's pram, boxes of Lego. The flotsam of abandoned childhoods. On the other side of the room, a door listed on its frame. She reckoned that was where the pipes would run. She put her shoulder to it and shoved it open. The light must have been on a sensor, because it flashed on when she stepped inside.

There was a pool of water where the soakaway had blocked, material clogging the drain – strands of hair on the surface scum. The water was repulsive and she did not want to touch it. She looked around for something to poke at the sludge. A stick lay in the corner. She picked it up and poked at the mess in the centre of the basement. The water gurgled and started to move, and stopped again. Bile rose in her throat at the smell. She needed something else. A heavy bookshelf stood against the inner wall; propped against it was a crowbar, a spade and a metal pole.

She picked her way through the water, but slipped on the slimy floor and fell hard against the bookshelf. Instead of toppling over, it slid away from her and she fell to her knees, hitting her head hard. The light went off and the cellar was pitch dark. She reached for the bookshelf to help herself up and the light triggered again, but the floor was so slippery that she stumbled once more and the bookshelf slid away even further, exposing a door.

The door was heavy oak with old-fashioned hinges; the plaster around it, however, looked recent. She got to her feet and tried the handle. The door was locked. She looked at the fittings. The large keyhole. Her hands trembled as she held the key she had taken from Yves' jacket in her palm. It was the right size. She hesitated for only a moment before she inserted the key into the hole and turned it. The door opened. A sigh of stale air touched her face.

'Hello?'

There was no response. She entered, triggering another motion sensor light. It blinded her for a moment. She waited for her eyes to adjust. The roof was higher than in the rest of the cellar and it had been painted white – floor, walls, and ceiling. There were no windows; the lights emitted a warm sunlit glow that was at odds with the iciness of the room. An orange sofa stood in the centre of the room, a table in front of it.

There were paints everywhere, canvases stacked with their faces to the wall, charcoal, paper – an artist's studio, hidden in the bowels of the house. Cora picked up the palette. The oils were still sticky. Recently used. She ran her expert fingers through the brushes – her familiars. She turned to the easel, lifted the muslin cloth covering the canvas and gasped. The painting was alive. Sinuous lines. A room filled with pulsating silence. A hotel room with the bland furniture that filled thousands of rooms the same as this one where a dark-haired girl was on her hands and knees. Her eyes were covered with a cat's-eye mask, but her full mouth revealed her terror. A graze on her elbow. Or a carpet burn. A man's belt buckle behind her. The girl's body braced in anticipation of the pain that was coming.

There was a separate pile of canvases on the table, weighted down by a rock. She picked the rock up, its heft a comfort as she turned over the canvases. Long, slow-motioned renderings of a girl in a hotel room. She laid them out, sequencing his vile display of her young flesh. Yves' muse. All the same girl. Clothed and afraid, her upturned face pleading in the first. In the paintings that came after that, she was naked and her face was lowered, a hand – fingers spread – a cage over it. Cora was lightheaded when she turned to the table and opened the ledger lying on it.

A list of titles. *Nymphets*. *The Lolita Series*. *First Buds*. Lists of dates. Lists of shipping addresses with anonymous post boxes. No galleries. Names that could have been collectors, connoisseurs of what Yves made. Pseudonyms – not uncommon in the world of art, where privacy was the ultimate marker of wealth, of taste. As she slammed the catalogue shut, dizzy with horror, she knew what she was seeing. This was what she had been asking for since Yves had brought her up here for the first time.

Cora looked up when she heard Trotsky bark. That could not be. Yves never came back before dark. He was back too soon, calling her name. Her heart lurched. The trapdoor. She had left it open. He would find her. She did not move. She could not – she was frozen. He would kill her, she was sure of it, if he knew. The thud of ski boots.

She thought of Freya and her promise that she would always return. *Breathe*, she said to herself. *Keep breathing and think. How do I get out of here? I must get out of here.*

Fight. She gripped the rough stone in her hand. *You must fight.*

The light came on in the room where the staircase was. Yves was coming down, down to where she was, Trotsky slipping and sliding down the stairs after him.

Yves was in the doorway, his skis weapons in his hands. He came for her, striking her with one and then the other, but she ducked and the blow glanced off her shoulder. He flung the skis aside and shouted her name, *CoraCoraCora*, as he reached out for her, but she was running at him, trying to get past him and out. He caught her and her heart was pounding, exploding in her, and then she was running past him. She was halfway to the stairs when he caught her again, but she shoved him and she made it up the second step and then the third. But he was behind her and he had his hands in her hair and one arm around her neck, choking her. The other hand was pulling her left arm back and up until she felt it would rip from its socket.

She stopped fighting and Yves dragged her back into his hidden chamber. Trapping her inside. She fought and he hit her and her legs buckled, but he kept dragging her.

He tried to kick the door shut, but the dog was inside too. She was barking, circling frantically and snapping. Desperate. The dog's teeth grazed Cora's wrist when it went for Yves. He let her go and kicked the dog, and Cora ran for the stairs out of the cellar, but he was bigger than her, stronger, and he came after her. She slipped, and they both fell. He got up and his hands were hard on her shoulders, turning her towards him, the expression on his face unreadable, telling her to listen to him. Telling her she had seen things wrong, yet all the time he was pushing her further and further into the hidden cellar and away from the light.

She thought again of her daughter and everything slowed down. She stopped pushing and instead stepped backwards towards the darkness. Her sudden acquiescence put Yves off balance. Her slight body seemed no obstacle to him. His guard was down. Big man, small woman, locked room. But she still had in her hand the rock that he had used to hold his sketches down. She lifted her arm as high as she could and brought it down on his head. He stumbled and fell against her, pushing her back into the table, his blue eyes boring into her. She lifted the rock again and struck him on the temple with all her force. He fell to his knees and reached for her ankle. She stamped on his hand and ran after Trotsky, slamming the door and locking him inside.

She listened for a moment for sounds in the cellar that he had built himself – the prison of his own mind. He wasn't dead, she was sure of that, but it was silent. She slid the bookshelf back again and wedged it into place with the crowbar.

It was hard to climb the stairs, but she managed it, dropping the trapdoor after her and then running, her breath tearing at her lungs and the injured dog loping alongside her. She slipped on the footbridge where the rat's corpse was embedded in the frozen eddy. She looked back at the cabin and saw the smoke from the dying fire curl out of the chimney, pale grey against the white sky. But there was her car and she was in it, driving away. Free.

FORTY-TWO

Freya opened the door and looked into the hospital room. Cora was lying exactly as she had been when she'd left the previous evening. 'Mum,' she said.

Cora turned towards her. 'I'm so happy to hear your voice.' Relief flooded Freya. 'Are you okay?' she asked.

'The nurses checked on me. I'm fine. I was looking forward to seeing you when the sun was up. Is it morning already?'

'Not really, I just thought I would come and be with you. I didn't sleep well and then I woke up and I couldn't move. It was terrifying, because I felt there was this presence in the room,' said Freya. 'For a moment, I thought it was you.'

"You must have been dreaming,' Cora replied. 'I've been lying here where you left me.'

'When I woke up I couldn't find my necklace. The butterfly. I've looked everywhere. In your bedroom and in your studio.'

'It's here.' Cora opened her hand. 'You must have dropped it.'

Freya reached for it, relieved. 'Who found it?'

'Shh now.' Cora gave a faint smile.

'I had these crazy midnight thoughts. I thought . . .' Freya broke off

'What did you think?' asked Cora.

'That if I didn't find it, you would die,' whispered Freya, fear catching at her voice again. 'It was so vivid.'

'Get into bed.' And so Freya took off her coat and boots and climbed onto the bed next to Cora. She put her arm carefully over her mother's body.

Sleep took Cora without warning and it was suffused with heat and the hum of insects and guinea fowl calling. She was a girl again and she was running through the veld. Running away from a man who could no longer pursue her, which is why he called *CoraCoraCora* until she could not hear him. Then the long grass, golden and dry, closed over her head. Her teeth and her claws perfect weapons now because, in her dream, she was a lioness hunting.

FORTY-THREE

There were few vehicles on the roads, none when Angel turned off onto the track that led through the woods to Yves Fournier's cabin. It was snowing lightly when she parked in a dense stand of trees. The clouds parted, revealing a canopy of stars. There were no lights on in the cabin, so she switched on her flashlight as she approached the building, went inside and pulled up the door to the cellar. The cold air fingered her face, and her fear of confinement rippled across her skin, raising the tiny hairs on her arms, the back of her neck, but she made herself go down the stairs.

In the first room was a washing machine, next to it, an old dryer. There was junk piled against the walls. Broken furniture, skis, abandoned toys. She called Fournier's name, but there was no response. All she could hear was the house's faint creaking. Timber and brick, protesting against the cold. She shone her torch around the room. In here, the insulated walls eliminated all sound. The silence was absolute. Instinct told her to get out; her will made her go forward.

She walked carefully. The surface was treacherous, a slick of water solid on the rough concrete floor, an abandoned spanner. She picked her way across the wet floor and pushed open the door that led deeper into the basement. The smell was stronger in here. A blocked drain. Bile rose in Angel's throat. She pierced the dark with her flashlight. There were art catalogues stacked in piles. On the opposite wall was the heavy oak bookcase. The books and art catalogues had fallen off the shelves and were adrift in the dirty frozen water. She picked one up. Yves Fournier's name on it. A book about an artist who only painted pictures of women without faces. Splayed bodies under merciless lights. It was hard to tell if they were alive or dead. Angel tossed it aside.

She put down the tarpaulin and the rope she had brought and put her shoulder to the shelves. The books tumbled off, and the bookshelf shifted a few inches before it stuck again. She crouched down. There was a groove in the floor. Next to it, a crowbar wedged between the wall and the shelf. She pulled it away and the bookshelf glided smoothly on its tracks, and there was the hidden door.

She fitted the key Cora had given her into the lock, turned it, and the door swung open. The hidden chamber let out a breath of stale air. Angel shone her torch around the room. It was painted white: floor, walls, and ceiling. A private gallery. There were only a couple of paintings left on the walls, but the bobbing torchlight made the masked child in them move. She stepped inside towards her own image, over the rock and his splintered skis lying on the floor near the scratched steel door.

Yves Fournier had tried to get out before he had given up and gone to lie on the sofa. She removed the pile of canvases he had covered himself with in an attempt to keep warm. The oil paint was not quite dry on one of them, and it had smeared green and yellow onto his red ski jacket. He was curled on his side, knees pulled into his chest, arms wrapped around them. She pushed back the hood of the red skiing jacket, his stubble rough on her fingers.

She held her fingers against the neck. A pulse, faint and irregular, but present. Breath on her fingers when she held them to his mouth. He was still alive. She knelt down, her mouth right up against his ear and whispered his name in his ear. No response. His fingernails were torn. He had tried hard to get out.

She stripped him – jacket, sweater, thermals, leggings, socks, underpants. Still no response. Angel stepped back and considered his naked body. The sinewy tattooed arms, the hollow belly, the flaccid, uncircumcised penis, the bony knees, and the misshapen toes. A few more hours. She reckoned that was the longest she would have to wait. This would be the second night she had endured with him. The first had been all those years ago in that hotel room. Not that he would ever know now – Yves Fournier was too far gone to recognise that it was she, Angel, who was the girl in the pictures. The paintings she was looking through that Fournier had used to cover himself. She found the first in the sequence that he had used to try and warm himself. To survive. It was of her, still clothed in pink shorts and a frilly white shirt.

Angel was back there again. It was stop-framed in her mind forever. She had been sitting on the edge of the hotel bed with her eyes lowered and her hands between her legs, her back ramrod straight, her only protection her arms crossed over her body. Yves on the webcam, directing. She'd known that the worst was to come. That was how she'd thought, back then. That things could be bad, could be worse, could be the worst. That was when she had still been innocent enough to think in degrees.

Angel checked Fournier again. His pulse was intermittent. Not that long. Nothing to do but to wait and let nature take its course. She was cold, so she wrapped Fournier's jacket around her shoulders. As she did so she saw an envelope lying on the floor. She picked it up – Yves' name written across it. She tore it open. A sheet of thick paper, which she unfolded. She read what Cora had written.

Yves
You broke my heart. You broke me in the process. You made me love you. You loved me, or so you said – until you were sure that you had me, and then you turned that on me as sharp as a blade. You used it to cut me and it gave you pleasure to do so, as it gave you pleasure to hurt me when we made love. That is not the right word for it, because there was no love in the act for you. I did not and could not resist. It was a desire for power, a punishment I did not understand, because I loved you. It was a hatred I thought I could soften. I had no defence against the blows you delivered one after the other, delivered with such precision that I can only believe that this cruelty is something you have practised all your life. I had glimpses of it in the beginning and I disregarded them. There, to my infinite shame, I am culpable. I did not believe

my own eyes. The deftness with which you deceive is astonishing, but what lies beneath is monstrous. I will never know what it is that you are hiding, but what I do know is that your heart is ice.

I am not, as you so often told me, delusional. I am not mad. I simply made the mistake of believing you when you told me you were a good man who loved me. Why would I not? You worked hard to create that illusion, but you punished me for my trust. You broke me. There is no point in pretending otherwise. In the strange terms you set yourself, you won. But the fight was not on terms I understand or accept. I don't know what this has made me, but it has not made me like you and for that I am grateful.

Cora

The silence was absolute. There was no need to check if Yves was still breathing. The smell of death was there on the ice of the basement air. He lay exactly where she had left him, but he was only a body now. She put her hands under his shoulders and rolled him onto the tarpaulin she had brought. She placed the paintings on top of him, threw in his clothes and the skis, tightened the straps around the tarpaulin and pulled him out of the secret room. She kicked the heavy door closed, turned the key, put it in her pocket and shoved the bookshelf back into position.

Angel hooked her arms underneath the body and hauled it through the next room and up the stairs. She paused in the hallway to catch her breath, shouldered the door open, manoeuvred him out and dragged him across the snow to the truck. She opened the back and hoisted Fournier in. It wasn't light yet, but the darkness was no longer complete, even though the snow was coming much faster now.

Angel climbed into the truck and drove back to the sanctuary, where the wolves were pacing their cages, hungry. They watched her, eyes gleaming.

She removed the tarpaulin from the vehicle and took it into the cutting room. She unwrapped it and took the clothes and the skis out of the cutting room to the furnace. She chopped the skis in half and shoved them in. She watched the flames lick hungrily at her offering and then she threw in some more wood and went back to the cutting room, switched on the machine. The steel blade whined as she efficiently dismembered him.

There wasn't much meat on the bones but she ran the more distinctively human pieces through the mincer. The skull and the bones she crushed and added the meal to the wolves' metal food bowls. Four. Enough food for them to feast themselves into a stupor. When Angel switched off the machine, she heard the sound of a vehicle.

Her heart was beating too fast and the blood was too loud in her ears. She checked the cutting room. No recognisable traces. She walked outside. The dawn was a crimson gash in the eastern sky and Jeb was getting out of the Search and Rescue truck.

'Angel,' he said, 'I heard you were back. Where have you been?'

'What's it to do with you?' she asked.

'Tina said family business?'

'That's what I said,' Angel replied. 'There's a reason you're asking me this?'

'Just curious,' said Jeb

'Curious is not a reason,' she countered.

'You're not curious about whether we found Mr Fournier?' he asked.

'Did you find him?'

'Not yet,' said Jeb. 'Everyone is out of ideas as to where to look.'

'I guess we'll all have to wait for the thaw,' said Angel. 'That's when the bodies turn up. Now, if you'll excuse me, I've got to get the animals fed.'

'Do you need a hand?' asked Jeb.

'No.' She turned her back on him, but he followed her back into the cutting room.

Angel picked up two of the four bowls of meat for the wolves and fitted them against her hips. She tensed when Jeb picked up the other two bowls, but there was nothing to be done about him, so she walked out into the snow.

Jeb followed her to the enclosure where the animals trotted up and down on the other side of the wire mesh. Eyes fixed, jaws open, pink tongues lolling. She set the bowls down. Jeb did the same. The animals huddled around the food.

Angel watched the wolves. Jeb watched Angel, but there was no expression at all on her face. The only sounds were the growls of pleasure as the wolves gorged themselves. When he left, the animals had finished eating and there was nothing left but a few bloody streaks on the snow.

Angel waited until Jeb's truck was out of sight before she released Trotsky from her kennel. Together, they walked across the empty lot to the cabin.

Angel locked the door behind her. She took the box of papers out from under her bed. The next file. Her next man. Fortyish, fair hair under the red baseball cap, blue T-shirt tight over his gut, shorts, trainers. Nothing out of the ordinary. His daughters, pretty little blonde girls, in matching green skater skirts which had the name of the alligator park where their father worked printed along the hemlines. His wife had sweat circles under her plump arms – it was hot in Louisiana. She was pretty enough.

Angel studied their innocent, smiling faces, wondering what they knew, what they had learned to hide, before she put the photographs back in the box. Put the box in her black duffel bag. Placed her sparse belongings on top of it. Twenty minutes was all it took to pack and remove any trace of her presence in the cabin. When she slung the bag over her shoulder, the dog whimpered. Angel knelt down and they touched noses.

'You're coming with me, girl,' Angel told her. 'You're mine now.'

The dog fell into step with Angel, and when she opened the door to the truck, Trotsky jumped in and Angel climbed in beside her. By the time they reached the highway, the falling snow had covered their tracks.

♥